Critical Praise for Corporate

Fre

"The story is fast-paced and the suspense doesn't let go until the final rewarding conclusion."

—*Mystery Sequels*

"[T]he pace is fast and Pen is an interesting character. Her injury is part of her life but doesn't define her. And yes, she has a rich, handsome boyfriend. One thread running through the excitement is Pen and Marsha's relationship, as they finally come to terms with the accident."

—*St. Paul Pioneer Press*

"[A] significant step forward for the series . . . readers will eagerly anticipate Lutterman's fourth adventure starring Pen Wilkinson."

—*Cedar Rapids Gazette*

"Pen must go in search of her missing nephew, a computer prodigy who may be able to prevent a cyber catastrophe that could destroy a major bank and send the world economy into, yes, freefall."

—*Crime Fiction Lover*

Windfall

"Pen Wilkinson is one of the most intriguing new characters on the Minnesota crime scene."

—*St. Paul Pioneer Press*

"A nicely written and taut book, *Windfall* would be a welcome addition to any library for fans of corporate thrillers . . . a fun read."

—*Reading Other People*

"With a fast-moving action-packed plot, this thriller has you jumping at shadows and considering keeping a gun on your nightstand, or better yet, under your pillow. Character driven and well written, you feel like you're in the middle of the action."
— *Sweet Mystery Books*

Downfall

"*Downfall* is an exhilarating, action-packed financial thriller . . ."
— Harriet Klausner, *Mystery Gazette*

"[A] fantastic read . . . an entertaining and engrossing book."
— *Charline Ratcliff Reviews*

"*Downfall* is a very intense thriller. Once I started reading, I couldn't put it down."
— *Mystery Sequels*

"*Downfall* by Brian Lutterman is a well-constructed thriller . . . an excellent read."
— Larry Krantz, *Readers' Favorite Reviews*

"[R]eplete with suspense made even more dramatic by the protagonist being confined to a wheelchair."
— John A. Broussard, *I Love a Mystery*

Bound to Die

Minnesota Book Award Runner-Up

"[A] taut, swift-paced and well-plotted debut thriller by a Minnesota author."
— *St. Paul Pioneer Press*

"[A] gripping, twisted, lethal saga, and one that quickly captures the reader's total attention and won't let go until the shocking climax..."
—*Midwest Book Review*

"An inexplicable quadruple murder, a duplicitous presidential adviser and a mysterious and deadly cult called the Bound bear mysterious connections to each other in lawyer Brian Lutterman's debut mystery, *Bound to Die*. Widow Tori McMillan wanders jungles, mountains and the nation's capital as she tries to find her best friend and a group of missing children, as well as to determine what actually happened to her husband."
—*Publishers Weekly*

"[B]ound to entertain...gets your interest from the get-go."
—Kristofer Upjohn, *Pine Bluff Commercial*

"With the help of an infatuated police officer and the hindrance of an FBI agent, Tori finds herself traveling from the Yucatan jungle into the mountains of Denver to the steps of the White House. Before it is over, Tori will question all that she believes to be good. Tori also puts her life on the line in order to solve the mystery that now threatens her sanity."
—Susan Johnson, *All About Murder*

Poised to Kill

"Author Brian Lutterman has proven himself to be a master storyteller in this masterfully woven tale of tycoons and terrorists. *Poised to Kill* is highly recommended reading, especially for enthusiasts of contemporary action/adventure thrillers."
—*Midwest Book Review*

"Lutterman keeps his readers on the edge of their chairs until the last page. The twists, chases, and shootings by professional terrorists keep occurring with increasing tension. Written in the first person, Lutterman draws his readers into the thriller. Lutterman is the author of *Bound to Die*, another taut, top quality thriller. This is a suspenseful, must read book."

—Marion Cason, *I Love a Mystery*

"[A] good, enjoyable read, with satisfying links to today's society. Lutterman should garner wide audiences for this story, and for those to come."

—Carl Brookins, *Reviewing the Evidence*

"Lawyer and author Brian P. Lutterman's latest novel, *Poised to Kill*, is an action-packed suspense thriller that's just simply enjoyable. Lutterman, who packed a punch with his debut novel, *Bound to Die*, proves that he is not just a flash in the pan or a one-book wonder with *Poised to Kill*… Highly recommended."

—*New Mystery Reader Review*

"[T]ightly plotted and has a fascinating take on an interesting scenario."

—*Books 'n' Bytes*

"Layers of betrayal is the name of the game in *Poised to Kill*. The plot ventures cross country and back around many twists and turns to uncover who might be behind the plan to cripple a nation, a major company, and ruin one man's life. *Poised to Kill* is very intriguing and full of unlikely suspects. It will keep you turning the pages and digging to find out which betrayal is the root, or are they all just pieces of one big plan."

—Joy Spear, *Murder and Mayhem Book Club*

Nightfall

Brian Lutterman

Conquill Press
St. Paul, Minnesota

NIGHTFALL

Cover Design: Rebecca Treadway

Library of Congress Control Number: 2018940936

Lutterman, Brian

Nightfall: a novel / by Brian Lutterman – 1st edition

ISBN: 978-0-9995385-1-7

Conquill Press/October 2018

Printed in the United States of America

10 9 8 7 6 5 4 3 2 1

For Jeanne

Also by Brian Lutterman

Freefall

Windfall

Downfall

Bound to Die

Poised to Kill

Chapter 1

Near Puerto Vallarta, Mexico
One year ago

Mark Tomlinson was in for the ride of his life. It would also be the last ride of his life. The Range Rover, its transmission in neutral, rolled slowly forward, beginning Tomlinson's journey from this world to the next. It was dark now, but in the moonlight he could identify the familiar scenery on the steep road leading down to the village, south of the big tourist city. But he wouldn't make it to the village, the adopted home he and Heather had come to love so much.

The Range Rover was rolling downhill now, but Tomlinson couldn't press the brake pedal. Both of his legs were broken, useless. He hoped the journey would end quickly, fulfilling his life's only remaining goal: making the pain stop.

Tomlinson had known that this man, or someone like him, would be coming. The calm, stocky figure with the New York accent had been waiting for him in his living room, in the dark, when he'd returned from town. His question had been predictable.

"Where are the copies you tried to give to the blogger, Mark?"

A single, straightforward question. There were any number of answers he could give. But none that would save his life.

The car was picking up speed, weaving but staying within the trench-like path that had been created for the road. Ahead lay a ninety-degree turn to the right, down to the village. But Tomlinson couldn't turn the wheel to stay on the road. Both of his arms were dislocated.

He had held out hope that the insurance policy he had left with his attorney, Dr. Cardenas, would preserve the evidence, if not his life. But the man had quickly qualified his question about the whereabouts of the copies he sought. "Other than the copy you gave to Dr. Cardenas, Mark. We've already retrieved that one. You should have paid him better."

And so the questioning had resumed. And a long night of unimaginable pain had begun. It would end soon.

"You have to have additional copies," the man had said. "Where are they?"

Tomlinson had tried several different answers. But none had been sufficiently convincing. Thus the journey. He had pleaded with the man to simply kill him, but his inquisitor had demurred. "Sorry, Mark. Even in Mexico, they might investigate a non-cartel killing. But not an accident." And in the unlikely event an autopsy was performed, Tomlinson realized, it would find broken bones, dislocated joints, and massive bruises—nothing that couldn't be explained by a car crash.

As the car rushed toward the sharp turn and the high cliff beyond, Tomlinson thought about Heather, his wife, who had died a month earlier. Would he be reunited with her at the end of the journey? And then he thought about the decision that had brought him to this point, made many years ago, to go into business with a man he had always known would turn against him. Against the world.

The tree cover opened up, and the black expanse of the Pacific stretched endlessly in front of him. The Range Rover left the road and soared off the cliff, toward the ocean, toward Heather. Toward the end.

Chapter 2

Long Beach, CA
Present Day

I felt the gun at my back, the barrel digging into my spine, prodding me forward in the near-darkness. I moved my wheelchair slowly forward toward an innocuous-looking household appliance. An upright freezer.

"Open it," the voice behind me commanded.

"No, please."

"Open it!"

I grasped the wheels of my chair with sweaty, shaking hands. "My God, no."

The gun jabbed at me again.

I maneuvered my chair to the side and gripped the freezer's handle. I opened the door to a sight I had somehow known would be there, and yet it shocked me to the core.

The naked body of a woman, now frost-covered, had been stuffed into the confined space. Against my will, my eyes moved over the torso to the face, a face I recognized.

Mine.

I screamed.

I was still screaming when I woke up. I looked around the darkened bedroom; I was alone. I struggled to a sitting position and clapped my hands twice, turning on the light.

Another night, another nightmare. But, looking at the empty space next to me in bed, I remembered that tonight, there was no one with me to share the experience. And that realization hit me with as much force as had the dream.

I looked at the mostly empty wine bottle on my nightstand. I had no idea what time it was, but I estimated that since my final, tearful encounter with James Carter, about one and three-quarters bottles had elapsed. That seemed as good a way as any to measure time.

I was free. And lost. And hung over. And alone, with my nightmares.

The body-in-the-freezer scene had, unfortunately, really happened to me. It hadn't, obviously, been me in the freezer—it had been another young woman. But without a last-second intervention by law enforcers, I would have joined her. Now, two years later, I relived the experience every few nights. Against all odds, I had fallen in love with a man who was willing to weather the nightmares with me. We both wanted the bad dreams to go away, but we couldn't agree on how to make it happen.

I checked my phone on the nightstand. It was 7:40 AM. I reviewed my options. I could stay in bed. Pointless, I recognized. I could get up. Equally pointless, since I had, these days, nowhere to go and nothing to do. And no one to be with. The awful reality rammed me in the gut, and I choked back a huge sob.

James and I had left the door open a tiny crack, separating rather than officially breaking up. But I couldn't even imagine everything that would have to happen to get through that crack, to get us back together again. I'd gotten tired of his nagging about my problems. He'd gotten tired of my stonewalling about my problems. And if he'd understood the full extent of my issues, he would have been even more tired of it.

The nightmares were bad enough, and I couldn't hide them from James, although I could, and did, fudge in telling him how often they occurred on the nights we weren't together. But I hadn't told him that during the last month, I'd begun to suffer anxiety attacks. Almost every day, I'd have an episode of shaking, sweating and hyperventilating, which seemed to be triggered by . . . nothing. I couldn't explain them. And two days ago, I'd had the worst experience yet: a full-blown flashback, in which I'd actually experienced, while fully awake, the scene of opening the freezer door and seeing the body. A waking nightmare, from which I couldn't escape. It had been terrifying, but it hadn't occurred again.

James's prescription for my troubles, repeated in too many fruitless conversations, was straightforward: serious therapy from a practitioner specializing in post-traumatic stress disorder. *Makes sense*, I'd respond.

"There are meds, too. Some of them can help quite a bit." I was willing to take his word for that. In any event, these drugs probably would have been better than my current medication of choice, which came in the bottles I now used to measure time.

So far, so good. But James could never leave well enough alone. He'd always add, in a tone he probably thought sounded like an afterthought, but which was always the real point of the conversation: "And of course, you've got to stop doing those . . . things you do."

Ah, yes. Those *things*. Those pesky extracurricular undertakings I seemed prone to getting involved in, the wrongness of which James saw as self-evident. That included the quixotic search for corporate saboteurs that had resulted, two years earlier, in my standing in front of a major appliance with a body in it. Another project, obtaining proof against a corrupt congressman, had ended in a shootout with a madman in an aircraft hangar. Then there was the search for my missing nephew, which had led to my near-death in the middle of a busy bridge in Minneapolis.

This last incident had been the final straw for my employer, the US Attorney's office in Los Angeles. Just too much distraction, they'd said. What they really meant was too much publicity, of a type that cast me in a favorable light but didn't benefit my superiors, or worse, reflected poorly on them. Distracting, indeed.

But actually getting me out the door had been a bit awkward, given that my job reviews had been, inconveniently, glowing, that I was both female and handicapped, and that I hadn't broken any laws or rules. But the US Attorney's office is run by, well, attorneys, so they'd found a way. And they'd prudently lubricated the process with a generous payout, taken from some obscure contingency fund. I'd been placed on a leave of absence, which would officially last for thirty days, but which in reality would last forever. And now I, along with my annoying distractions—those *things* again—was supposed to quietly go away.

Looking around my bedroom, I decided to get up, which for me means maneuvering myself into my wheelchair. That done, I went to the bathroom and then rolled out to the kitchen and looked in the refrigerator. There wasn't much there—no bodies, thankfully—but what I did see looked revolting.

I returned to the darkened living room and carefully opened the blinds. Daylight. Another day, which I couldn't face. A glance at my phone told me I had received a text message. I thought about more wine, but I figured I might as well look at the text.

It was from James and had been sent last night. My hand tightened around the phone as I read the message's five words, which made no sense to me: "Pen, please hear her out."

Hear who out? What the hell was this? After all James and I had been through yesterday, he was sending me mysterious, cryptic messages? I tossed the phone onto an end table.

I'd been at rock bottom before. Four years ago. I'd woken up in a hospital bed after a car accident and learned that I would never walk again. It wasn't until two days later, after my increasingly urgent inquiries, that they'd told me the fate of my six-year-old niece, who had been with me in the car I'd been driving. She had been killed. Within months, my fiancé and my employer had both dumped me.

That was pretty low.

And now I was testing the bottom again.

I decided against resuming my appointment with the wine bottle just yet, forcing down some coffee and Advil instead. Then I went back to the bedroom, cleaned myself up, and got dressed, mostly just for something to do. My morning routine was a pain, but after four years as a paraplegic, I was used to it, and I was learning to value the familiar. In due course, I returned to the living room and faced the emptiness.

Disabled, broken-hearted, unemployed . . . was I missing anything? It didn't matter. I had more than enough material for a massive pity party. And I now faced a day of pain a lot worse than the headache had been. At least, I did until somebody knocked at the door.

I figured it must be either my landlady, Eleanor, or Publishers Clearing House with a check for $10 million. Either way, worth answering. I glanced through the peephole I'd had installed at my eye level. The person outside was not Elvis or the Queen of England, but someone whose presence was even more improbable. I opened my door to Anita Smith Woodruff, ex-wife of James Carter, with two thoughts:

What the hell . . .? Why . . .? and

Please hear her out.

She walked in, a trim, elegant figure, fashionably dressed, with smooth mocha skin. She and James mostly got along now, with James living half a continent away, although he had never backed off his description of his ex as "a pit bull." I had met her just once, during a handoff of James's and Anita's daughter, Alicia, who was now fourteen. Now we just looked at each other for a long moment before I had the presence of mind to ask her to sit down. I realized as she took a chair that the apartment was a mess. And I, of course, looked like complete hell.

"Hi," she said, studying me, giving no hint of what had brought her to LA from her home in Minnesota.

I nodded.

"I was sorry to hear about you and James. I hope you'll be able to put it back together."

I didn't say anything.

"It's just a separation, right?"

"Right."

"Alicia was really upset." I had grown close to Alicia, who lived with Anita and her current husband, Andre, in a Minneapolis suburb.

She continued to study me. *Hear her out.*

"You don't know, do you?" she said.

"Know what?"

"I didn't think so. I guess maybe you've been . . . upset."

"Yeah."

She took a breath. "My husband, Andre, is in jail for murder."

For the first time, I felt fully awake. "*What*?"

She forced the weakest of smiles. "I guess I'm bad luck."

I stared at her, dumbfounded. Earlier in the year, James had also been accused of murder here in California. I had helped to clear him.

"A pretty nasty coincidence," I said. "What happened?"

"The man he's accused of murdering was his boss, the CEO of his company. His name was Blake Lofton."

The name sounded vaguely familiar, I thought.

"It's kind of complicated," Anita added. "Blake was also his brother-in-law. He was married to Andre's sister, Simone."

"Okay."

"And there's a further complication. Blake Lofton was a nominee for governor of Minnesota."

"Holy—" I cut the thought short. "How strong is the case against Andre?"

"Very strong, unfortunately. Blake was stabbed in his home, probably by someone he knew." She left it at that.

"How is Alicia doing?"

She sighed. "About like last time. It doesn't get any easier."

Alicia had taken it very hard when James had been accused. "Is he going to make bail?" I asked.

"Yes. He'll be out today. In the meantime, I've hired the best criminal defense attorney in Minnesota. His name is Lars Hankinson."

I'd definitely heard that name. Hankinson was a colorful figure with a flair for publicity and courtroom theatrics. His nickname was "Mr. Scorched Earth." I decided it was time to get to the point. "James said I should 'hear you out.' What do you want to tell me?"

"I'd like to hire you."

"To do what?"

"To be one of Andre's defense attorneys. But you'd have only one function: to investigate the murder. To find out who killed Blake."

"I . . ." I paused to collect my thoughts. The idea was ridiculous on so many levels, I didn't know where to begin.

Hear her out.

"The police—" I began.

"The police are done investigating. They think they have their man."

"But Hankinson . . ."

"Uses investigators sometimes. Does some fact-finding. But he is wary of too much investigating, especially if the facts might conflict with the story he wants to spin. I want you working directly for me, to learn the truth."

"Why would Hankinson agree to that?"

"He bitched and moaned about it, but I'm not giving him a choice, and he won't pass up the chance to handle a juicy case like this one. He'll be in charge of the actual defense. You'll investigate for me. You won't have to work with him at all. Just stop in and touch base with him first."

So she had already talked to him about me. She'd prepared an answer to every objection, except the biggest one of all. "Anita," I said, "I'm flattered that you think I could help, and that you flew halfway across the country to ask me, but I'm not an investigator. And I've never worked in homicide, or even in criminal defense. You need to hire a pro."

"You have a talent for uncovering the facts. From everything I've heard, you're resourceful and dogged. But the main thing is, we don't have to worry about your loyalties or priorities. You'll be working for us, and you want to help Alicia, just as we do." She was being unfair, using my fondness for Alicia to soften my objections. And she was catching me off guard; I was exhausted, emotionally spent, and unable to think of a good response to her well-prepared arguments.

I may have been distraught, but I wasn't an idiot. Anita was looking for more than competence; she was looking for control. She thought, or at least hoped, that anything damaging I might learn could be buried under layers of personal loyalty and attorney confidentiality.

"What does James think?" I asked.

Her voice softened. "He still loves you, Pen. He wants what's best for Alicia. But he wants what's best for you, too."

I stifled a sob. "I'm not in great shape, Anita."

"You'll be okay. And we need you."

"I'd have to think about it."

She stood up. "We need you," she repeated. "Don't think too long."

She left, and the apartment was silent. I had no doubt that James still loved me. But it was tough love. Really, really tough. He had encouraged his ex-wife to recruit me for a project that had all the makings of a fiasco. But he knew I needed to be working, not wallowing in self-pity. And, not coincidentally, he was trying to prove a point by involving me in exactly the kind of undertaking that had caused so much conflict between us.

Were there times when I was tempted by the prospect of cozy domesticity? Just the two of us, safe, secure, and happy? Of course there were. It exasperated and mystified James, as well as my two closest friends, Pam and Cassandra, that I had rejected that scenario. Steering Anita to me wasn't revenge on James's part, exactly, but I could well imagine his thought process. *You want interesting, honey? You want to help people who really, really need help? Well, here you go.* I could visualize his smile. But it was his knowing smile. A loving smile. I felt a crying jag coming on and quickly stifled it.

It shouldn't have been like this. And yet it had to be. And that our decision to separate was truly mutual mattered not at all. James and I had come together as wounded people, and we had healed together. But the healing process had worked too well. We had become, or were now revealed as, different people. Now relatively whole and healthy, we wanted different things, and envisioned different futures, than had the broken souls who'd encountered each other nearly two years ago. And now we were both headed back down toward broken.

James had let me go, sent me on my way, acknowledging that the life he had imagined for us was never going to happen. But, at age thirty-seven, I'd seen a lot. I had survived. And I could do it again. I couldn't give up my independence. I couldn't be reined in, constrained from doing what I needed to do.

And what, exactly, *was* I doing?

It's your life's work, asserted a voice from somewhere inside me.

Right, my conscious, rational self replied. *Sounds like a hell of a job.* What that job was, I couldn't describe exactly. It didn't have a title, or an office, or a dental plan. It was risky, messy, and occasionally even dangerous. All I could say was that I felt compelled, and at least somewhat qualified, to help people in sticky, high-stakes situations who needed to learn the truth. It was important work.

And terrifying.

I needed to do the Andre Woodruff job for myself, it was true. I needed to get on with life. And I found it hard to resist a challenge, or to ignore a mystery. But most of all, I needed to do it for a young girl whose stepfather faced life in prison, a girl who'd been through too much already.

Chapter 3

Minneapolis-St. Paul, MN

Brilliant bands of October were draped across the Mississippi River valley as my plane descended toward the Twin Cities airport. My stomach gave a lurch as we touched down, giving me a sharp, grounded reminder that the party was over. My grieving process—and my vacation from reality—had been brief and unsatisfying, thanks largely to the efforts of James Carter.

I gathered up my belongings as the other passengers filed past me to the jetway. For better or worse, here I was, chasing halfway across the country to try to prove the innocence of a man I had never met. The venture sounded dubious enough. But if I'd had even the slightest idea just how risky and complicated it would prove to be, I would have tossed my Life's Work into the dumper, gotten back onto the plane, and gone home to resume the pity party.

I proceeded through the terminal and rolled out into the pickup area, breathing in the chilly vehicle exhaust until my rented handicapped van appeared. It was similar to my own vehicle, except that I needed to get out of my wheelchair and transfer to the driver's seat. My own van enabled me to simply roll up to the steering wheel and clamp the chair into place.

My first item of business was to check in with Lars Hankinson, Andre's attorney, who had a large reputation and an ego to match. According to Anita, he was unhappy about my involvement in the case, and not surprisingly, he hadn't returned my phone calls. He was a formidable man, potentially able to cause problems for me, so I'd decided to do as Anita had asked and reach out to him. As a maverick criminal defense attorney,

Hankinson didn't maintain his office in one of the swanky high-rises in the heart of the business district. His building, an older, two-story structure, was located on the southern edge of downtown Minneapolis, near St. Mary's Basilica. I found a handicapped parking spot, but then I had to take a side entrance and ride up half a floor in a creaky old elevator to reach Hankinson's office.

The door to the offices of N.L. Hankinson & Associates, LLC, was stubborn, taking me three tries to pull open and scoot through. The reception area was surprisingly spacious, apparently to accommodate two large vanity walls. A lot of the pictures were of Hankinson and people I didn't recognize—clients or local celebrities, I supposed—but there were a couple of vaguely familiar faces. A perky young receptionist told me Hankinson was with a client. I offered to set up an appointment and come back, but she encouraged me to wait. I sat for more than an hour, surfing idly on my phone.

The great man finally emerged, alone. If there had been a client with him, he or she had left by another exit. Hankinson was, if not larger than life, a large man, about six-foot-six, his height accentuated by cowboy boots and the vertical lines of his suspenders. He looked at me as if I were a long-lost daughter. "Well, well. It's the famous . . . Pen!" He held his arms out expansively, as if he was going to hug me, but fortunately he settled for pumping my hand and ushering me into his private office. The inner sanctum was a continuation of the reception area, with still more vanity-wall photos. I recognized several movie stars, a governor or two, and a vice president of the United States.

"Thank you for stopping by," the attorney said. "Can I get you anything?"

I didn't respond.

"No?" He walked around behind his enormous desk. "I can't tell you how excited I am to finally meet you, somebody with your *vast* experience and towering reputation."

So that's how it's going to be, I thought. Extreme sarcasm. He probably used the tactic in court to destroy prosecution witnesses.

"Now, I have to apologize," he continued. "I've been calling you Pen, but I just learned that your correct name is Doris. And with your devotion to the facts, that must bother you a lot."

Again, I didn't respond, even though I disliked my given name and had gone by Pen since childhood.

He sat down behind his desk. "So, Doris, I have to admire the way you avoided any conflict of interest in this case by resigning your job as a prosecutor. Now, I know some reports indicate that the US Attorney's office out there on the coast let you go, but I don't believe that for an instant. All these people saying you're a showboat and a publicity hound—outrageous. Frankly, it takes a lot of gall for people to criticize you, Doris, after all you've been through."

So he'd been ticked off enough to make some calls to check me out.

"That accident in Florida, for example, the one where your niece was killed. A lot of people might conclude that you were negligent—in effect, that you killed her. Of course, no charges were filed, so I suppose people just say that you skated somehow." He shook his head. "The things people say. So unfair."

"Could we talk about the Andre Woodruff case?"

He nodded somberly. "Of course. That's why you're here, after all. I'll tell you, I've just been at a loss as to how to handle this one. I'm really relieved to have you here—I know you'll get to the bottom of this. Now, I think—"

I turned and headed for the door.

"Leaving already? I really need your input."

I didn't look back. He caught up to me at the creaky old elevator in the hallway and stepped in front of me as I approached the elevator door. I absolutely, totally hate it when someone intentionally blocks my path. I looked up at him.

"I'll only say this once," he said, his tone now deadly serious. "This is my case. And it's a hell of a case. You do anything to fuck it up—*anything*—and I'll make your life a living hell. Guaranteed."

I guess I was supposed to cry or wilt or flee, and yesterday I might have done all three. But somehow, amazingly, I was back in the saddle now, doing what I do. And that included dealing with assholes. I smiled. "Sure, Lars. And you can take your sarcastic bullshit and blow it out your ass."

His expression showed momentary shock, which quickly morphed into disgust. "Just get the hell out of here." He walked away.

As a litigator, I was a little disappointed to be watching a big, challenging trial from the sidelines. But what Hankinson did—tell tales, push conspiracy theories, and put prosecution witnesses through undeserved hell—bore little resemblance to the kind of law I wanted to practice. I was fine with sitting this trial out.

But I'd do my damndest to make sure the trial didn't happen.

Chapter 4

The next governor of Minnesota got up from his desk and looked around his spacious office. Tony McCort's domain was lined, floor to ceiling, with hundreds of books. They were the instruments of his rise in the world, compensating for the high school education he had barely finished and the college education he'd never had at all. At forty-eight, he was a wealthy man, but unlike his now-deceased gubernatorial opponent, Blake Lofton, McCort had built his fortune from scratch. He had grown up poor in north Minneapolis, the son of an absent father and an alcoholic mother, and made his own way in the world. Surprisingly, he had made no effort to exploit his humble beginnings in his political campaign, even though his Horatio Alger success story contrasted nicely to his opponent's narrative. Harvard-educated Blake Lofton had inherited a large fortune, which included part ownership of his family's Fortune 500 company.

Self-reliance was more than a concept that explained McCort's inspiring personal story. It was his guiding principle, the bedrock of his political and moral philosophy. He had lifted himself out of poverty. If he had done it, so could anyone. So *should* everyone. It took character, courage and hard work. If people didn't have those virtues, they deserved to be poor. McCort was only weeks away from implementing his own vision for the state, to transform it into a place where independence and personal responsibility ruled. Those who didn't share that vision, especially those who preferred to be dependent, who felt they had a claim on their fellow citizens, would no longer be enabled by the state. They would be encouraged to leave the state.

Above all, McCort believed in action. The Blake Loftons of the world could afford to sit back and wait for success to come to them. Not Tony McCort. He believed in action that was direct, forceful, and unrestrained. Nietzsche's will to power. Rules, niceties, traditions — those, too, were luxuries reserved for the Loftons and their like. McCort simply did what was necessary to further his own interests.

Always.

He walked out from behind his desk, left his office, and walked down the hallway. As CEO and majority owner of Together Fitness, a nationwide chain of workout and tennis centers, he was an enthusiastic and conscientious user of his own facilities, with a chiseled physique and an easy gait. He had been up since 4:30 AM and by nine in the morning had already put in half a day's work in the office, in addition to a vigorous workout. He was spending more time on political matters than business now. The murder of his opponent in the upcoming election had been a gift, likely to hand him the governorship. But he couldn't forget about the hidden trap, the potential pitfall that could derail everything.

Halfway down a long hallway, he punched in the code on a numeric keypad next to an unmarked door and walked through. Inside, a staff of half a dozen people worked at computer terminals. Television screens tuned to news channels hung from the ceiling. This room housed the intel center, an operation that reported to McCort personally, and the existence of which no manager, director, shareholder, regulator, or campaign staffer was aware.

He stood for a long moment, surveying the operation. All of McCort's reading over the years had taught him that information was power. Not just management information, or market information, or financial information. All that was critical, of course, but it was his determination to go beyond these standard categories—far beyond—that set McCort apart from his competitors, that put him on a different plane.

The intel center closely monitored the world, national, and local news, a summary of which was sent to his iPad every morning. But the intel operation monitored more than just the news. It monitored people. People who might be helpful, but mostly people who might stand in the way of McCort's reaching his goals. These subjects included politicians, donors, regulators, competitors, investors, and bankers. The intel center monitored people in a different way, going far beyond information that was in the public domain. Four of its employees were experienced hackers, who regularly reviewed internal files, travel reservations, surveillance footage, and confidential emails. Nor was monitoring confined to cyberspace. The center's manager, Ivan Bolger, and another operative, a woman, regularly conducted physical surveillance and in-person interviews to gather information on its subjects. If McCort believed in unrestrained action when necessary, he felt that way about information-gathering in particular. And, as always, he'd acted on his belief.

*   *   *

Ivan Bolger looked up as Tony McCort appeared at the door of his glass-walled office in the intel center. His boss was a tanned, muscular figure of medium height with a thick head of silver hair. Bolger himself was about the same height but stocky, with slightly crooked teeth and thinning hair.

Bolger and McCort had become so tight, and spent so much time together, that there were even some whispers about the relationship between these two single men. The rumors were false. Bolger, who had been married and divorced twice, was more than content with the single life. And McCort, Bolger knew, had a healthy interest in the opposite sex, but had never married.

Bolger suspected that while his boss valued his independence, there was another reason he had remained unattached, a reason that must go back a long time.

Bolger had come to work for McCort after twenty years with the New York police department, much of it spent in the intelligence division. He had quickly come to enjoy working with Tony and especially appreciated the lack of rules, bureaucracy, traditions, and other restraints, all of which had served as roadblocks to doing his job at NYPD. Tony McCort was the most strong-willed person Bolger had ever known. He had decided he wanted to be rich, and he had simply gone out and done it. One day he had determined that he should be governor of Minnesota. He would accomplish that, too.

But politics, unfortunately, required public approval to achieve success. That was a difficult change for McCort, who prided himself on not caring what people thought. For Bolger, the challenge was to manage the outward stream of information, limiting the flow to items that would enhance public approval. In this campaign, there existed a single, explosive item of information that had thus far resisted management. Bolger wouldn't rest until it he had brought it under his control.

McCort entered the office, shut the door, and remained standing. "Anything on Andre?" he asked.

"He's out of jail, but on monitoring," Bolger replied.

"Are the cops looking for anybody else?"

"Not really. More to the point, they're not looking at us. Unless something else happens to stir things up, we should be in the clear."

McCort sat down. "Everything could still blow up."

"Especially if Andre knows something about you."

"He doesn't, not for sure. He wouldn't be able to prove anything. But even if he knew—well, it doesn't have anything to do with his defense. He's sure as hell not thinking about the election when he's got a murder rap hanging over his head."

Bolger nodded.

"Speaking of the election, has Barb sent those new poll numbers over from the campaign office yet?"

"No, she says they won't be available until this afternoon."

McCort's face assumed a completely blank expression, which meant he was pissed as hell. "Stay handy. We'll need to look at those numbers."

"Right. By the way, another attorney has filed to represent Andre."

"To work with Hankinson?"

"We don't know. Her name is Pen Wilkinson. She was involved in the North Central Bank scandal a couple of years ago."

"The James Carter thing?"

"Correct. After that, she moved out to LA and worked as a federal prosecutor. She's the one who nailed Larry Shields."

McCort lifted his eyebrows. "Taking down a crooked congressman—that was her? A busy lady."

"And then," Bolger continued, "she was involved in that incident on the Hennepin Avenue Bridge last summer."

"*That's* where I've heard the name. The chick in the wheelchair, right?"

"That's her."

"So what is she doing on the Andre Woodruff case?"

Bolger hesitated before giving the answer an intel man dreaded having to give. "I don't know."

Once again, the blank expression.

Bolger went on: "I confirmed that Anita Woodruff flew to LA four days ago, then came right back. She probably recruited Wilkinson on the trip—her boyfriend is Anita's ex-husband. I wouldn't think she'll be actively involved in the defense. Hankinson wouldn't share the limelight with anybody."

"Then why is she here?"

"Hankinson already has a couple of junior associates in his law office, so I don't think she'll be assisting at trial. Maybe she'll be investigating."

McCort nodded slowly. "That's possible. And if she is, maybe we can use her to find what we're looking for."

On the other hand, Bolger thought, maybe she'll find what we *don't* want found.

Chapter 5

After meeting with Lars Hankinson, I figured the next logical step would be to confer with my client. I had never met Andre Woodruff, but James's less-than-objective comments about him were, predictably, unflattering. Two years ago, during a tense period when we had feared for Alicia's safety, James had assured me that Andre's personality alone would be unpleasant enough to drive away a hired killer.

I'm pretty sure he was kidding.

After meeting with Anita, I had gotten curious and Googled her current husband, discovering that Andre and James had more in common than I'd realized. Besides having married the same woman, both had enjoyed great success in the corporate world. At the same time James had served as a top executive in the banking industry, Andre had been climbing the corporate ladder, finally becoming CFO at AgriMinn, the Minneapolis-based agribusiness conglomerate owned by his brother-in-law, Blake Lofton, and the Lofton family. James and Andre had been two of the nation's highest-ranking African-American business executives.

Andre, now forty-eight, had grown up in north Minneapolis, the son of Carl Woodruff, a prominent minister and civil rights leader. Carl had been shot and killed more than thirty years ago by a police officer during a routine traffic stop. The policeman who shot Carl said he thought the minister had a gun. He didn't, and the killing had set off a wave of protests by the minority community in Minnesota. Young Andre, eighteen at the time, had been in the car and had witnessed the horrific scene.

Andre's mother had died when he was twelve, leaving an older brother, Isaac, and a younger sister, Simone, as well as Andre. He had married video and television producer Anita Smith Carter, four years younger, eight years ago, not long after she and James Carter had divorced.

Anita and Andre Woodruff lived to the west of the city on the southeast shore of Lake Minnetonka, a huge lake lined by enclaves of serious wealth. I drove west on Interstate 394 and Highway 7, then along winding, wooded roads resplendent with fall color, through the small, exclusive suburb of Deephaven. There was no problem identifying the Woodruff residence; two television trucks were parked on the road outside. The vehicles' occupants looked up with interest as I drove up to the gate. I lowered my window, ignored the reporters' shouted questions, and pressed the button outside the gate.

"Yes?" a male voice answered.

"It's Pen."

"Come in and park over on the right side."

The gate slid open, and I pulled ahead into a paved courtyard. The main house, a large, Prairie-style structure of wood, stone, and glass, was straight ahead of me. To the right, flanking a screen of shrubbery, was a parking area and a path leading to a small guest house, similar in style to the main structure. After parking, I transferred to my chair, opened the door, extended the ramp, and rolled out.

Andre came out through a side door of the main house to meet me. He was tall—about six-foot-two—and had maintained the slender build of the state tennis champion he'd been in high school. He wore his hair closely cropped and looked scholarly, with black-framed glasses and a graying goatee. "You shouldn't have come," he said without preamble.

"Look, Andre—"

"You're here, so come in, I guess."

24

I gestured back toward the road. "Are those media types ever going to go away?"

"Oh, sure. In a couple of days, I'll be yesterday's news and they'll move on to the next murder or riot." He gazed out at the road, hands in pockets. "Anita says she feels uneasy about all the publicity and all these people around—wants to put in a surveillance camera out here. I told her to forget about it. Who's going to sit and monitor the screen? I sure as hell don't want to look at these people. We've got a good security system for the house, and of course we've got the fence and gate." I glanced at the simple wrought-iron fence, which didn't look as though it would be very tough to scale.

"How is Alicia holding up?" I asked.

He held his palm out flat in a so-so gesture. "It's wearing on her, I think. I hope you'll have time to talk to her tonight."

"Of course. How are *you* doing?"

He gave me a sour look. "I'm having more fun than should be legal. Fortunately, I'm not on house arrest. But I am on monitoring, and I've got to be back here by nine every night." He lifted his pant leg, revealing a monitoring bracelet. "And a surveillance cam is sort of what got me into trouble in the first place. I'll explain that later. Anita invited you to stay with us?"

Anita had extended the invitation to me in an email, offering me the use of the guest house on their property. I had accepted. Although James owned a condo downtown that I'd used on previous visits, and I had a key and figured I was probably still welcome to use it, I couldn't bring myself to stay there now.

"Yes, if it still works for you, I'll be staying here, thanks."

He paused and then shrugged. "Come on in. I'll have your things taken inside." I followed him back to the side door, which, to my pleasant surprise, was equipped with a ramp. We proceeded into the house, and Andre led me down a short hall-

way to a great room that overlooked the lake. The room featured a massive fireplace, North Woods decor, and huge picture
windows. I declined Andre's offer of refreshments, and he sat
down.

"So," he said, "Anita tells me you're going to figure out who
killed Blake." His tone wasn't scornful or even skeptical, but
somehow still expressed how preposterous the thought was.
Maybe no inflection was needed; the idea was just ridiculous on
its face.

"I think she's oversold me a bit, Andre. I just agreed to do
some digging. Maybe I could develop some leads that might
help the police or Hankinson."

His tired, skeptical look told me what he thought about the
police or his attorney following up new avenues of investigation. "Based on what I've heard about you, I can't expect you to
listen to this, but I feel obligated to tell you anyway. You should
walk away from this case, right now. I can't claim to know how
it's going to turn out, but it won't end cleanly. Even if I'm acquitted, I will be soiled by the process. So will everyone associ-
ated with the proceedings. There's no shame in deciding you'd
rather not be a part of it."

I thought I understood what he was saying. The bad things
he warned against were a feature of almost every murder case.
"I'll stay," I said.

His nod was slow and weary.

"Maybe you could just give me a little background on the
players," I said, opening up the note-taking app on my phone.

He leaned back in his chair and crossed his legs. "Blake
Lofton and I were high school friends. We both went to the
Talmadge School in Minneapolis. He and I were doubles part-
ners on the tennis team, and we won a state championship. We
were an odd couple, of course. He was rich and I wasn't. He
was white and I wasn't. My sister and I were two of only four
black students at Talmadge. To most kids, we were probably

curiosities. Maybe they thought it was trendy to hang out with us."

"What happened after high school?"

"Blake went off to Harvard. I went to Macalester, over in St. Paul. We stayed friends, and of course we became even closer when he married my sister, Simone. Each of us got an MBA. After that, Blake worked for the family business, and I took a job with a big retailer. About ten years out of college, he invited me to come over and work for him at AgriMinn. It was a good offer, and I took it. He made his way up to CEO, and I went along for the ride."

"He made you his chief financial officer," I said. "How did the two of you get along?"

He stared out at the lake for a moment before answering. "We got along well. We were friends. But I had to understand and accept that he was the boss and that I served him."

"You couldn't challenge him or criticize him?"

"Sure I could. In fact, he expected me to. He had a very strong ego and insisted on hearing the bad news. But it was always understood that I was never to engage in any self-promotion, or to expect to advance beyond where he wanted me. For the most part, I was fine with that. But . . ."

I waited.

"When Blake resigned earlier this year to run for governor, I saw myself as his logical successor. So did most people. But he gave the job to a guy from outside the company, from Cargill."

"Why did he do that?"

"Two reasons. First of all, Blake had everybody slotted. Everybody in their place. He had me slotted as a number-two guy."

"What's the other reason?"

"He expected me to stay on as CFO, to be his eyes and ears, to help the new guy, and to make sure everything was run the way he wanted."

"Why wouldn't he just give you the job?"

"I know it's hard to understand. But like I said, Blake had a category for everybody, and his opinions hardly ever changed."

"We need to talk about the murder," I said. "What happened the night Lofton was killed?"

He looked me squarely in the eye. "Are you sure you really want to know the truth?"

"Hankinson didn't?" I guessed.

Andre shrugged. "When he came to see me in jail, he told me to think hard about my version of events, and that he'd come back the next day to hear my story. Draw your own conclusion."

I wasn't surprised. If a client was guilty, most criminal defense attorneys didn't want to know it—too many potential ethical problems. They would rather work with the lie. Anita understood; she wanted to get Andre acquitted and to know what happened. The goals weren't always identical, and she'd hired two different people to pursue them.

"I want the truth," I said.

Chapter 6

One week earlier

The next governor of Minnesota exhaled and tightened the sash of his bathrobe. It was, as always, hard to get good help, and for Blake Lofton, heir, CEO, and future governor, the help included just about everybody, including family members. There was an order to the universe. Everybody had to understand that, or nothing worked. People needed to occupy their space, understand their place, play their role in the scheme of things. Nearly all the world's—and more to the point, his— problems and annoyances arose from people who couldn't or wouldn't assume their role.

Lofton left his bedroom and trudged down the stairs. He wasn't actually governor yet. There would be an election in another month. But that was a formality as far as he was concerned. To serve as governor—well, that was his function. Some people might envy him and his life: his wealth, his successful career, his beautiful wife and children, and now, his political success. These people didn't understand that it was simply the role he had been placed in, and it was often a burden.

Others' lives revolved around his, which meant he had to be involved with them. Which was why he was now getting up in the middle of the night to deal with yet another person's need for stroking, hand-holding, butt-kicking, or whatever. It wasn't the first time for this person, and it wouldn't be the last. Yes, good help was hard to find.

Lofton admitted his visitor, and they went to the living room, where the supplicant paced the room. "We need to talk."

Lofton sank heavily into a leather chair. "No, we don't need to talk. You need to be an adult. You need to get over it."

"Get *over* it?" The response was shrill and indignant. "You're delusional, Blake."

The confrontation that followed was protracted and unexpectedly stormy. Lofton never would have expected such discontent, such disharmony, such displacement. If this person's function, at this point in time, was to serve the next governor of Minnesota in the expected capacity, what was so hard to understand about that?

At length the argument subsided, and Lofton suggested a drink. His companion grudgingly agreed but didn't sit down. Lofton walked toward the drink cabinet in the corner of the room. Why did he have to deal with this clueless person's petty complaints? And why was he now about to take on the neediness and cluelessness of an entire state? It would be tonight's grievances times five million, for all of Minnesota's inhabitants.

He sighed. It was his role.

He fixed his own drink first. Still facing the wall, he said, "I never expected a stab in the back from you."

"I'm sure you didn't," said the voice from directly behind him. And with that, the knife entered Lofton's spine. Lofton sank to his knees in unimaginable agony. Then the knife ripped into him again. And again, severing nerves, slicing through bone and flesh and arteries.

And upending all order in the universe.

Chapter 7

"The police figure that's how it happened," Andre said. "Blake let somebody in late at night and he was stabbed in the back, so it was almost certainly somebody he knew."

"So where were you that night?" I asked.

Andre stood up and walked slowly across the room. "Blake and I had been going back and forth about the CEO job ever since he was nominated for governor in August. The new CEO started September first. It wasn't much of a discussion; Blake pretty much brushed off my complaints and assumed things would go on as he'd planned. I told him I was going to leave AgriMinn and move on. He said it was 'out of the question.'"

"Sounds like a man used to getting his way."

"You think? Anyway, I'd had enough. On the night he was killed, I was at home, and yes, I'd had a couple of drinks. I decided to resolve this thing once and for all. I went over to his house."

"Where's that?"

"He has a mansion on the lake a few miles from here, in Wayzata. But like me, he has a place in the city, too. I had a plain-Jane condo a couple of blocks from AgriMinn headquarters downtown. The company provided it. But the Loftons have a big house in the city. It's in the Kenwood neighborhood, a couple of miles from downtown. It's been in Blake's family since— I don't know, statehood or whatever. Anyway, I went over there at about 11:30 and woke him up."

"Was he there alone?"

"Yes. Simone stayed out at the lake that night. I got Blake out of bed, and when he came down to let me in, I told him off. I said I was fed up, that I'd deserved the CEO job, and I was leaving the company. He started with his usual condescension— told me I just needed to cool down and pointed out that I'd been drinking, which was true. But I wasn't having any of it. I told him he could take his CFO job and shove it, and I was gone, effective immediately. He called me ungrateful, and that's when I lost it. I hit him. And he hit me back. Then we both sort of lost our anger and had a drink."

"So how did you resolve things?" I asked.

Andre paused, arms folded, and leaned against the wall by the fireplace. "We didn't. He wanted to get Simone involved to mediate between us, but I didn't want to drag her into it. We just grudgingly agreed we'd meet the following day. We didn't make up or shake hands or anything. I just finished my drink and left. Look, this whole incident was as notable for its unlikeliness as it was for its stupidity. I just don't *do* shit like this. I'm the steady, cautious one. Blake paid me well for a lot of years to put out fires and calm things down. It was embarrassing as hell."

"What happened next?"

"I stayed in the city that night, and early the next morning the police rousted me and took me down for questioning. That's when I learned Blake had been murdered. They arrested me on the spot."

"What did they have?"

He resumed pacing in front of the picture window. "What didn't they have? They found Blake in the living room where we'd met, stabbed in the back. They found no signs of forced entry, which means the killer was probably somebody he knew. They found signs of our altercation. They found my fingerprints and DNA all over the place. They even found some of my blood—Blake had managed to land a punch to my nose. But worst of all, they found security camera footage of me arriving at the front door a little after midnight and leaving about forty minutes later. You see? I told you a security camera got me into trouble. The housekeeper, Bonnie, found him at eight the next morning."

"Wouldn't they have had footage of a second person? The actual killer?"

Andre shook his head. "They don't. Which means the killer had to have come in through the back door, where there's no camera."

"Why isn't there a camera?"

"I honestly don't know, although Blake always resisted security measures. You'd tell him to hire six security people for a rally, and he'd cut it back to three. Too late to ask him now."

I studied him for a full minute. Was he telling the truth? Experienced observers looked for "tells"—body language, speech patterns, mannerisms, and so on—that indicated lying. I'd had a bit of experience, and I didn't sense any deception from Andre. But even for an expert using the latest techniques, lie detection was more an art than a science. And now the reality was setting in: the case against Andre Woodruff was devastating, nearly airtight. I could see why Lars Hankinson might not believe his own client.

I wasn't sure I did, either.

"I know how it looks," Andre said, pacing some more. "But I'm innocent."

"So who killed him?"

He stopped pacing, put his hands in his pockets, and blew out a long sigh. "I've thought a lot about it, of course. And you know what? I don't have a clue. Blake was a pain in the ass. But he tended to exasperate, not infuriate. He handled people well and had an appealing personality, which even included some ability to laugh at himself. It was hard to stay mad at him." He shook his head. "Even after the falling-out we had, I miss him. He was my closest friend."

"I'm sorry."

He walked over and sat down next to me. Outside, the fil-tered autumn sunlight was fading, and rogue leaves swirled down from massive oak trees. "Unfortunately," Andre said, "I know how this whole thing is going to play out."

"What do you mean?"

"We have racial problems, Pen."

"I breathe and watch the news at eleven, Andre. You want to shock me with something else?"

"In the past year there have been three police shootings of unarmed black men here in Minnesota. Two were killed. One survived. Whose side are you on?"

"Whose . . . *side*?"

"Were the police at fault?"

"How would I know? Only the legal system could decide that."

He shook his head at my naiveté. "Come on, everybody's got an opinion. They conduct public opinion polls about these cases all the time. Every jerk on a barstool is sure who's at fault."

"I don't know, Andre. Can't we just talk about your case?"

"We are."

"You're black and Lofton was white. That doesn't seem to have much relevance that I can see."

"Then you're not thinking hard enough, Pen. Look, that's all I'm going to say about it."

I decided to leave it at that, but he'd piqued my curiosity. "Just one more question: Could this murder have been political somehow?"

"I doubt it. It's true that Blake was probably going to win, and that the lady replacing him on the ticket is a weaker candi-date. But his opponent, a guy named Tony McCort—I can't see it. He's a very aggressive and competitive person, but . . ." He shrugged.

"Thanks, Andre. I have to get going."

"Where to?"

"I'm meeting with Simone."

His features softened at the mention of his sister. "Thank God for her. I know she's got my back."

"How did she and Lofton get along?"

"Their marriage was okay. I wouldn't say they were an unusually close couple, and of course Blake could be difficult. But she was a devoted wife, and—well, you'll see when you meet her. She takes everything in stride. Now she has to cope with being a widow."

I thanked him and left.

The television trucks were still in place, ready to film me as I left. I stared straight ahead as I drove past them.

My phone rang, and I clicked on the speaker; it was Anita.

"Just checking in," she said. "Did you see Hankinson?"

"Yes."

"He was supposed to give you some information. Did he?"

"No."

A pause. "Sorry about that. I'll take care of it." We chatted for another minute and agreed to meet back at the house that night.

I thought about Andre, who hadn't been a terribly friendly person, but was, unsurprisingly, hardly the ogre James had made him out to be. Though dubious about my purpose here, he had answered all my questions. I hoped he had answered them truthfully.

Chapter 8

Following my phone's GPS directions, I drove north around the lake toward Wayzata. I noticed a gray Audi SUV behind me for about two miles, through several turns, but then it disappeared. I wasn't concerned; Audi SUVs were probably the official vehicle of Lake Minnetonka. I was in a seriously wealthy area, where the residents had names like Dayton and Pillsbury, families that sometimes supplied governors to the state of Minnesota.

Simone Woodruff Lofton was, according to Google, two years younger than Andre. She had pursued her own career as an accountant and was now a senior partner with a large CPA firm in St. Paul. I had looked at a picture of her on her firm's website, and it had nearly taken my breath away. Even at forty-six, Simone was extraordinarily beautiful, with smooth, light brown skin and large, dramatic eyes. It was a natural, unaffected beauty, a face that projected warmth.

The Lofton estate—for that's what it was—was far more impressive than Andre and Anita's place. It was a massive Tudor-style house, flanked by spacious lawns and surrounded by forest. The front gate opened automatically, and I drove up a long driveway, pulling up in a circular cobblestone drive in front of the house. Simone was waiting for me as I came down the van's ramp, looking every bit as striking as she had in the online pictures I'd seen.

"Welcome," she said. "I'm Simone." She shook my hand in both of hers.

"Pen Wilkinson," I said. "I'm sorry for your loss."

"Thank you so much." She looked genuinely shaken and grief-stricken, even though Andre had said she and Blake hadn't been unusually close.

"Have you seen Alicia?" she asked.

"Not yet."

"She's told me about you. Come in."

I followed her a long way around the house to a delivery entrance, which was equipped with a ramp. We went through a kitchen bigger than my entire apartment, finally ending up in a library. With its light-colored woodwork and furniture, I suspected the room was Simone's domain. A large desk contained stacks of papers and files, along with a computer, signaling that this was a working office. Perched on one corner of the desk was a photograph of Blake Lofton, a classically handsome man with a full head of graying hair, an aristocratic nose, and a narrow mouth, with a smile that looked understated but genuine. He was flanked by Simone and two tall, handsome young men. Their sons.

"Your sons are a couple of good-looking guys," I commented.

She smiled. "Yes. I just wish they lived closer. They've already gone back to their lives on the coasts. Tyler works in software in the Seattle area, and Aidan is teaching in a poor neighborhood in Washington, DC."

"They don't work for AgriMinn?"

"Not yet. Of course, Blake fully expected them to return someday to take over the company. Maybe they will."

She took a side chair in front of a window with a lake view. "You just saw Andre?"

I nodded.

"How is he doing?"

"I don't know him, but he seemed very calm."

"He usually is. It's hard to tell when he's under stress. I know he's a little aloof and doesn't come off as a warm and fuzzy person, but believe me, he's not a killer." She shook her head. "This is all so unreal. The murder, and then Andre being charged. Either one would be hard to believe, but both . . ."

"Tell me about your husband," I said.

She collected herself. "He was an unusual man in some ways. He had narcissistic tendencies, but somehow he knew and even understood it. That isn't really supposed to be possible, I'm told. He wasn't thoughtful or considerate, but he was never cruel or abusive. He used people, but not for enjoyment or for the sake of using them. He simply assumed they were there to be used."

She leaned forward, elbows on knees. "And yet, people loved him. I loved him. I think it's because he was genuine. He never pretended to be anything other than what he was. He could make people laugh, and he at least acted as though he didn't take himself too seriously, even though he did. We have two wonderful sons. Now that they've moved on, I'm just rambling around in this huge house." She sat up. "I'm sorry—that sounds self-pitying, and there's no cause for it. I've had a good life."

There was always cause for self-pity, I thought. And it was never a good thing. Nobody knew it better than I did.

A uniformed maid appeared with tea, and I rolled over closer to the coffee table to accept my cup.

"I imagine you were questioned about the murder," I said when the maid had left.

"Oh, yes. The same officers who came to tell me Blake was dead began asking questions. Where I was that night? Were we getting along?"

"Were you?"

"Yes, we were, at least as well as we usually did. He was running for governor and things were hectic, but no more so than when he was a corporate CEO." She set her teacup down. "I won't try to mislead you, Pen. We weren't an exceptionally

close couple. We each pursued our own careers, and we regularly spent time apart. We were comfortable with that. It's no
secret that I wasn't thrilled about his going into politics."

"But you went along with it?"

"I did. I tried to see it as an opportunity to support issues
I'm passionate about, mostly women's issues. Trafficking and
abuse, chiefly. But I also saw it as a chance for racial healing.
We've had a black president, but seeing the governor of this
state, especially one from an old, wealthy family, with an inter-
racial marriage—I think that would have made a powerful
statement. And Minnesota could use some healing right now.
We've had several recent police shootings of young black men,
and things are very tense."

"Andre felt that somehow race will become an issue in his
case, too."

"Race is always an issue," she said, her voice and expression neutral. "That's just the way it is. Especially for Andre and
me. People are always asking us about it because of our father."

"He was a civil rights leader."

"And he was killed by the police—pulled over for having
a broken taillight. A classic pretextual stop. These issues won't
go away, Pen."

She was right, of course, but I still couldn't see what race had
to do with my job: to help find out who had killed Blake Lofton.

"Let's talk about the night of the murder," I said. "Where
were you that night?"

"Right here. But unfortunately, I can't prove that. My cell
phone was here, but I have no witnesses. No phone calls or electronic connections. None of our staff stays here overnight."

"How often did Blake spend the night in the city?"

"I'd say about third of the time. It went in stretches. One
advantage of his being governor is that we could have lived
in the governor's mansion in St. Paul. We could have been
together, and it's close to my office. Instead we've got this huge

place way out here and that big old house in the city. But they've both been in Blake's family for a long time."

"I'm told there was no sign of forced entry."

"That's correct. The odds are that Blake knew the killer and let him in."

"Presumably through the back door?"

"Correct. There's no camera there."

"Who knows that?"

"I don't know."

"Is there any other way into the house?"

"Just through the garage. I can't imagine how Blake could have let anybody in that way. You actually have to go through the basement to get there. And how would the person have gotten into the garage to begin with?" She paused. "Why don't you go down—say, day after tomorrow—and see the house with me? Just give me a call tomorrow to set it up."

"Sounds like a good idea," I said. I looked at my notes again. "The police have apparently let you off the hook. No offense, but why?"

"The spouse is usually the top suspect, of course, and they've investigated thoroughly. They've looked through our finances, our phone records. They've questioned our neighbors and friends. I suppose they'd still be on my case if the evidence against Andre wasn't so strong."

"One obvious suspect would be Blake's opponent in the race for governor."

"I'm sure they investigated Tony McCort thoroughly. It's my understanding that he has an alibi."

"Do you know him?" I asked.

"Yes, he actually grew up in our old neighborhood in north Minneapolis. Both Andre and I remember him."

"What did Blake think of him?"

"Blake obviously didn't grow up in our old neighborhood." She gave me a small smile; north Minneapolis was a largely black area with a high poverty rate. "Blake encountered Tony over the years, and they didn't seem to like each other very much. They were political opponents, from starkly different backgrounds, and they were both alpha males—very competitive."

I looked down at the list on my phone; I'd asked all my questions. "I appreciate your time," I said. "Who else should I be talking to?"

"You'll probably want to talk to some people Blake worked with. The two that come to mind are Ellie Ostlund, his campaign manager, and Lauren Jorgenson, his personal assistant, who now works full-time for the campaign."

"Thanks." I wrote down the names. "How about your other brother?"

Her face showed instant skepticism. "I doubt if Isaac would be able to help you. Andre and I have very little contact with him. He's gone his own way, and he's . . . had personal problems." I wanted to know more, but she obviously didn't want to talk about Isaac. I thanked her, and she saw me out.

As the ramp extended from my van, she hugged me. "Good luck," she said. "If there's anything—and I mean anything—I can do to help, please let me know. Do you think you'll be able to find out who killed Blake?"

"Yes," I answered without thinking. *Now why did I say that?* I wondered.

*   *   *

After Pen had left, Simone returned to the library and sat down. She hesitated, reaching twice for her phone but thinking better of it. Finally, she pulled it from her purse on the desk and punched in a number. Andre answered on the first ring.

"Yeah, Simone. Did you meet with Pen?"

"I did. She just left."

"How did it go?"

"She asked pretty standard questions for the most part. But then she started asking about Isaac."

"What did you tell her?"

"Just what we talked about, that we don't have much contact with him, that he's had personal problems, and so on."

"You think she bought it?"

Simone blew out a breath. "I don't know. She seemed pretty sharp."

"Yes. I think Anita was right about her. Look, it's possible she could talk to Isaac and not get into our . . . area of concern."

"Yes. But the fact is, we have no control. Isaac is a wild card. Should we try to talk to him and head this thing off?"

"We might make it worse," Andre said.

"We could throw some money his way."

"What if Pen throws more money? And it would be only a short-term fix. I don't know, Sim. If Isaac blows the whistle, he's implicating himself."

"Probably, but it's not much of a whistle for him. Not compared to you, anyway. I guess we just ride it out, deal with it if and when it happens."

Andre chuckled. "I knew you'd have a plan."

Chapter 9

I headed back to Anita and Andre's. Neither of them came out to greet me, but a friendly young maid named Cristina gave me a key to the guest house, where my bag had been brought in. A few minutes later, Cristina reappeared with a tray of food for me.

"Will you be needing anything?" she asked. "I don't stay over on weekends."

"Thanks. I'll be fine." As I situated myself in the small kitchen, I noticed a large envelope from Lars Hankinson's office, addressed to me, sitting on the table. Inside was a stack of papers—police reports, fingerprint and DNA results, and even a couple of photographs—relating to the Blake Lofton murder. Some of the items might have been obtained through the official discovery process from the county attorney's office, but others had to have come from unofficial sources. This was, it appeared, what Anita had expected Hankinson to give me. Maybe the attorney had gotten a sudden attack of cooperativeness. Or maybe Anita had torn him an auxiliary rectal cavity.

I looked through the information as I ate. What I saw contained little I hadn't already learned from Andre and Simone. Lofton had been stabbed six times in the back with a long-bladed knife and had died almost instantly. The murder weapon, likely a kitchen knife, was never found. Neighbors hadn't seen anyone going in or out of the Loftons' Minneapolis house that night except for Andre. The estimated time of death was consistent with the time of Andre's visit, and his arrival and departure had been captured by the front door surveillance camera.

The body had been found by a housekeeper named Bonnie, who had quickly been cleared. Extensive efforts had been made, without success, to establish an alibi for Simone, whose cell phone had been at her home all night. Authorities had made a thorough search of the Wayzata mansion, as well as the Lofton family vehicles, finding no physical evidence linked to the crime. Anita's alibi had been provided by a household staff member, along with cell phone location records and internet use. Lofton's top staff members had been interviewed, and two of them, Ellie Ostlund and Lauren Jorgenson, had been asked to account for their whereabouts. Ostlund couldn't provide confirmation that she'd been at home the entire night. Jorgensen, who for unexplained reasons had gone over to the house and seen the body the next morning, did. I made a note to check out the reason for her visit to the crime scene.

One interesting item was the summary of an interview with Tony McCort, Blake's opponent in the gubernatorial race. The police had confirmed from multiple sources that he'd been out of town, in Phoenix. Even more interesting was the interview with a guy named Ivan Bolger, who was identified as the director of security for McCort's company. When asked to provide an alibi, he claimed to have been at a regular poker game at the home of a police officer, who had been present along with three of his fellow officers. All confirmed Bolger's presence until approximately 3:30 AM. I made another note to find out why the police might have considered him a suspect.

I finished my dinner and the packet, returning the papers to the envelope. The police had thrown considerable resources into the investigation—not exactly a shock given the prominence of the victim. I knew I wouldn't get far retracing or second-guessing their work. I needed to explore other avenues—long shots, hunches, and people more weakly related to the crime.

I heard a knock on the front door. "Pen?" a young voice called out.

"Come in, Alicia." The now-tall fourteen-year-old walked in and had to really bend down to embrace me. We just hugged for a long time, and when she sat down across from me, her cheeks were wet.

"Thanks for coming," she said.

"How's it going?"

She forced a smile, showing big, beautiful teeth. She was growing into a lovely young woman, having exchanged her dreadlocks for shoulder-length hair. "I know the drill," she said.

I didn't know what to say. First her father, then her stepfather, accused of murder. How could anyone explain or understand that? "You got through it last time. You can do it again."

"Last time you helped figure out who the real killer was." She hastened to add, "I know that's not fair. That's a lot to expect from you."

"I'll try my best." We were silent for a while.

"I'm so sorry about you and Dad," she said at last. "So disappointed."

I steeled myself and then, working hard to keep my composure, described what had happened between James and me.

"He told me basically the same thing." She shook her head. "He loves you so much, Pen."

"So much that he doesn't want me to take risks."

She smiled through the tears. "You have trouble with that. There's still hope, isn't there, Pen? That you still might stay together?"

"Sure," I said, feeling guilty as hell for lying to her.

"And you and me . . ."

"BFFs. That will never change, Alicia." I gripped her hand tightly.

She came around and sat next to me. "I can't believe it only happened Friday night," she said. "Only a week ago. I was in bed—Mom lets me sleep in on Saturdays. Anyway, Cristina woke me up and said Mom was on her way downtown. She'd gotten a phone call from the family attorney, saying Blake was dead and Dad was in jail. She almost fainted. It was unbelievable. I almost fainted."

We talked for a few more minutes. Then she said goodnight and went back to the main house.

I looked at my watch; it was now a little after nine. It was time to make a call I'd been putting off. I pulled up the number on my phone. A female voice answered.

"Pen?"

"Hi, Lexi." I had met Lieutenant Lexi Candiotti of the Minneapolis Police Department earlier in the year, when she had helped me locate my missing nephew here. We had hit it off and stayed in touch.

"I'm in town," I said.

"Great. Let's get together."

"I'm afraid that's a problem." I explained why I was in Minnesota.

After a brief silence she said, "That makes it a little awkward."

"I'm working for the other side on this one." Lexi didn't work in Homicide, but she had to be careful about fraternizing with a defense attorney who was trying to prove the police wrong in an active case. She had once been the Minneapolis homicide commander but had been reassigned to a low-key position after being involved in the controversial shooting of a black teenager.

"It's really not an ethical concern," she said. "More like a political problem."

"I know. I shouldn't be working on it for long, and when I'm finished . . ."

"Give me a call." We disconnected. She didn't wish me good luck.

I then texted my nephew, Kenny Sellars, who was a student at the University of Minnesota. I told him I was in town and hoped to get together in the next few days. I put the phone away and looked at the blank TV screen and then down at my hands. They were shaking. I thought about James and tried to offset that by thinking about nothing. It didn't work. I felt panicky, my breathing shallow.

I went out to the little kitchen and found a bottle of wine in the refrigerator. Then I looked around for the wine glasses, spotting them on a shelf up too high for me to reach. At that moment, I was tempted to swig from the bottle. Instead, I found a glass in the bathroom. After gulping down a couple of glassfuls, I felt better. I knew I should sleep, but I didn't want to face the nightmares.

I got ready for bed and turned on the ten o'clock news. Within minutes, I began to see evidence of the charged racial climate Andre and Simone had warned me about. There had been a rally at the state capitol in St. Paul, protesting the recent shootings of young black men by the police. I turned up the sound.

One protester, a representative of the group Rights for People of Color (RPC), speaking through a bullhorn, denounced the murder of Blake Lofton. I was confused; I couldn't see what that had to do with police encounters with young black men. But both the speaker and the crowd sounded passionate about it.

"Not only has Blake Lofton, an advocate of police accountability, been brutally murdered," the speaker shouted, "but these same police have wrongfully arrested the son of *Carl Woodruff* for the crime! Have they no shame?"

In that instant, I began to see what I'd gotten myself into. In particular, I could see why it had felt so awkward talking to Lexi. The police had strong reasons to dislike Blake Lofton, who'd supported efforts to reform their department. But they were also trying to prove the guilt of Andre Woodruff, the black man who'd allegedly killed him. For the black community, it had to seem like a lose-lose proposition. On the screen, the camera shots became jerky as a tussle broke out between demonstrators and police. There was screaming, fighting, and general chaos. I shut the TV off and stared at the blank screen for a long time.

*   *   *

Ivan Bolger walked through the now-deserted offices of Together Fitness to the Intel center and let himself in. He nodded to a lone employee who sat in front of a screen, then walked through the darkened suite to where a shaft of light from an open door spilled out into the corridor. Tony McCort sat at a conference table inside the room.

Bolger entered and pressed two buttons on the wall. The door hissed shut, and a faint hum could be heard inside the windowless room, which had now been secured against any form of electronic penetration.

"Have you seen the polling numbers?" McCort asked.

Bolger sat down. "Yeah, I saw them. Too early to panic."

"No, it's not. We're going in the wrong direction." McCort stood up. "According to Barb, there's still no question we're facing a weaker candidate now, but we've lost ground because of sympathy for Lofton. Sympathy. For *Blake Lofton*." He shook his head. "Never saw that one coming."

"Just temporary," Bolger said. "We're still in the lead."

"We can't take that chance. We need to reassert control over the situation."

"The way we talked about?"

The next governor of Minnesota nodded. "Yes. It's what we need to rally our forces, energize our base, reassert control."

"Right," said Bolger. "We've been playing defense since the murder."

"Meanwhile, don't let up on Pen. She just might find what we're looking for."

"She's a cripple in a wheelchair, Tony. She doesn't live here. She's not even an investigator. What can she do that we can't?"

"She's a human being. We rely too much on technology. We need to get the answers from people, in person. Pen might be able to do that. And let's face it, your bedside manner is nothing to write home about."

Bolger managed a faint, crooked-toothed smile. "I'm hurt."

"Whoever has the package might not know they have it. That makes the information even more dangerous." He rose from the table. "Do it."

Chapter 10

At eight the next morning, I drove east on I-94 to St. Paul, reviewing in my head what I'd managed to learn about Eleanor "Ellie" Ostlund, Blake Lofton's campaign manager. A former state auditor and party chair, she had run for governor four years ago, losing in the primary to the current governor, who was stepping down. Earlier this year, she had run again, this time losing the party's nomination to Blake Lofton. But Lofton had persuaded her to run his general election campaign against Tony McCort, promising her a top job in his administration. Ostlund, forty-five and never married, had come from a family of modest means, the daughter of a warehouse worker and a homemaker. She had worked her way through college, eventually earning a PhD, and served on the faculty of a private college in Minneapolis. When party leaders convened later in the week, they were set to select her as their replacement candidate.

The Lofton/Ostlund campaign headquarters was located in a shabby building on University Avenue, about half a mile west of the state capitol. I found a handicapped spot on University as a light rail train zoomed by in the middle of the street. Inside, a tiny reception area was situated in front of a large, chaotic open area filled with people sitting at folding tables, working on computers and shouting on phones. After a ten-minute wait, I was directed to an enclosed office in the back of the open area.

I knocked, pushed the door open, and rolled into the office. An intense, rather plain-looking blonde woman stood next to a filing cabinet, reading a document. She wore a blue business pantsuit, her face framed by stylish glasses.

Ostlund looked up. "I don't have much time."

"As I explained on the phone, Ms. Ostlund, I'm working for Andre Woodruff's defense, and I have some questions."

"Okay." She stood there, waiting.

"I'll make it as quick as I can, but you might want to sit down."

Ostlund shrugged, walked behind a battered desk, and sat down. With exaggerated patience, she leaned forward, hands clasped on the desk. "You're from California?" she asked.

"Right. This is just a temporary job, working for Andre. I'm acquainted with his wife and stepdaughter. In fact, I'm staying with them."

"What do you need from me?"

"Things look busy in here," I said.

"As of Thursday, I'll be the candidate. Unofficially, we've been assuming it will be me. We never stopped the campaign after Blake's death. You can bet Tony McCort never stopped, either."

"Are you going to win?"

"Yes." She checked her phone.

"The pundits seem to think you'll have a tougher race than Lofton had."

"Women always have it tougher. It will be close. I can't pull in the big donors the way Blake did. But I'll win." The office door opened. A man looked inside, apologized, and closed the door.

"Was Lofton confident of beating Tony McCort?"

"Overconfident, I thought. He wasn't leading by that much. But he acted as though he had it in the bag."

"Why?"

"He made a couple of references to an October surprise."

"What does that mean?"

"Some kind of ace in the hole he could pull out late in the race if he needed it."

"Damaging information about McCort?"

"Probably something like that, but he never told me what it was."

"What did you think of Lofton?" I asked.

"Blake Lofton was the worst kind of asshole, the type who poses as a nice guy. He would listen politely and nod sympathetically. Then he'd proceed to do exactly what he wanted to do."

"Why did he feel entitled to do that? Because of his supposed superior wisdom?"

"No, because of his spot atop the pecking order. He thought that by definition, he always knew best."

"That sounds like kings who used to think they had the divine right to rule. Usually they were tyrants."

"Oh, but our Blake saw himself as a benevolent ruler. Always did what was best for his subjects."

And that, I thought, meant that Blake Lofton was a man capable of immense self-delusion. "If Lofton was so bad, why did you work for him?" I asked.

"Politics is all about picking the lesser of multiple evils. As bad as Blake was, Tony McCort is a whole lot worse, as far as I'm concerned."

"Could McCort have killed Lofton?"

"No. Not that he's not evil enough, but supposedly he was out of town. He's an asshole with authoritarian tendencies whose chief goal in life is to hose the poor, the sick, and the black. If I were the cops, I'd be looking at his security guy, Bolger—now there's a man who'd shoot somebody for a twelve-pack of cheap domestic beer. A little crazy, everybody says." A phone on her desk buzzed. Ostlund looked tempted but ended up ignoring it.

"Bolger has an alibi, too," I pointed out.

She shuffled through papers on her desk, stopping to read one of them. "Sure, but who's providing it?"

"Cops."

"Exactly."

"So?"

"Blake opposed racial profiling and pushed for more police accountability. How do you suppose the cops felt about that?"

"You're saying that because of a policy difference, they'd lie to protect Lofton's killer?"

She looked at me pityingly. "Look, if you're going to be investigating this, you need a reality check. The conflict between the police and the minority community isn't just a policy dispute. Both sides see it as existential. It's a defining issue."

Indeed it was, I thought. Everybody was telling me the Lofton murder was about race, and I seemed to be the only sentient being on the planet not to understand it.

"I assume the police questioned you about the murder," I said. "What was the outcome of that?"

"Inconclusive, I'd say. I have a partial alibi. My boyfriend left my house on Cathedral Hill at 1:30 AM. The police think the murder was committed before that, but they don't know for sure. Yeah, I had something to gain, so they had to put me through the wringer. But I had no personal animosity toward Blake. He was straightforward. You knew where he was coming from."

"He defeated you in the primary election."

"I didn't take it personally. He didn't run a dirty campaign— not like McCort. He just won because he had more money."

I wasn't sure about that. Ellie Ostlund seemed smart and capable, but she didn't impress me as a polished, appealing candidate. "Did you ever go to his house?"

"Sure. Both his houses. So did Lauren."

"That's Lauren Jorgenson, his personal assistant?"

"Listen, I'm kind of a busy person. I really don't have time to give you an education on everybody who worked for Blake."

"I'm busy, too, and you're wasting my time with your snotty remarks and multitasking. I could have been done by now."

"You want me to have you tossed out of here?"

"Sure. And I'll make sure there's plenty of news footage of you throwing an unresisting handicapped woman, who works for Andre Woodruff, out of your office."

She closed her eyes, took a deep breath, and let it out. "Lauren works for the campaign now—director of advance and scheduling. Blake promoted her a couple of weeks before he was killed."

"I need to talk to her, too."

"Her office is across the room. Check with her when we're done."

"Did anyone else in the campaign ever visit Lofton's houses?"

"I doubt it. Blake usually didn't deal directly with the lower-level campaign people."

"Who knew he was going to be at the Minneapolis house on Friday night?"

"I'm not sure. I didn't, but I didn't really need to know. Maybe Lauren. Probably Simone. His volunteer driver would have known. He'd planned to spend the night out at the lake but changed his mind. He would have been here in the city on Saturday night, anyway, so I guess he decided to make it a weekend."

"Why would he have stayed in the city on Saturday night?"

"He was going to Duluth on Sunday morning and was driving. It's a closer drive from Minneapolis than Wayzata."

"But no one knows why he stayed there on Friday night?"

She shrugged. "There was probably no specific reason. He was probably just tired and didn't want to make the long drive."

I put my phone away. "Thank you for talking to me."

She stared at me, finally giving me her full attention. "I've got an election to win. Don't waste my time again." She returned to her work.

I rolled out into the main area and nearly ran into a young man. I asked him where Lauren Jorgenson's office was, and he pointed to a room on the opposite wall. I threaded my way through the rows of tables to a closed door and knocked.

"Come," said a voice from inside.

The office was an oasis of calm in the hectic campaign head-quarters. An attractive dark-haired woman in her early forties sat behind a largely clear desk, reading from a loose-leaf notebook. She was dressed conservatively, wearing black-rimmed glasses. "Hi," she said.

I introduced myself and asked for a few minutes of her time.

Lauren glanced around uncomfortably, as if unsure she should be talking to me.

"Would another place be better?" I asked.

We agreed on four o'clock at her house, and I left her office. But not before gazing out over her left shoulder, through a window, at the gray Audi SUV that was parked on a side street. I found a door at the rear of the office and rolled down a short corridor to a side exit. I pulled the door open and saw that I was in luck. The door led to a delivery entrance, which could be accessed via a ramp to the sidewalk. I rolled through a parking lot across the rear of the building to the side street where the Audi was parked, then behind a parked car to the street itself. Then I pulled out my phone, placed it on my lap, and rolled up toward the SUV. I went up to the driver's door. He wouldn't be able to pull out of the space without running over me. I reached up and rapped on the window. When the surprised-looking man with close-cropped hair rolled down his window and looked out at me, I took his picture.

"You didn't get my good side," he said in a thick New York accent. A cool character, I thought.

"I could show this picture around," I said, "but you could save me some trouble by just telling me who you are."

The man looked at me, stone-faced, totally unreadable. "My name is Bolger."

Tony McCort's director of security. I wasn't surprised. "Why are you following me?"

"Following you? Must be some misunderstanding."

"You were on a roll for a minute there, Mr. Bolger. Why don't you be honest with me? I'm not recording you."

He held up a small electronic device. "You certainly aren't."

"Why don't we call the police and you can explain it to them?"

"Nothing to explain." He didn't look the least bit worried.

"Then maybe your boss, Mr. McCort, would like to explain it to the media."

His features tightened ever so slightly. "Do you have a problem with Mr. McCort?" The menace was clear.

"I didn't until he sent you to follow me."

"Why don't you take it up with him?"

"I'd be happy to."

Bolger handed me a card. "Here's the address of our corporate headquarters. Come on over at seven tonight and we'll get you in."

"Make it eight," I said.

He lifted an eyebrow. "Sure."

"Now I've got you stalking me at two different locations," I lied, since I hadn't actually photographed him at Andre's house. "I don't want to see you again, and if I do, it's three strikes and you're out. I don't care how chummy you are with the police— they won't be able to ignore my complaint." I started to roll away, then turned back. "And when I file for a civil restraining order against you, your boss may not enjoy the publicity."

I rolled around the corner to University Avenue, got into my van, and started it. As I pulled away, I glanced down the side street to where Bolger had been parked. He was already gone.

Chapter 11

I drove toward Minneapolis, anything but sure I had lost Bolger. I couldn't see him, but he could easily have planted a GPS tracking device on my van, and I couldn't check for it. I scrolled through my phone and found the north Minneapolis address I'd looked up last night, then programmed my navigation app to take me there.

Both Andre and Simone had assured me that their older brother, Isaac, wouldn't be able to tell me anything useful. That was precisely why I wanted to talk to him. I was always suspicious of attempts to downplay or suppress information. But more than that, I knew the police had covered all the high-probability routes. If I was going to clear Andre, I'd need to explore the less-traveled byways.

I exited I-94 and drove west, then north for a couple of miles through older, dilapidated neighborhoods, past boarded-up store fronts, check-cashing places, pawn shops, and scruffy liquor stores. I wasn't far from where Prince had grown up and begun his musical career. I realized I hadn't seen a white face for a long time, and I suddenly felt foolish. Why would these people trust a blonde lawyer? I might not have, if I'd been in their shoes.

I parked a couple of houses down from Isaac's address and rolled out of the van, and the freak show was on. People on the street stopped talking, raking leaves, or whatever they'd been doing to look at me. I smiled to a couple of the people; one of them smiled back and the other scowled at me. Isaac's address belonged to a substantial but shabby two-story house on a corner lot.

I rolled up to the front; there were three steps leading up to the door. I pulled a telescoping pointer from my purse, extended it, and leaned as far forward as I could, barely managing to press the doorbell. A loud buzzer went off inside, but nobody answered the door. I could hear the faint sounds of a TV, so it seemed safe to assume somebody was home. I pressed the buzzer three more times as the neighbors looked on.

Finally, a large figure slowly approached the door and opened it. The man who looked out in astonishment was in his fifties, weighing close to three hundred pounds, with a bloated face and thinning hair. But I could clearly see the resemblance to Andre, and even a little to Simone.

"Isaac?"

He squinted at me. "Maybe."

I introduced myself and said I was working for Andre's defense. That didn't seem to impress him. But he hadn't gone back inside.

"I wonder if you could give me a few minutes?"

"Why? I don't know anything about the murder."

"I'm just looking for some background information."

"How do I know you're working for Andre?"

"Call him."

He hesitated. He clearly didn't want to contact his brother. "All right," he said. "Come in." He glanced at the wheelchair and caught himself. "Oh . . ."

I didn't want this out-of-shape man trying to pull me up the steps. "Maybe you'd like to just come out and sit on the steps."

Isaac took a sideways glance at the neighbors, then shrugged. He closed the door, left, and returned a minute later wearing a shabby denim jacket. He eased his considerable bulk onto the top step and leaned forward. "So, is Andre going to get off?"

"It doesn't look good."

He nodded. "You can have all the money and power in the world, but you go up against the cops and you just another . . ."

He refrained from dropping the n-bomb.

I shouldn't have been shocked that he saw the case in strictly racial terms, but I was struck by the similarity between his response and Ellie Ostlund's. Didn't the merits—the strength of the case—matter at all?

"What do you do for a living, Isaac?"

"Not much right now. I worked for the post office for some years. Then I worked for UPS for a while. Hurt my back, had to go on disability." He shrugged. "Andre got the brains. Simone got the looks *and* the brains."

"And you?"

He managed a weary smile. "A sparkling personality and sunny disposition." He guffawed. "Naw, I got jackshit."

"Do you see any way Andre could have committed a murder?"

Isaac shook his head firmly. "No way. Most people, you'd say they get mad enough, they can do a guy. Not Andre."

I felt I wasn't getting anywhere with Isaac, which wasn't surprising, since I wasn't sure what I wanted from him. "Do you know Tony McCort?" I asked.

"Oh, sure. All of us knew him."

"I understand he grew up around here."

"He was the white kid."

"What was he like?"

"He knew his way around. He got into a few fights but could take care of himself, and after that they mostly left him alone. It wasn't easy. It was a bad neighborhood. Still not great. His family was . . . well, nobody knew anything about them. Hell, he didn't really seem to have a family. At times, I think he was living on the street. He'd show up at our house once in a while and my dad would feed him or slip him a few bucks or hire him to do some odd jobs around the church."

I was fascinated. "Did you have any inkling that he'd be such a success?"

"You know, I did. There was just something about him."

"Are you still in contact with him?"

He laughed at the thought. "Not likely. I'm just one of those dependent losers, stealing from the decent, hardworking folks. I'm the type's gonna get my fat ass whipped into shape or booted out of the state when he's elected."

"You think he'll win?"

"Tony McCort ain't going to lose."

"Do you think he killed Lofton?"

He shook his head. "He'd find another way to get what he wants."

I was pondering that when Isaac added, "You're not the only one asking about him."

"Really? Who else has been around?"

He sized me up. "You know, this information might be valuable. My time is valuable."

"How valuable?"

"Enough so a nice, well-dressed lady like you might be glad to compensate me a little for it."

I dug through my purse and took out $130, which left me with about a buck and a half. He looked disappointed, but he took the money and went into the house. A minute later he reappeared, carrying a business card, which he handed to me. The card belonged to a private investigator named Jack Schott.

"What did this guy want?" I asked.

"Pretty much anything he could find about Tony from the old days."

"And what did you tell him?"

"I'd rather not go into that."

I wondered if he was being coy or just holding out for more money. I snapped a picture of the business card and handed it back to him. Then, as I was putting my purse back in order, I asked, "Do you live here alone, Isaac?"

He nodded.

"No one visiting right now?"

"No."

"Thanks for your time." After a quick glance at the still-watching neighbors, he lumbered back up the steps and into the house.

I rolled back toward the van, thinking about what I'd seen in the driveway of Isaac's house: a shiny new Nissan SUV.

*   *   *

Tony McCort checked his buzzing cell phone: Bolger. "Yeah?"

"This Pen has been busy," the security man said.

"Doing what?"

"Talking to Isaac Woodruff."

"Holy crap. Did Isaac call you?"

"Yeah. He did his duty."

"How did she get onto him?"

"Isaac didn't know," Bolger said. "Maybe she just had some extra time or didn't have anything else to do."

"Or maybe she knows something we don't."

"I don't see it, Tony. She's been in Minnesota all of a day."

"Do you think Isaac told her about Schott?"

"He says he didn't, of course. But whether he's telling the truth—that depends."

"On what?"

"On whether she had a few bucks in her pocket."

"Right," McCort agreed. "What's she doing now?"

"Talking to Lauren Jorgenson."

"Nothing to learn there."

"Not as far we know. And anyway, you can ask Pen yourself in a couple of hours when she comes in."

"I just might do that."

Chapter 12

Lauren Jorgensen lived in a modest two-story house in the Longfellow neighborhood in south Minneapolis. I found a parking spot right in front of the house but found myself looking at two sets of steps leading up to the front door. I called Lauren and explained the situation.

"No problem," she said. "My husband is home."

Five minutes later I had been pulled up the steps by Justin, a big, agreeable man with thinning hair who described himself as a real estate investor ("I flip houses," he said). Justin then disappeared while I followed Lauren to a small sun room at the rear of the house. Lauren got me situated at a wicker table, then brought out coffee, and we sat, looking out over the leaf-covered back yard. Based on her attractive appearance and friendly, unassuming personality, Lauren might have made a better political candidate than her new boss, the abrasive Ellie Ostlund.

I explained in greater detail who I was and what I was looking for.

"Ellie said it was okay to talk to you. I'm not sure I can add much, but I'll try."

"Tell me about yourself," I said.

"Let's see . . . Forty-three, married eleven years, no kids, law school dropout, Lutheran, and Pisces. Have I missed anything?"

"How about campaign worker?" I said.

"That's recent. For two years I was Blake's personal assistant. My biggest job was scheduling his non-AgriMinn activities—political, civic, charitable—and handling his dealings with all those organizations."

"How did you get the job?"

"I was a legal assistant in AgriMinn's general counsel's office. That's where I came to his attention."

"What kind of man was he?"

"He was . . . He was . . . I'm sorry." She reached for a tissue and wiped her eyes. After composing herself, she said, "A lot of people only dealt with him in a business context, or in a political setting, or at a social gathering. I saw him in all those different ways. He was a complex man."

"I'm told he tended to categorize people, to assign roles to them."

"Yes, he did. But you know what? He was usually right. He was good at sizing people up and figuring out what they were good at, what their potential was."

"How did he categorize you?"

"I guess I'm proof that he wasn't always rigid in his evaluations of people. He promoted me just a couple of weeks ago. He said he hated to let me go, but it was going to be a tough campaign, and he'd need me there to oversee scheduling and advance. And after the campaign—we never talked about it, but I might have had a job in the governor's office. The promotion was a nice thing. And he was a nice man . . ." She broke down again.

I waited, reflecting that while both Ellie and Lauren acknowledged Lofton's faults, Lauren still seemed to have some positive feelings for him. "I'm sorry, but we need to talk about the murder."

She hesitated, then nodded.

"The housekeeper found the body," I said. "But I understand you were at the crime scene, too."

"Right. The housekeeper's name is Bonnie, an older woman who's worked for the Loftons forever. She wasn't actually supposed to be there that morning. She thought Blake would be staying in Wayzata Friday night. But he'd changed his mind the previous afternoon."

"Who knew that?"

"I'm not sure. I didn't, but I didn't need to. We had a volunteer driver, and Blake had called him. I don't think Ellie knew, either. I imagine Simone knew. But that may have been it. He hadn't told Bonnie, so she showed up to clean. Anyway, Bonnie called me, all panicky, and said she'd found him and that he might be dead."

"She called you? Not 911?"

"She said later that she did it out of instinct. She thought somebody must be on the way there to pick him up for the Duluth trip and that I might know what was going on. She thought that because Blake was there, she must have gotten the day of the trip wrong."

"Who picked the day of the trip?"

"Blake and I did. I'd talked to the Duluth people, and they said either Saturday or Sunday would be fine. We decided on Sunday."

"What happened after Bonnie called?"

"I rushed over there and found her outside. We went in."

"You had a key?"

"Yes, although I didn't need one then, since Bonnie had already used hers. Blake gave me one shortly after I started working for him. I was always running over there to pick up a fresh suit or some papers or whatever. I had a key to the Wayzata house, too."

"So you went in," I prompted.

"Right. And then . . ." She stopped, steeling herself. "He was in the living room, face down, with his robe on, with blood everywhere. I could tell right away he was dead." She stopped and took a couple of deep breaths. "It was awful."

"What happened next?"

"I'd called 911 on the way over, and the police and ambulance arrived just a minute or so after I did. The police started questioning us right away. They let Bonnie go after only an hour or so, but I was at the station until around noon."

"They suspected you?"

"They seemed to, yes. Fortunately, I'd been home all night."

"And Justin was able to vouch for you?"

"Not Justin—he was up north hunting with some buddies. I had a friend who stayed over that night. And she's actually a police officer, so I had a credible witness. And then I found out they'd arrested Andre and that they'd really thought it was him all along."

"Who do you think killed Blake?"

"I don't know. I hope it wasn't Andre. I like him."

"You knew him at AgriMinn?"

"Yes. He's a nice guy. A little distant, maybe. I find it hard to believe . . ." She shook her head. "I just don't know."

"Do you think Andre was capable of murder?"

"They say anybody is, if you put them under enough pressure. And things were really strained between him and Blake. I hate to say it, but Blake really treated Andre unfairly."

"You think Andre should have gotten the CEO job?"

"Of course. Everybody thinks that. I really liked Blake, and I owed him a lot. I knew him better than most people, I think. But as you said, he did tend to categorize people."

"Do you think Tony McCort could have had something to do with the murder?"

"He's mean enough. Determined enough. But supposedly he's been cleared."

"He was out of town," I confirmed.

"He's strong-willed to the point of fanaticism. But I guess he didn't do it."

I thanked her for talking to me, and Justin was summoned to help me down the steps. Lauren stood on the sidewalk and waved as I pulled away. She was crying again.

Chapter 13

The corporate headquarters of Together Fitness was located on a two-building campus in Eden Prairie, south and west of Minneapolis. It wasn't far from where I had once lived for six months when I'd worked at a bank in downtown Minneapolis. Signs at the entrance directed people either to the headquarters or to an adjacent fitness club. Nightfall had descended over the city at eight as I followed the signs to headquarters visitor parking and found a handicapped spot in the mostly-empty lot. I rolled up the long sidewalk, stopping to pull my coat up more tightly against the chilly fall wind.

Inside the darkened lobby, I had to show my ID to the guard, who gave me a badge displaying my picture to wear on my lapel. Then I had to wait ten minutes until Ivan Bolger appeared. The security man greeted me with a curt nod and said nothing as he led me to the elevator. On the mostly-dark third floor, I followed Bolger toward a light coming from a corner office. We entered the room, and I looked around at walls lined with hundreds—maybe thousands—of books. Tony McCort was seated behind his desk, wearing reading glasses as he peered at a computer screen. He looked up, removed his glasses, and then studied me as he slowly stood up. He was a striking figure, silver-haired, wearing neatly-pressed slacks and an open-necked shirt, still looking fresh at the end of the day.

"Pen Wilkinson," he said. He walked slowly around a huge desk, came over, and shook my hand, never taking his eyes off me. Bolger took a side chair. "Welcome," McCort said. He perched on the edge of his desk. "What can I do for you?"

"You could start by telling me why Mr. Bolger is following me around."

"I didn't get where I was by being ignorant of the people working against me."

"What makes you think I'm working against you?"

"Are you a strong supporter of mine?"

"No."

"Then as far as I'm concerned, you're my enemy. There aren't a lot of people who are neutral about me, Pen. Or about my philosophy. In this world, you're either a producer or a taker. Either you understand me and support me, or you don't."

"The polls show that about half the people of Minnesota support somebody else for governor," I said. "Are you going to tail five million people?"

He smiled. "If I could, I would. But Ivan is stretched a little thin as it is." I glanced over at Bolger, who watched me with his piggy eyes but said nothing.

"Mr. McCort, I'm going to at least give neutrality a shot here. I'm just trying to find out who killed Blake Lofton. I'm sure you want that, too." He didn't react, so I went on. "If we want the same thing, why should I be your enemy? Unless you go out of your way to antagonize me."

"Ivan does that without even trying." He laughed, and even the granite-faced Bolger cracked a thin smile.

McCort stood up, put his hands in his pockets, and stood next to me, a little too far into my personal space. I didn't back down. "Why don't we cut to the chase?" he said. "I know a lot of people would like to pin the murder on me. Sure, I'm a logical suspect. But, unfortunately for my political opponents and the media, about a hundred people saw me that night at a fund-raiser in Arizona. And Ivan's got four cops vouching for him. He doesn't have to worry about it either."

"If you both have ironclad alibis, why would you worry about me?"

He stepped away from me and sat on the edge of his desk again. "Because I checked you out. You're a fighter. You're handicapped, but you support yourself without any government benefits. I respect that. It's rare in this age of dependency."

I felt heat rise to my face. Had McCort been snooping in my bank account?

"You're persistent," he continued. "If you decided you wanted to pin this crime on me, you might be able to do a lot of damage."

"I'm not out to damage anybody."

McCort looked exasperated. "You're not getting it, Pen. Unless you're here to help me, I consider you a threat. And I will act accordingly."

Now it was my turn to be exasperated. Everybody was trying to force me to pick a side. For the police or against them. For Tony McCort or against him. In my experience, the truth usually resided somewhere in between the polarized extremes. So did most of life's interesting stuff, including the interesting people.

"Don't you think you're going to win the election?" I asked.

"Yes, I will win. I would have beaten Blake, too, but it would have been tougher. Ellie—well, she's smart. She's got twenty IQ points on anybody in Minnesota politics. But she's not very likable. Not like me." He smiled, showing a toothy grin.

"Who killed Lofton?"

"Who knows? Plenty of people had reason to dislike him. I hope it wasn't Andre."

"Why?"

"Because I like him, or at least I did when we were kids. I don't really see him anymore. And I admired his father. He was a strong man—capable. And then there's Simone . . . what a sweet lady. I wouldn't want her to be hurt. Andre hitched his wagon to Blake's star, but he's a guy who could have made it on his own, without patronage or affirmative action."

"Do you know Isaac, too?"

He shrugged. "I remember him a little. Basically a loser."

"Thank you for meeting with me, Mr. McCort. I'm going to have my vehicle checked for a tracker. I hope I don't find one."

"They're cheap, easy to use, and widely available," he said. "If you do happen to find one, it wouldn't necessarily have come from us."

I turned and rolled toward the door. Bolger got up to open it for me.

I turned back. "I came in here wanting to give you the benefit of the doubt," I said. "I guess I can't do that now, can I?"

Bolger followed me to the elevator. "You remember the way, don't you?" he asked.

"Yes."

"Then I'll leave you here. Goodbye."

I rolled onto the elevator and pushed the button for the lobby. I began to descend, but the elevator lurched to a stop a few seconds later. Then the lights went out. There were no emergency or panel lights. I was in total blackness. *What the hell* . . . I waited. Nothing happened. I felt for my phone, pulling it from the outside pocket of my purse: zero bars, and the battery was almost dead. I shined the phone's light around the elevator. There was an alarm button, which I pushed. Nothing happened. There was a box with an emergency phone. I couldn't get it open. I tried every button I could reach and used a key to try to pry open the telephone box. Nothing worked. My light was starting to dim, and I shut the phone off. Already it felt like a hundred degrees, and I was sweating, my hands shaking. An anxiety attack.

I yelled, screamed, and banged on the door, to no avail. It was late, and the office had looked deserted. There was a security guard at the reception desk, but that was two floors down and across the lobby. There were McCort and Bolger, but to try to attract their attention was not only futile but beside the point; they were responsible for my being here.

I took deep breaths, sweating in the dark. It had been a couple of days since I'd had a real anxiety attack, but now I felt the walls closing in. I had to get out of there. *Now.* I banged on the walls with slick hands and yelled some more, my chest heaving. How long until morning? Maybe some janitor or security guard would come along. I felt for my phone, pulling it out and flashing the dimming light around the elevator again. I stabbed at all the elevator buttons. I tried making a call and then sending a text, which only used up dwindling battery power to no effect.

I shut off the phone. I couldn't see my hand in front of my face, and the elevator felt like a sauna. I tried to calm down, to settle in for a long wait. How long? I might have to wait until morning. *No way*, I thought. I couldn't take it for another five minutes. Why on earth was McCort doing this?

I was sobbing, near a breakdown, when the lights went on and the elevator began to move. I didn't know how long I'd been trapped. My eyes hurt from the lights, and I was soaked with sweat. The doors opened onto the darkened lobby, and I gulped in fresh air. I managed to get myself out of the elevator and then spent a couple of minutes pulling myself together. I checked my phone again; as best I could tell, I had been in the elevator no more than twenty minutes. It had seemed like all night.

I rolled tentatively through the lobby. The reception desk was unoccupied. I headed for the door as quickly as I could. The automatic door opener wasn't working, so I had to push my way through two heavy doors to escape the building. Outside, the wind felt like ice on my sweat-covered skin, and I rolled toward the parking lot as fast as I could. Inside the van, I started the engine, turned the heat up, and plugged in my phone.

I nearly launched through the roof when somebody rapped on my window. Bolger. I slammed the van into reverse, but in my mirror, I could see an SUV blocking my exit. I reached for my phone to call 911.

"Don't bother," Bolger shouted through the window. "The police always check with us before responding."

I glanced around; I was parked against a curb, with a handicapped sign squarely in front of me. There was no escape.

I cracked the window. "You'd better let me out of here, right now, you son of a bitch." I reached for my phone, figuring I would tape our conversation.

He shook his head and wagged his finger, holding up the same electronic device he'd used to jam my phone during our previous encounter that day.

"You shouldn't have threatened us," he said. "And it wouldn't hurt you to show a little respect, either."

I just glared at him.

"Heard you screaming and squealing in there," he said. "I'll bet before you were a cripple, you liked it a lot."

"You *bastard!*" I screamed, pounding on the window in fury. He laughed and returned to the SUV.

Bolger left, and I tore out of the parking lot, made my way to Highway 5, and pulled in at a busy, well-lighted gas station. It didn't look as though I'd been followed. For ten rage-filled minutes, I visualized all the police reports I'd file, and the lawsuits I'd bring, and the restraining orders I'd request. Finally, I calmed down. I wouldn't do any of those things. But I would do exactly what McCort, for whatever reason, didn't want me to do: keep digging.

Chapter 14

A s I started the van and prepared to pull out, I spotted a noti-fication on my phone. There was a message from Lieuten-ant Lexi Candiotti. I called her back.

"Pen?"

"Hi, Lexi."

"What are you doing right now?"

"I just finished meeting with Tony McCort."

"Interesting—you'll have to tell me about it. I'm wondering if you'd like to stop over tonight?" she said.

I was puzzled; I had been all but radioactive during our call yesterday. "Are you sure that's a good idea?"

"Don't worry—it will be fine."

"Okay, then." I was cheered by the thought of her friendly presence, and it didn't hurt that she was a cop.

"If you're free, just come on over. You can park in the gar-age." She gave me the code.

"See you in a few minutes."

I clicked off and set out for her apartment, which was located in a high-rise building on the northern shore of Lake Calhoun, in the Uptown neighborhood. I found the garage entrance, en-tered the code, and drove in, finding a handicapped spot near the elevator. Then, after glancing warily around the dimly-lit garage, I rode up to the eighteenth floor.

The lieutenant let me into her apartment. She was of me-dium height, with dark, curly hair, equipped with a no-nonsense wardrobe and attitude. We embraced briefly. "What's going on?" I asked.

"I have somebody here who wants to meet you."

I exhaled. "Sure." I'd have to wait to unload my troubles onto her. I followed her into the living room, where a figure was seated on the sofa. He stood up, and I recognized a tall, handsome man with an impressive head of curly hair. He was the mayor of Minneapolis.

"I'll leave you two," Lexi said, disappearing back into the kitchen.

The mayor greeted me with a politician's easy grin and practiced handshake. "So pleased to meet you, Pen."

"Mr. Mayor." No one considered Grant Palmer, a lawyer and former state senator, a policy heavyweight, and he was often said to be a good fit for the city's "weak mayor" form of government. But even his opponents conceded that he had the best hair of any Minnesota politician.

"I'm having a drink," Palmer said. "Join me?" I wanted one badly, but I declined.

The mayor sat down. "Thanks for coming over," he said. "Sorry about the cloak and dagger, but I'm sure you understand the need for discretion. Lexi has told me what you're doing here. It's quite an undertaking."

"I have a client," I said. "I can't tell you anything about it."

"Sure. But there's nothing to prevent *us* from telling *you* something."

I was confused. "Why would you—"

"Look, I understand you have a duty to try to clear Andre."

"And it's your job to convict him."

"Not exactly. That's the county attorney's job. I have a larger responsibility to the city."

He took a swallow from his tumbler, then leaned forward. "We're on the precipice, Pen. This racial conflict is ready to blow everything to hell. The Lofton murder is uniquely dangerous."

"How so?"

"Look at the possible outcomes of this case: If Andre is found guilty, north Minneapolis could explode in flames. We'd be convicting a prominent, successful black man, the son of a revered civil rights leader who was shot by the police."

"And if he's acquitted?"

"Pretty much the same result. We'd be letting the murder of a liberal politician, a man sympathetic to the black cause, go unpunished. The liberals would be enraged. But the conservatives would say we're letting a killer go scot-free. The city is screwed no matter what happens. But the worst part of it would come from the way Andre would be acquitted. You know how that would happen, don't you?"

By now, I had figured it out. Race, as Andre and Simone had intimated, was at the core of the case. "Hankinson is going to use the O.J. defense," I said.

"Of course he is. What else can he do? It's a gamble—a real Hail Mary—but it worked for O.J. Simpson. You get as many minorities as possible onto the jury, or at least people sympathetic to minorities. Then you go after the police. And there are plenty of people who, rightly or wrongly, want to believe the worst about the police right now. Lots of people—including potential jurors—could imagine the police conspiring to frame Andre Woodruff for the murder."

I nodded, really wishing I had a drink.

"That's the worst-case scenario," Palmer continued. "The O.J. defense is designed, using minimal actual evidence, to slander and fan hatred against the police force. If that happens, I'm not exactly in a good place."

That was putting it mildly, I thought. The O.J. scenario would, regardless of how it played out, leave the police department, the city—and of course, the reputation of the mayor—in tatters.

"What do you want from me?" I asked.

"There are only two scenarios I can see that allow the city to avoid disaster. One would be if Andre would admit to the murder and plead guilty."

According to Andre, that wasn't going to happen, but I couldn't tell Palmer that. "What's the other one?" I asked.

"If someone else is found to have committed the murder. Of course, that would leave egg on our faces for arresting the wrong guy, and people would still be upset that Andre was charged. But that would be a small price to avoid having the city explode."

"I'm already doing my best to find the actual killer."

He fortified himself with a long pull from his glass. "I have to be careful here. You understand that, don't you?"

I was beginning to. He was going to let Lexi help me on the sly, which would enrage the police and prosecutors if they found out about it. The powerful police union would oppose him for re-election. But Palmer was right. Unlike the police, his job was bigger than obtaining a conviction. He needed to see that justice was done and the city protected. And the best way of preventing violence—maybe the only way—was to make sure the trial of Andre Woodruff never happened.

"I understand," I said. "What do you expect from me?"

"Nothing, except your discretion. We know this is the longest of long shots. But the police have had their chance. We need to try every possible option to resolve the Lofton murder without violence. We understand you'll do what you have to do. But if there's anything Lexi can do, secretly and within reason, to help you learn the truth, we'll consider it." He stood up. "Find me another killer, Pen." He gestured vaguely and smiled. "I'll give you a medal or the key to the city or something." Palmer shook my hand and left.

Lexi returned. "I'll take that drink now," I said.

She had anticipated that and had brought a bottle of Sauvignon Blanc. She poured out the wine, and we sat back for a minute, looking silently out her picture window at the darkened landscape of south Minneapolis. "No offense," she said, "but you look like hell. What's going on?"

I opened my mouth, intending to update her on my encounter with McCort and Bolger. Instead I blurted out, "James and I separated."

The story came spilling out, along with the tears. We talked about it for a while, and finally I was able, with the aid of additional wine, to pull myself together to deal with matters at hand. I told her about my meeting with Tony McCort and the elevator episode that followed.

"I don't get it," she said. "He thought trapping you in an elevator for a while was going to intimidate you?"

"It did intimidate me. It shouldn't have, but somehow he seemed to know I would react poorly to it tonight. It wasn't rational, but I was scared to death." I didn't want to talk about my anxiety attacks in general.

"Bastard."

"No argument there. But why did he do it? If both he and Bolger have alibis, why is he worried about me?"

"He can't control you."

"He's giving it his best shot."

We both sipped from our glasses. "How confident are the police about their case against Andre?" I asked.

"Very confident. They've got means, opportunity, and plenty of motive. Their main concern is the trial. They worry that Hankinson would shift the focus away from Andre to the police. They'd be the ones on trial. And in this climate, who knows what would happen?"

"Nothing good."

"For sure. Another concern is Andre himself. He's an articulate and intelligent guy—he'll make a great witness."

"What do you think of McCort?" I asked.

"He's a tough SOB—grew up in the mean streets of the north side. But we'd better get used to him. He'll probably be the next governor."

"And the police are pleased about that?"

"Mostly, yes. McCort is our guy. Most of us didn't care for Blake Lofton. On the other hand, McCort is security-conscious—even a bit paranoid—convinced that liberals and media are out to get him."

"That kind of belief tends to become self-fulfilling. Bottom line, do you think he had any involvement?"

"No."

That was good enough for me. I emptied my own glass and wanted a refill, but I decided against it, thinking of the long drive back out to the lake. "Let me run a name past you," I said. "Jack Schott." I explained how the private eye had visited Isaac Woodruff, asking about McCort. "Do you know anything about this guy?" I asked.

"I met him a couple of times. He worked in various detective jobs for the St. Paul police until he was forced out."

"Why did they get rid of him?"

"He was a thumper. The city paid out well into seven figures in damages to all the people he tuned up over the years. Finally he had an especially bad case, a kid who ended up losing the sight in one eye. It's tough to fire a cop, but that did it. So then Schott went private. He probably did okay; his police connections were still good. He was always fairly popular among the rank-and-file cops, at least the whites. The minorities thought he was a racist."

"You said you met him. What did you think?"

"He was a pig. But apparently you don't know the most interesting fact about him."

"What's that?"

"He's dead."

Schott, Lexi said, had drowned next to the dock at his cabin in northern Minnesota, near Grand Rapids, four months ago.

"Are they sure it was accidental?" I asked.

"No signs of foul play. The local sheriff and state Bureau of Criminal Apprehension handled the investigation. Schott was staying there alone, so there were no witnesses, and the cabin is isolated."

"So we may never find out who hired Schott to investigate McCort, or why."

"It's a can of worms," Lexi said. "What if Lofton hired him? And what if McCort was afraid of what he'd find?"

I shook my head, too exhausted to puzzle it out.

"The case of Schott's death has been closed," she said, "but I'd better let the BCA guy know he was questioning Isaac and make sure the detectives working the Lofton case know, too."

"Thanks."

"We probably won't meet again until this is over." She reached into her purse and produced a prepaid cell phone. "Use this if we need to communicate."

I took the phone.

"If you're ever subpoenaed or questioned, none of this ever happened," she added.

I nodded. Like the weaselly secretary on *Mission: Impossible*, they'd disavow me, leaving me hanging out to dry if anything blew up.

"This was a brief social call," she continued, "and the mayor was not present. Unfortunately, McCort knows you were here tonight."

"How?"

Lexi reached back into her purse and produced a plastic bag, which appeared to contain a small electronic device. "A GPS tracker. I took it off your van while you were talking to Palmer. I'll go through the motions of dusting it for prints and tracing it, but it will be a dead end."

"What can you tell me about Ivan Bolger?" I asked.

"He's been on my radar for some time."

"Why?"

"Because since he arrived here from New York, he's been busy making friends on the Minneapolis police force."

"He's an ex-cop himself?"

"Yes. He put in his twenty for the NYPD. Then he moved out here and took the Together Fitness job and started ingratiating himself with key members of our department."

"Nothing necessarily suspicious about that," I noted.

"True. But I made some discreet calls to check him out. Turns out he barely made it to twenty in New York. They were glad to see him go."

"Why?"

"He was in repeated hot water for excessive force complaints, even after he moved off the streets and worked in intel. The word was that he was more than a garden-variety thug—he's smart. But he's also a little crazy—something just not right about him. My source said: 'Bottom line: watch your back.'"

We were silent for a long minute. I said, "What are we doing here, Lexi? It's hard to see how this ends well for either of us."

She didn't answer.

"I'd better get going," I said.

She smiled. "Let the fun begin."

Chapter 15

It was past eleven when I got back to Andre and Anita's place—too late to see Alicia, even though, being a teenager, she was probably still on her phone in bed. Once in the door, I made a beeline for the kitchen and the wine bottle. It had been a hell of a day. Tonight, a glass had been placed down on the counter, where I could reach it. I had just gotten settled with my pinot noir when I heard a knock at the door.

"Come in."

Anita entered. "You look like you've had a rough day. Is there enough of that for two?"

"Sure," I said, although I probably would have consumed the rest of the bottle by myself.

She went over to the kitchenette and returned with another glass. I filled it for her. "Cheers." We clinked glasses, and she took a chair across from me.

"How's life?" I asked.

"I'm holding my own. Fortunately, I've got an assistant who can keep the show going while I'm taking care of things here." Anita owned her own television production company, which put out a popular, nationally syndicated home-and-garden show.

"How about Alicia?"

"Not great. There have been some incidents at school."

"Other kids picking on her?"

"A group of them, the little shits. If it keeps up, we've talked about sending her out to California to finish the school year."

"Oh, Anita, I'm so sorry." I wouldn't be unloading my own problems onto her now.

"How's it going?" she asked.

I gave her an edited version, covering my interviews with Ellie Ostlund and Lauren Jorgenson. I briefly described my meeting with McCort and Bolger but omitted any mention of the elevator incident. I told her nothing about meeting with the mayor or Lexi Candiotti. But I did mention interviewing Isaac Woodruff.

She was instantly wary. "Isaac? Why did you talk to him?"

"Why not?"

"Well, he just—he and Andre just don't get along great. Isaac hasn't had a good life, and the comparisons to Simone and Andre aren't too flattering. He lost his mother at an early age— he seemed to take that the hardest of the three kids—and then Carl's death . . . Even though Andre actually saw the shooting, Isaac was the closest to his dad and was by far the most upset. In some ways, he never really recovered. Isaac is secretive and suspicious—and more like Carl than anyone would like to admit. Andre and Simone are more like their mother."

"He didn't say anything bad about Andre. In fact, there's only one interesting thing he told me." I described Isaac's encounter with a now-deceased PI.

"Schott," Anita said. "I haven't heard that name. If he was investigating McCort by talking to Isaac, that would be going back a long way. I understand McCort knew the Woodruff kids when they were young, but I haven't heard anything about their being in contact after that."

"We'll need to check with Andre about that."

"I'll ask him in the morning."

I changed the subject. "I enjoyed meeting Simone."

"She's the real deal, Pen. Downright saintly, if you ask me. She puts up with everybody, genuinely cares about other people. She still goes into the city every Sunday morning and attends services at her father's old church. She puts everybody else first—but it works for her, I guess. We've become close over the years—we talk on the phone just about every day." Anita's description of her sister-in-law sounded grudging, as if she found it difficult to believe anybody could be that genuine.

"Do you know Ellie Ostlund?" I asked.

"Oh, sure. She's an egotistical windbag like Blake, but not as smooth and not as condescending. Just not as good at it."

I'd never had an extended conversation with Anita, and I could see how her blunt style would have clashed with James's, which was much the same. The more low-key Andre was undoubtedly a better fit for her.

She took a sip from her glass. "What did you think of Hankinson?"

"As a human being, not much."

"I didn't hire him to be Mother Teresa. I hired him to be what he is: the nastiest, most ruthless junkyard-dog SOB I could find."

"You succeeded." I knew Hankinson was an intuitive, emotional lawyer who wasn't into detailed or methodical collection of facts. I'd been up against a couple of attorneys like him, and I knew they could be very dangerous. You couldn't prepare for them by marshalling facts—they played a different game. Maybe that was what Andre needed, since the facts weren't with him.

Anita took a long gulp from her glass. "Hankinson has encouraged Andre to take a deal." She must have noticed my shocked expression. "So I guess Andre's prospects aren't looking great."

"You know how Hankinson's going to handle the defense."

She looked at her glass. "I could use a little more. How about you?"

"Sure."

She retrieved the bottle, refilled our glasses, and returned to the couch.

"I know Hankinson will go after the police," she said, "and I can see you disapprove."

I didn't respond.

"I get it, Pen. The results for the city won't be pretty. There might be violence. But that could happen either way. I suppose it's fair to ask whether Andre is behaving responsibly by letting Hankinson do an O.J."

"What do you think?"

"Andre is aware of the risks for the city—the entire state, actually—but he's not in a mood to take one for the team. Not after being booked, cuffed, fingerprinted, photographed, and thrown into a cell that smells like piss. Not after having his daughter watch while every moron and racist on TV or the Internet calls him a murderer and worse. Andre has some very definite feelings about the police. That comes not only from watching them shoot his father, but from the times he's been stopped and harassed over the years. DWB."

I nodded. James had had his share of stops for Driving While Black.

Anita went on. "If people are inclined to believe the worst about the cops, as far as Andre is concerned—and I agree—the police brought it on themselves." She leaned forward, glass in hand. "We're not going to quietly lie down for this one, Pen. The media and Tony McCort would love to blame the victims. Minorities have always been mistreated by the police, but when we complain about it and the rage explodes after the latest episode, well, then the whole thing's our fault. You know this."

I did. Dating a black man for two years had given me an occasionally unpleasant primer on race relations. But I also knew it wasn't that simple. I'd worked with a lot of law officers who were honorable people, who treated others fairly and resented being blamed for the actions of a few of their colleagues who didn't. My friend Lexi Candiotti was Exhibit A.

Anita went back to the main house, and I got ready for bed, finding some late news on TV. Protesters at the state capitol had established an encampment, vowing to stay until actions were

83

taken to improve police accountability. Counter-demonstrators had thus far been kept at a distance. It was a tinderbox, just waiting for a spark.

*   *   *

"Andre?"

"Hi, Simone. Just wanted to let you know Pen talked to Isaac."

"How did you find out?"

"Pen told Anita."

"I thought you asked her not to talk to him."

"I did. I probably shouldn't have. My disapproval could be the very reason she did it. Damnit, I wish I could have talked Anita out of hiring her. I just knew she was going to be trouble."

"What did she find out?"

"Not the big thing, thank God. But she did find out something else interesting. A private eye named Schott talked to Isaac not long ago. He was looking for dirt on Tony McCort."

"Not us?"

"No," Andre replied. "But of course he'd be going back to the day. Back to the relevant period."

"I guess. So who's this Schott? I've never heard of him."

"I haven't either. Do you suppose Blake could have hired him?"

A pause. "I guess it's possible, if he was looking for dirt on McCort. But we'd never find out. Blake never would have left his prints on it. Maybe he had somebody like Ellie set it up."

"The time frame is wrong. Schott talked to Isaac before the primary, when Blake was Ellie's opponent."

"Then I just don't know."

"We may be reaching the point where we have to just shut Pen down."

"I hope that's not necessary."

Andre chuckled. "Better than feeding her to McCort."

Simone's response was deadly serious. "She'd better hope she doesn't get in Tony's way."

Chapter 16

June 3, 1989

A ndre Woodruff and Blake Lofton walked down the front steps of Holt Hall, the impressive, castle-type building that had housed the Talmadge School's original class of sixteen students when the institution had been founded nearly a hundred years ago. Blake and Andre, ties loosened and suit jackets slung over their shoulders on the warm June day, began the long trek across the parking lot and soccer fields to the tennis courts, where Blake's BMW was parked.

"Your father was in fine form," Blake said.

"Oh, yeah. 'Amen' and 'Hallelujah' and the whole nine yards," Andre replied. The boys had attended a luncheon given for the students who were graduating with top honors. The Reverend Carl Woodruff had been invited to give the invocation and had delivered a masterful performance.

"Your dad seems determined to be liked and accepted by the rich white men who run this place," Blake observed.

"I guess so."

"And yet he won't take their money."

Andre gave him a curious look. "What do you mean?"

"I'd be surprised if you and Simone didn't qualify for scholarships. Yet you don't receive any."

"We don't?"

"Nope. I asked my father." Charles Lofton was chairman of the school's board of trustees. "You look surprised."

"Shocked is more like it," Andre said. "We don't have the money to pay for Talmadge."

"Apparently you do."

Andre wondered where the money came from. Carl had founded his church two decades earlier, but it wasn't huge, and many of its congregants were poor. The Woodruffs lived modestly; Andre had always assumed that he and Simone attended Talmadge on scholarship. "I'll see if Simone knows what the hell's going on."

"She won't know," Blake predicted.

"Probably not."

"You should know that scholarships are basically never enough. They expect a family to borrow and impoverish themselves if they take the school's money."

"I don't think we've borrowed," Andre said. "I'm not sure where we'd borrow from. As far as scrimping, we're reasonably frugal, but not impoverished. There's enough for tennis lessons and equipment, and Simone's music lessons." He wondered why Blake had brought this up the day before they were scheduled to graduate.

The boys instinctively slowed as they reached the tennis courts, where they had spent hundreds of hours together during their high school careers. "So when is Simone going to go out with me?" Blake asked.

"I don't know."

"I don't take it personally. She doesn't date anybody. She does hang out with an eclectic group of people."

"Like Officer Dave?"

"A friendly policeman. Sort of a strange friendship, don't you think? But then, of course, there's the *really* strange friendship."

"That scrawny white kid—Tony. I don't know that it's a friendship. He hangs around Simone, and she's nice to everybody."

"I don't think he goes to school at all," Blake said.

"Maybe not. He's too busy mooning over Simone."

"But he actually seems somewhat smart. What does he *do*, exactly?"

"Nobody is sure. Seems to be a street kid. Dad gives him a little money once in a while, pays him to shovel snow at the church—stuff like that."

"He seems to hang out with your brother a little."

"I've noticed that, too. Probably to have an excuse to visit Simone."

They had entered the tennis court, where vigorous games were under way in the courts at either end. They paced idly around an empty court in the middle.

"Are you still going to work at Best Buy this summer?" Blake asked.

"I guess. An electronics store should be better than fast food. You going to do anything?"

"Oh, my father will find something for me to do at the company."

"You'd better take it. You've got those cousins to compete with." Blake had two cousins who were potential rivals for the future leadership of family-owned AgriMinn, one of the country's largest privately-owned companies.

Blake picked up a stray tennis ball and tossed it back to the players. "I'm not worried about the cousins."

Andre nodded. Blake never seemed to worry about much of anything.

"Does Simone know I'm going to marry her?"

"Aw, come on, man. That's not even funny anymore."

"Am I renowned for my sense of humor?"

"Blake, I know you and your old man have this thing going. You hung around with the token black kid for four years. You even supported Dukakis instead of Bush for president. Haven't you jerked his chain enough?"

"It's not even remotely about my father."

"Yeah, right. A rich, white tight-ass like you is going to marry a poor, churchgoing black girl?"

"Who happens to be beautiful, smart, and unnaturally nice? Why not?"

"That's not the world we live in."

Blake smiled. "It will be the world *I* live in."

Andre studied his friend, and for a brief, transcendent moment, a crack in time seemed to open up before him, revealing a future in which Andre's fate, and his family's, were inextricably wound up with Blake's, but in which he, Andre, would never understand Blake or the world he inhabited.

The temporal crack closed. Andre shook his head to clear it, and the boys resumed their trek to the car. And Andre thought again about how his Talmadge School tuition was getting paid. *What kind of world am I living in?* he wondered.

Chapter 17

Tony McCort and Ivan Bolger met in the secure room in the intel center a little after eight in the morning. "Anything on Pen?" McCort asked as he took a seat.

"First the bad news: we lost the tracker."

"What the hell did you expect? You knew she suspected one."

"Right. But it's where we lost it. It stopped transmitting at a building just north of Lake Calhoun."

"Okay."

"I had intel check out the residents of the building. One name stood out: Lexi Candiotti."

"Who is—wait, the police lieutenant?"

"Right."

"Not a supporter of ours."

"Not a supporter of Lofton, either. But I've confirmed that she's a friend of Wilkinson's."

"Let's think this through," McCort said. "Pen is representing Andre. Candiotti is on the other side, pretty much. That's interesting, but what does it mean?"

"Maybe just a friendly get-together. Or maybe Pen went there mostly to have her vehicle checked."

"No, I smell something more going on, somebody else involved. A faction in the police that opposes us, maybe. Or even the mayor—who knows?"

"Wouldn't that be special?"

"Oh, yeah. If the union knew Palmer was flirting with the opposition . . ."

"He'd be finished," Bolger said flatly.

McCort leaned back in his chair and ran a hand through his hair. "I think you're right. But we need to prove it."

"Won't be easy. They know we know about the meeting. They'll be careful."

"True. But first things first. Tonight's the night."

*   *   *

It was nearly noon by the time I'd hauled myself out of bed, gotten ready, and driven into the city. The Loftons' city house was located in the Kenwood neighborhood—venerable, expensive, wooded, and now brilliant with fall color. The big old house wasn't too shabby for a second residence. In fact, it was palatial, worth at least a couple of million. As Simone had instructed, I parked in the alley behind the house, went up to the back door, which was equipped with a ramp, and pressed the bell. I unconsciously looked around for a security camera, knowing that none existed at this door. Simone admitted me with the same warmth she'd treated me with at our first meeting. "Come in," said the new widow, exuding more passion, intensity, and people-oriented enthusiasm than had her brother. "This is the door the killer went in."

"And out, if he or she didn't want to be picked up by the camera."

"That's right. They could have known there was no camera here, or just gotten lucky."

"Is the camera in front visible?" I asked.

"Yes, but by the time you see it, it would pick you up."

"What about the security system?" I asked. "Do the people who have keys know the code to disarm it?"

"Yes, but there's a loud beep when it disarms that goes through the house's intercom system. Anybody entering the code would have woken Blake up."

I pondered this as Simone led me through the rear entrance, down a hallway, and to a large front sitting room. "Have you had breakfast?" she asked.

"Yes, thanks."

"Coffee or tea?"

"I'm fine," I said. "I appreciate your coming into the city to see me."

"Not a problem. I need to think about what to do here— maybe clearing some things out."

"The police believe that Blake knew his killer."

She nodded. "Why would he have let someone in the back door if he didn't know them? He didn't give a lot of thought to security, but it was late at night. He wouldn't have left the door unlocked or the security system unarmed."

"Andre went to the front door. Not too smart if he knew there was a camera and planned to kill Blake."

"That's why they'll have trouble proving premeditation. Andre says he didn't specifically notice the camera, that he never thought about it."

And I suspected the lack of premeditation had been a factor in the decision to free Andre on bail—that plus a million bucks in cash. "Obviously the police have checked out everybody who was in and out of the house regularly."

"There weren't many to check. Andre and me. We have a small staff for this house—just a maid, Bonnie, and a caretaker, who was out of town the day of the murder. Then there's Ellie Ostlund and Lauren Jorgenson. They cleared Lauren and the staff without difficulty. Ellie and I don't have any alibi, but with what they have against Andre . . ."

"How many visitors use the front door as opposed to the back door?" I asked.

She frowned. "Probably about fifty-fifty, I guess."

"Not much help there. Hypothetically, what if Ivan Bolger showed up at the back door?"

"That's Tony's security man?"

"Right."

"I'd guess Blake would have let him in. He knew Bolger. You'd see him at every debate and political event. Blake would have had no reason to fear him."

"And presumably Bolger would have had a good story—a good reason to ask to be let in."

"I suppose."

"Let's shift gears a bit, Simone. Have you ever heard the name Jack Schott?"

"No, I don't think so."

"He was a private investigator, a former police officer."

She shook her head. "Sorry."

For the first time, I had the feeling that Simone might not be telling the truth. Had Andre called her? "Schott visited Isaac earlier in the year—about four months ago. He was asking about Tony McCort."

I saw a brief expression of doubt cross Simone's face at the mention of Isaac. "I doubt if Isaac has seen Tony McCort in a long time. Maybe since we were kids. What did Schott want to know about McCort?"

"According to Isaac, pretty much anything negative."

"Do you think Blake or his campaign might have hired this man to dig up dirt on McCort?"

"The thought crossed my mind."

"I guess it's not inconceivable, but it sounds unlikely to me. I don't remember Blake ever investigating his opponents."

"Why not? It's pretty common. It's called opposition research."

"It's just that—how do I explain this? Blake's actions generally weren't driven by other people. He did what he wanted. Other people didn't often figure into his decisions."

"How about someone else in the campaign—say, Ellie?"

She gave me a hopeless shrug. "I don't know."

I paused, trying to think of other explanations.

"You're frustrated, aren't you?" she said.

"A little," I admitted. "But my expectations are limited, Simone. I hope yours are, too. I'm pursuing low-probability ideas."

"I understand. But based on what I've learned about you, and what Anita has told me, I think you can find Blake's killer."

"That's nice of you to say."

"I mean it. What you've done in your life is extraordinary — just overcoming the accident and functioning with a handicap."

"Lots of people do it. Maybe millions."

"Yes, there are some remarkable stories. But yours is one of them. Pursuing a demanding career, fighting corporate saboteurs, prosecuting crooked public officials, stopping a big-time hacker. I'm glad you're on Andre's side."

"That's very kind of you." I meant it. I'd worked hard and been through a lot, and not many people seemed to appreciate it.

"I heard about you and James," she said. "I've never met him, although of course I know who he is. I'm so sorry."

"It's all right. It's — it's just that . . ." And with that, I broke down. I was embarrassed to death, but I couldn't help myself. Simone came over and embraced me as I blubbered for a good five minutes. I looked up slightly and saw that the new widow had joined in the weeping. Finally she let me go, and I wiped my face. "I'm so sorry," I said.

She brushed back her own tears. "Don't be. It has to be really hard."

I managed a smile. "With your husband dead and your brother being prosecuted for murder, how did this conversation become about me?"

She returned my smile. "Better you than me."

Chapter 18

In the van, I spent another quarter-hour pulling myself together. Then I drove to Ellie Ostlund's campaign headquarters. I was surprised when she had me shown into her office without delay, but after talking to Simone, Ellie was like a bucket of ice water thrown into my face. "Make it quick," she said.

"Have you or the campaign ever had any involvement with a PI named Jack Schott?"

For the first time since I'd met Ellie, I felt as though I had her full attention. "I haven't," she said. "And I can't believe the campaign would have before I got here, not without my knowing about it. What was this guy doing?"

"Investigating Tony McCort."

I saw her foot tapping restlessly under the desk. "We've done the usual opposition research on McCort. We've searched all the public records, dug up all his speeches, gone over all his votes in the Legislature, and so on. But we haven't hired detectives to dig into his past, and I don't have any plans to."

"If it wasn't you or the campaign, who do you think could have hired Schott?"

"Why are you assuming his hiring had anything to do with politics? A business competitor or jealous ex-girlfriend could have retained him."

"Schott went back a lot of years with his inquiries—back to McCort's old neighborhood."

"That makes some sense, since not a lot is known about Tony's early years. He appeared to have a pretty hardscrabble childhood, but he never talks about it. "

"Have you found anything damaging on him?"

"Not really." Her disappointment was evident. "He's never been married—that's a little unusual for somebody who isn't closeted, and he isn't, as far as we can tell. We've looked into his business. He's been sued a number of times, but that's normal. He had a female employee charge him with sexual harassment once. We don't know whether it was legit or not—they settled it quietly. He's used some tax loopholes, but he stayed within the law. There are all kinds of other rumors, but when it comes right down to it, there isn't much McCort could have done that would shake his base of support."

"Schott sounds like a thug," I said. "Would Lofton hire somebody like that?"

"Yes, if he was the most effective candidate for the job. Blake wasn't impressed by expensive suits, fancy titles, or polished manners. He wanted results."

A private eye with flexible ethics might fit the bill, I thought. "Do you think Lofton could have done this on his own, without telling anybody from the campaign?"

"Possibly, but I doubt it. Not his style."

Maybe not, I thought. But I thought of the new SUV in Isaac's driveway. That had cost a lot of money. Lofton-type money. "Let's assume hypothetically that for whatever reason, Blake did hire Schott. Could he have used Lauren Jorgensen as a go-between? To pass money or instructions?"

Ellie hesitated, glancing at the closed door. "That kind of thing might have been a little sensitive for Lauren. He did trust her. She's very loyal and efficient, and he promoted her to a higher position in the campaign. But something cloak-and-dagger like that—it might have been a little heavy for her. If something had gone wrong . . ."

"Could you ask around and see if anybody has heard of Schott or knew what he was up to?"

"I guess so, if I have time." She sounded doubtful.

"Thanks."

I left, thankful that Ellie had been surprisingly cooperative. Maybe she was as intrigued as I was.

I wheeled across the room to Lauren Jorgensen's office and knocked.

"Come."

I pulled the door open, and she smiled. "Pen."

"Do you have a minute?"

"Sure." Compared to Ellie's office, her abode was an oasis of calm. Her hair and makeup looked freshly done, and her smile was impressive. I thought again that she would have made an attractive candidate herself.

I wheeled in, closing the door behind me. "I just have a couple of questions," I said.

"Okay."

No, she hadn't heard of Jack Schott. No, she hadn't been involved in any opposition research by the campaign, and she hadn't noticed any research on McCort being done by Lofton himself.

"You knew Blake reasonably well," I said. "Do you think it's possible he could have been involved in something like this? Gotten his hands dirty?"

"I don't think he would have hesitated to investigate McCort, or to go more deeply than standard opposition research," she said. "He wouldn't have had scruples about that. I do think he would have kept his fingerprints off it. He would have been too astute to let it be traced to him. If he'd done it through the campaign, that would have run the risk of a leak."

All of which pointed to his using an independent player like Schott, I thought. "But he never mentioned anything like that to you," I said.

"No, he didn't." I saw a peculiar look pass over her face, and it took me a few seconds to identify it. She was hurt. She'd been kept out of the loop.

"Did he, as far as you know, have any contact with Isaac Woodruff?"

"No. Even though Isaac was his brother-in-law, there was no contact that I recall. Even Andre and Simone tended to keep their distance from him."

"If Blake had wanted to pay somebody like Schott on the sly, how would he have done it?"

"I'm not sure. But I do know this: People like Blake Lofton have no difficulty doing it. They have access to funds in all different forms and places." She smiled. "The rich are different."

"They sure are." I thanked her and left.

Back in the van, I noticed that a message had come in on the burner phone provided by Lexi Candiotti. I returned the call.

She answered. "Hi, Pen. I mentioned Jack Schott to the investigators working the Blake Lofton homicide. They weren't overly impressed, I guess. They say it's possible Lofton had McCort checked out. Candidates investigate each other all the time. But they're satisfied McCort's alibi is solid."

"What about Bolger's?"

"He was at a poker game with four cops."

"So, case closed?"

A pause. "It's a bit troubling."

"Why?"

"This group of officers has a nickname. They're called the Friday Night Group—they have a regular game on Friday nights. They're cops who are white, active in the police union, politically conservative, and prone to complaints for excessive force."

And that, I realized, played into Lars Hankinson's narrative, that a cabal of racist cops had conspired to cover up Lofton's murder. And the conspiracy theories wouldn't stop there. Given the political climate, and Lofton's perceived anti-police policies, his murder might conceivably be spun as an actual assassination by rogue cops. Calling the poker game "troubling" might be the understatement of the year.

"By the way," Lexi said, "I talked to the BCA guy who looked into Schott's death. His name is Wigginton, and you have an appointment at four."

"Okay."

"He's not terribly happy about meeting with you."

"Why not?"

"Pen, you're not a prosecutor anymore. You're a defense lawyer. To a lot of law enforcement types, you're basically pond scum. You'd better get used to it."

I sighed, thanked Lexi, and disconnected.

*   *   *

The Minnesota Bureau of Criminal Apprehension was located on the east side of St. Paul, past downtown, in the Phalen neighborhood. I found the building and took a handicapped spot. Ten minutes later, I was seated in a conference room with investigator Sam Wigginton, a lanky man with gray, brush-cut hair and a neatly-trimmed mustache.

"Lieutenant Candiotti told me you were interested in Jack Schott's death," he said. Wigginton's voice was excessively patient, his smile forced. He was barely tolerating my presence here.

"Right."

"So were we. The local sheriff asked for our help. He just wanted the death checked out, Schott being a former cop and all. Our regional BCA guy up north called me in. So I went up and looked at what the investigators had found and then came back down here and made some calls."

"And?"

"I found nothing wrong with how the locals had figured it. A neighbor found Schott's body in the water near his dock. The ME estimated he'd been there about twenty hours. There was evidence of drinking, but it was hard to tell how much he'd had.

There was a bruise on the side of his head, but that was consistent with hitting his head on the dock when he fell."

"Was it also consistent with somebody hitting him over the head?"

Wigginton exhaled. "I asked the same question. The ME's answer was that he 'couldn't rule it out.'"

"Are all his conclusions that reckless?"

Wigginton shrugged. "The death was ruled a drowning."

"The sheriff must have investigated further."

"He did. He couldn't find any witnesses who'd talked to Schott or been in the area, although it's a pretty remote cabin. No tire tracks or footprints, but there'd been rain later that night. The deputies searched the cabin thoroughly and couldn't find any drugs or contraband. No suicide note. Nothing that was inconsistent with an accidental drowning, possibly alcohol-related."

"So that was that?"

He gave me a tight smile. "They don't bring us in just to nod and rubber-stamp the obvious conclusions. When I got back, I did some digging. I called Schott's girlfriend, a lady named Lynda Parrish. She wasn't up there with him when he died. She didn't care for the place—it's a little rustic—so Schott often went up there alone."

"What was her take?"

"Lynda didn't really want to talk to me, but of course that's not unusual. I did get her to say that Schott wasn't depressed. In fact, he'd seemed a little more optimistic about his finances, which had been tight for a while."

"Did you look into his money situation?"

Once again, Wigginton gave me a strained, I'm-not-an-idiot smile. "I checked his bank accounts, which had modest balances. His credit report showed some recent late payments, but nothing too serious. He didn't leave a will. He appeared to have no other assets except the cabin."

"Who handled his estate?"

"His sister, Catherine, who lives in Michigan. There wasn't much for her to do. Catherine wasn't really satisfied with the investigation into his death, but she couldn't say what more we should have done."

"What about his business?"

"I took a quick look through his files. He had maybe half a dozen open cases. I didn't see anything controversial or dangerous. I checked his phone records—nothing out of the ordinary."

"Was there any sign that he had worked for the Blake Lofton campaign, or was involved in any investigation involving Tony McCort?"

"I didn't see anything like that, but I didn't go through all of his files in detail."

I exhaled, frustrated. "Was there anything else out of the ordinary, anything suspicious?"

The small smile reappeared. "I know it's boring as hell, but sometimes—maybe most of the time—things are just what they appear to be."

Chapter 19

On the way back to Andre and Anita's, I decided to stop by Isaac Woodruff's house. I had stopped at an ATM, but I hoped to pry a few more answers out of him without resorting to further bribery. The issue seemed moot when I pressed the doorbell at his house. Nobody answered, and the new SUV wasn't in his driveway. I pressed it a couple more times, then headed back to the van. Damp leaves covered the grass and sidewalk, and a faint smoky scent filled the chilly autumn evening.

I had opened the van's door and extended the ramp when I heard a voice behind me.

"Hi, there."

I turned around. The greeting had come from an older black woman, trim and handsome in a blue sweat suit. She'd been standing outside, raking leaves, during my first visit to Isaac.

"Hi," I said, uneasy. She'd probably want to know what I was doing in the neighborhood.

"Saw you at Isaac's house."

"Right. I talked to him yesterday and wanted to follow up with him. I'm an attorney, representing his brother."

The woman's features softened at the mention of Andre. "He's such a nice man. I'm sure he didn't kill anyone."

"I'm trying to prove that."

She held out her hand. "My name is June. Would you like to come in?"

Five minutes later, I sat in June's kitchen while she made coffee. Her sullen grandson had pulled me up the three steps to their side entrance while June held the door. That done, he'd helped me into the small but tidy kitchen and then disappeared.

June set the steaming mug in front of me, then sat down at the table. "I knew the Woodruffs in the old days," she said. "I didn't go to Carl's church, but I'd run into them from time to time. I didn't know the mother—she died fairly young. But I remember Carl." She smiled. "Such a handsome man. Such a great talker, so friendly and caring. He was a great man. He knew everybody. The whole community was up in arms when he was killed."

"There were riots," I said.

"Oh, yes. Riots don't make any sense, of course. It's just destruction. But people get so mad, and there's nothing they can do, and . . ." Her voice trailed off.

I pulled out my phone and showed her the image of Jack Schott's business card. "Has this man ever been around, asking about Tony McCort?"

June shook her head. "No, I don't remember this man, or anybody like him."

"How long have you been a neighbor of Isaac?" I asked, sipping the coffee.

"Oh, a long time now. We'd lived here for about five years, I think, when he bought the house next door. So that would have been about 2003."

"Where did he live before that?"

"I really don't know, truth be told. I believe he lived here in the city somewhere. I heard he hadn't been doing well. Drug problems. Maybe drinking. His problem was, he never got married. A good woman would have helped him stay out of trouble. There were women, but none of them stayed."

"He bought a pretty big house," I noted.

"Yes, he did. It's a nice house, although he's neglected it. I really don't know why he moved here if he had that kind of money. The years haven't been kind to this neighborhood. We've had some gang problems—things like that."

"Do you suppose he came into some money?"

"I guess he must have. He never had money before then." She paused. "And actually, he hasn't seemed to have much money since then, either. I guess he must pay the bills, but he always seems short."

"Looks like he bought a new vehicle."

Her lined face wrinkled further as she considered this. "Yes, and I don't know where the money for that came from."

"Do you think he still uses drugs?"

"I heard he was clean. I haven't seen anything tells me he's not, except his usually being short of money."

"Do his family members come to visit?"

"Never, as far as I can see." She shook her head. "Poor Isaac. He hasn't had an easy life. His mother died young. Then his dad got killed, and he seemed to take that harder than the other two kids did. And his brother and sister being so successful." She got up and poured herself some more coffee after I'd declined. "Now, tell me about Andre."

For the next few minutes, I told her what little I could about Andre's case. She seemed fatalistic about his being convicted. "I didn't know him as well," June said. "He was quiet, and always off playing tennis. But whenever I saw Simone, she'd always talk and ask how we were doing." She shook her head again. "Such a shame."

As I drove back to Lake Minnetonka, I kept thinking about Isaac Woodruff's finances, which didn't appear to make much sense. He'd apparently come into some kind of windfall around 2003, which he'd used to buy a relatively expensive house. Since then, he'd been receiving some income, but barely enough to scrape by. Where did he get that income? It seemed logical that Simone and Andre, his wealthy siblings, might support him. If so, why hadn't they done so more generously? And was it Schott who had bought him the new SUV? But, more to the point, what did Isaac, or his finances, have to do with anything?

*   *   *

For once, the road in front of Andre and Anita's house was devoid of media vehicles. Back inside, I looked at my notes for a while, then gazed out at the lake and the Minnesota autumn, wondering where to go from here. It was tempting to conclude that the Schott angle was a dead end. Professional investigators had looked at the PI's death and found nothing. But how closely had they looked at his life? What had he been doing in Tony McCort's old neighborhood? And who had hired him? I wanted to find out.

After I ate the delicious dinner Cristina, the maid, had brought for me, Alicia came over from the big house. We avoided talking about any of the problems we faced at the moment, including my investigation, her difficulties at school, and the ruptured relationship between her father and me. Instead, we just hung out, watched a movie, and made popcorn. It was all we could manage tonight.

After Alicia left, a little after ten, I thought about looking further into Jack Schott's activities. When it came right down to it, I had few other options. Like the police, I had found no meaningful leads to any suspect other than Andre, and in the back of my mind, I couldn't shake the nagging thought that he might be guilty. After all, as Wigginton had pointed out, the most obvious explanation is often the correct one. And, as Lauren had noted, almost anyone could kill if put under enough pressure. Still, I had to proceed on the assumption that he was innocent.

Andre was my client, and he seemed, somewhat surprisingly, like a good guy. But I knew the real reason I was pressing forward was a future conversation I'd be having with Alicia. I needed to be able to tell her I had done everything in my power to find a killer who was not her stepfather. And, after getting to know the family better, I wanted to be able to tell Anita and Simone the same thing.

*   *   *

It had been a long day for Officer Richard "Duke" Sorrel. He'd been working patrol for nearly twenty years, and it wasn't getting any easier. He walked out of the south Minneapolis bar into the cool night, feeling a little better after a couple of beers. He never drank more than two. He liked the bar because it wasn't a cop hangout. He did spend time with his fellow officers and enjoyed their company, but after his shift, he needed a break from his blue brethren. He turned a corner from Lake Street onto the quiet, dark side street toward where he had parked.

Today's shift had been a bitch. Three domestics. *Three.* The streets were dangerous, and cops armored up. But it was the domestic calls that really scared Duke. And sure enough, in one of today's incidents, the girlfriend had been wielding a knife. Duke had been able to talk her down and arrest both her and the boyfriend, but his hands had been shaking afterward.

As if all this wasn't bad enough, he now had to contend with being second-guessed every minute of the day. Cameras in his car, and on his body, recorded everything. He had to remember to shut the damn things off when he took a leak. Any encounter on the street might be caught on video by a bystander. He couldn't even roust loitering punks on the street, who wouldn't be involved in anything good. He might get sued, or recorded, or denounced at a news conference. Street trash could mouth off all they wanted, get away with whatever they wanted. It wasn't just disheartening; it was disgraceful. Thank heavens there were at least a few politicians who got it, who weren't beholden to community activists, who didn't care about political correctness. There was hope.

As if on cue, a man appeared on the sidewalk ahead of him, a familiar figure, getting out of a car.

"Hey, Duke," said his friend. "How's life?"

Sorrel's face lit up. "Hey. What are you doing here?"

"Just came to see you," said the man. And with that, a hand came out of his pocket, holding an object.

A gun. Aimed at him.

Duke's mouth opened. "What the hell—"

The pistol fired.

Chapter 20

June 7, 1989

A ndre Woodruff watched as the last of the crowd left the small, nondescript building, once occupied by a funeral home, that housed the North Community Bible Fellowship. The Reverend Carl Woodruff stood outside greeting his flock, a few of whom lingered as they left Wednesday night services on a warm evening. Carl was a confident, gregarious figure, forty-six years old, a shade over six feet, with short hair, horn-rimmed glasses, and a narrow tie that gave him a faint Malcolm X vibe. He had been born in rural Arkansas but had moved to Minnesota with his family after World War II. After high school he had worked as a bootblack, newspaper carrier, and door-to-door salesman before starting his own church in 1970. He had never attended college or divinity school.

Carl was a powerful presence on the pulpit but also charming in one-on-one encounters, a talent he now displayed in a conversation with an older couple outside the church. Andre waited patiently. It was always like this after services. He had locked the doors, put the stray hymnals away, extinguished the candles and lights, and locked up. Most importantly, he had helped count the contents of the collection plate, prepared a deposit slip, and transferred everything to a pouch for night deposit on the way home.

His brother Isaac appeared beside him.

"Hey," Andre said.

"Hey. Want a ride home?"

"Nah, I'll ride with Dad."

"Fine."

"Who's your buddy with the Nissan Maxima?" Andre asked.

"Dude named Aaron."

"Dad has to know you weren't inside during the service."

"Yeah, well . . ."

"Where'd you meet Aaron?"

"At work. He's a lab guy." Isaac had graduated from high school three years earlier. Since then, he had attended several classes at community college and now worked as an orderly at the hospital downtown.

"What's Aaron doing here?"

"Just stopped by to say hello. He lives up toward Dowling."

"He was here last week, too."

"Works late on Wednesdays."

"He has a nice set of wheels," Andre said.

"Yup. Better than that piece of shit I got."

"It has Illinois plates."

Isaac shrugged. "He's been up here a while but doesn't want to register it. He had some legal problems down there— doesn't want it to come up."

Andre nodded. After a minute he said, "Haven't seen the white kid around here tonight."

"Tony? He probably knew Simone wasn't going to be here."

Carl completed his conversation with the older couple, turned toward Andre, and nodded.

"See you," Andre said.

Isaac grunted.

Andre followed Carl toward the latter's car, wondering who Aaron was and why Isaac had lied about him. He found his brother's statements troubling. It wasn't just that he had lied— Andre had always been able to detect that. It was that the lies had been so elaborate and practiced. Who the hell was this guy, and why was he turning up on Wednesday nights? And what was in the packet he had handed Isaac?

When they were belted into Carl's Honda and under way, Andre said, "Nice sermon tonight."

"Thanks. It seemed to go over well. How'd we do?"

"A shade under eleven hundred."

Carl made a face. "We need to do better on Wednesdays. We have expenses."

Andre saw his opening. "I'll get my first paycheck in a week and a half."

"Better watch the pennies carefully. Macalester came through with a nice scholarship, and there's that federal loan, but . . ."

"Dad, how are you paying for Talmadge?"

Carl didn't answer right away. "It hasn't been easy," he finally said.

Andre waited, but Carl said nothing further. He obviously expected Andre to accept his statement as an answer. "I know what Talmadge costs," Andre said. "I know it couldn't have been easy. Simone still has a couple of years left. I know what comes in from the church. Why aren't we on scholarship?"

Another pause. "Scholarships don't cover everything, and I don't want us beholden to the people who run the school. It's our responsibility to pay. You don't need to worry about it, Andre. You don't know everything about our finances. Your mama left some life insurance. And we've got some generous benefactors in the congregation. We got you through school, and Simone will be fine, too."

Andre decided not to press it. But he knew his father, a man who took his faith seriously, with a reputation for truthfulness, was lying. Andre had filled out the financial aid applications for college and seen his father's tax returns. There was no nest egg sitting around, from life insurance proceeds or any other source. And he would have bet there were no "benefactors." There were none in the congregation, for sure. Carl never would have taken gifts from people in his own congregation for personal use, and most of the people were poor, anyway.

And outside the church? Theoretically possible, but almost certainly not. Carl Woodruff was a respected figure in the Twin Cities civil rights community. He was known as a moderate voice on the North Side, a go-to resource for city leaders needing to solve racial problems. In this role, Carl had made a number of white friends, including some wealthy ones, such as Blake Lofton's father. But Carl knew that to be beholden to, or dependent on, such people would be to forfeit their respect, and the esteem of most of his congregation and community. Andre knew that his father's deepest, most secret desire was to be accepted by these establishment figures. That was understandable, Andre figured, for a black sharecropper's son, and it explained why Carl had done whatever it was he had done to send his children to an exclusive private school.

But what *had* he done?

Chapter 21

I rolled out of the bathroom at eight, toweling my hair, and saw something on the TV screen that made me stop. I found the remote and turned up the volume as the news showed a residential street lined by emergency vehicles with flashing lights. I listened. A veteran off-duty Minneapolis officer named Richard "Duke" Sorrel had been shot to death at close range, around the corner from a bar he frequented on Lake Street. I rolled closer and turned the volume up higher. An email sent to news organizations claimed the shooting was a retaliatory assassination, done on behalf of the group Rights for People of Color (RPC), which vehemently denied sending the message or committing the murder. The email hinted that two more assassinations would follow, to avenge the police shootings of three young black men in recent months.

The rest of the news segment was all anger. Anger by politicians, police, and citizens on the street at the cold-blooded murder of a well-liked officer. Mayor Grant Palmer, his voice shaking, denounced the killing. The police chief went further, attacking RPC. He claimed that even if the group was not responsible for the murder, it had created a climate of hatred and violence that had encouraged the killer. Gubernatorial candidate Tony McCort adopted an I-told-you-so tone, claiming the murder was an inevitable result of restrictions placed on police. His opponent, Ellie Ostlund, denounced the murder in more measured tones.

I didn't know what to think. I turned on the national news, which was featuring the story prominently, playing the same video clips from the same people. I picked up the cell phone Lexi had given me. She answered without a greeting. "We don't know what's going on."

"Did you know this guy? Duke?"

"I'd met him, that's all. Everybody liked him."

"Could this be what it looks like? An assassination by this RPC group?"

"It was an assassination. The RPC claim is probably bullshit. Their leaders are well known. Why would they claim responsibility?"

"So it's a false-flag crime?"

"Probably, but we don't know who it is. It could be a more radical anti-police group that doesn't get along with RPC."

"What a mess."

"I guess there's only one thing we know for sure about the murder," Lexi said. "It's going to escalate the tension and conflict, and probably the violence."

"True," I said. "And who's going to benefit from that?"

We left the question unanswered and agreed to talk later.

*   *   *

Tony McCort walked out of his strip-center campaign headquarters in Bloomington to the gray Audi SUV, where Ivan Bolger waited. He got into the vehicle. "Any blowback on Sorrel?"

"None. Nobody's really buying the RPC claim, but we didn't expect that they would."

"Right. It just casts confusion on it. But as far as the . . . thing itself?"

"We're clear, Tony. Nobody's got a clue. I planned it out and I did it right."

McCort nodded.

"How did it go?" Bolger asked. McCort had met with his pollsters, consultants, and campaign managers.

"Looking fine. We won't know specifics until we get the flash poll results tomorrow, but there's every indication we'll get the boost we need. Barb predicts four points."

Bolger pulled out of the parking lot and started back toward Together Fitness headquarters in Eden Prairie.

"We'll have a series of messages to roll out," McCort said. "Basically one per week. Right now we'll stick with the need to take the shackles off the police instead of pandering to interest groups concerned with criminal rights. After that we'll go with re-introducing the death penalty."

"Ellie will be expecting all that at the debate."

"Sure. But what can she do, defend RPC? She's nowhere, Ivan. She tries to move to the right and her own people won't turn out to vote. Bottom line, we've regained the initiative, and we're set up to execute the rest of the way."

"Do you have a contingency plan in case there are problems?"

McCort gave him the blank look. He always had a contingency plan. "Everybody will be on edge, waiting for two more revenge killings. We won't do that if we don't need to, but if our lead starts to falter, RPC may have to get naughty again."

Bolger nodded.

"I assume you're back on Pen's trail."

"Sure. We replaced the tracker the same night."

"So what's she up to?"

"She hasn't met with the police again. She met with Simone at the Minneapolis house. Then she went over to BCA and probably met with the guy who looked into Schott's death. And this morning she's meeting with her nephew."

"The hacker?"

Bolger turned onto the interstate and headed west. "Yep. Want to bet she'll be after Lynda next?"

"Lynda won't tell her anything. But Pen's on the trail."

"She is, but of course this is a long shot."

"Sure it is."

"Even so, we have to be ready to move in case she actually finds something."

"Hell, yes. If she finds it, we're on her instantly. If not, we're dead." He looked out the window at the passing urban landscape. "This is dangerous business, Ivan. We need her looking hard, but in the right direction. I think we may need to do some fine-tuning."

*   *   *

I finished getting dressed, packed my purse, and rolled out to the van. I didn't see any of the Woodruffs around. I set out for the city, thinking again about Jack Schott. Blake Lofton seemed the most logical person to have hired the deceased private eye to dig up dirt on Tony McCort. There seemed a decent chance that Schott had in fact found damaging information on McCort, since he'd seemed supremely confident about the election, talking about an "October surprise."

So far, so good. But what had happened next?

Schott had died. There was no real evidence he'd been murdered, but it was possible. Why would he have been killed? Presumably he'd already given the damaging facts to Blake Lofton, who'd planned to make use of it against McCort if necessary. But what if Schott had gotten greedy and gone into business for himself? What if he'd tried to shake down McCort to benefit himself? That would have made him a logical candidate for elimination by McCort. But how did it explain the murder of Lofton? Maybe, I thought, McCort hadn't taken kindly to having Blake snoop around in his past. But without more facts about Schott, it was all speculation.

I took the exit for the University of Minnesota and drove into the Dinkytown neighborhood just north of the campus. After circling the block a few times in heavy traffic, I found a lot with a handicapped spot. Light rain was beginning to fall as I rolled along the busy sidewalks to the small diner on Fifteenth Avenue. After waiting a few minutes, I managed to secure a small table near the front of the restaurant. With great effort, I maneuvered a chair out of the way, then rolled up to the table, got situated, and ordered coffee.

Ten minutes later, a handsome young student with dark, curly hair walked through the door and spotted me. His face broke into a smile. "Aunt Pen." Kenny Sellars came over, embraced me, and sat down, carefully placing a heavy backpack at his feet. Kenny, my sister Marsha's son, had moved to Minnesota from Florida the previous year to live with his father and stepmother. He'd gotten involved with some nasty people, and I'd come out to help him. Kenny's younger sister had been killed in the same car accident that had left me a paraplegic. I'd last seen him two months ago when Marsha had remarried in Tampa.

"How's college?" I asked my nephew, who ordered coffee and pancakes.

"I'm just plowing through the typical freshman classes. Nothing too exciting."

Translation: He was bored to death. For Kenny, that might be dangerous. I hoped the transition from the adrenaline-charged life of high-stakes, illegal hacking to that of an ordinary college student would go smoothly, but I wasn't optimistic.

"How's Sierra?" I asked, hoping he was still dating his high school classmate.

Another smile. "She's great. We're—you know, taking it slow."

"Sure."

We chatted for a while about his mother and about his father, who was unemployed, about to be divorced, and facing serious financial and legal troubles, all of which he richly deserved. "I really don't talk to him," Kenny said, making his way through the stack of pancakes.

"I suppose you wonder why I'm here," I said.

"I know you're close to that girl—James's daughter—what's her name?"

"Alicia."

"Right." Giving little detail, I explained my involvement in the Lofton murder case.

His eyes widened. "You're involved in *that*? Wow. That's huge news."

"I'm just a bit player," I said, "trying to find anything I can that might help Andre Woodruff."

He finished his pancakes and reached for his coffee. "How can I help?"

"Well, you obviously can't get involved in . . . the type of thing you were doing before."

"You mean illegal hacking."

I involuntarily glanced around the restaurant. "Yes, that's what I mean. But I need some research. I'm not strictly sure about the legality, but I'm comfortable with the ethics." I may have been comfortable, but Kenny's mother, my sister Marsha, would have wrung my neck if she'd known what I was asking him to do.

Kenny didn't appear surprised or worried. "Go on."

"I need you to find everything you can about this man." I slid a sheet of paper containing Jack Schott's name and address across the table. "He's dead."

The teenager nodded. "So no invasion of privacy. *His* privacy, anyway. Anything in particular I'm looking for?"

"Mostly financial and legal information, I guess. He was a private investigator."

"What if I find stuff about his clients or his cases?"

"If you see anything about his cases, let me know, and we'll decide whether or not it would be kosher to proceed further."

"Sure."

"I'd also like to have you check out the finances of another guy," I said. "But a public search only. Databases available to banks and credit bureaus and so on. No snooping."

"No problem," Kenny said, taking a second slip of paper on which I'd written Isaac Woodruff's name.

"I appreciate it, Kenny. And for heaven's sake, be careful."

He managed to avoid rolling his eyes. "Don't worry."

I wasn't really concerned. My request was truly kid stuff compared to the type of thing he'd been involved in when I'd come to Minnesota to help him out of a jam. He was good. Really good.

*   *   *

Kenny left. The restaurant had cleared out, and it was now quiet enough for me to make a couple of phone calls. I ordered another cup of coffee and called Jack Schott's sister, Catherine Dahlen, who lived in Ann Arbor, Michigan. I had some trouble explaining my role.

"You're looking into Jack's death?" she said.

"No, not really. But he may have been connected to a current case of mine."

"I don't know what to tell you, Ms. —"

"Wilkinson."

"Right. Jack and I weren't close. His death didn't seem to make much sense to me, but the police explained everything they'd done to investigate, and it looks like he just got drunk, hit his head, fell in, and drowned. Nobody's come up with a better explanation."

"Did Jack have a drinking problem?"

"I doubt it. He liked to knock a few back on a regular basis, especially with his cop buddies. But I don't think it was excessive. Lynda wouldn't have put up with that."

"What kind of cases did Jack work on?"

"Typical private eye stuff. Work for insurance companies. Background checks. Tracking down cheating spouses. A little skip tracing."

"Do you know Lynda?"

"I've met her a couple of times. She seems more agreeable than his wife was."

"How long was he with Lynda?"

"A few years, I guess."

"Did he have any financial problems?" I asked.

"Off and on. He wasn't great with money, and his ex took most of what they had when they were married. He gambled some. And there were periods when business was slow. He paid his bills. Sometimes it took a while."

I looked at my notes. "I understand you handled his estate."

"Such as it was. I flew out for three days to take care of things. Lynda wasn't much help. She arranged for his service and burial and left me with pretty much everything else. I talked to a lawyer, had him file the paperwork for the estate. There wasn't a will. Jack's bills were pretty much up to date, but there was nothing extra. No life insurance."

"What about his business?"

"There weren't more than three or four active cases. I just called the clients and explained that they'd have to find a new investigator. I wrote a couple of small checks to refund fees for those who had paid retainers."

"Did he leave a computer?"

"Yes, but I don't think he used it much. I gave it to Lynda."

"Any files or papers related to his cases?"

"There were some files," she said. "I didn't go through them in any detail. I put them in storage along with the rest of his stuff."

"Why storage?"

"I thought it was too soon to just get rid of everything. Maybe Lynda, or even his mother, Mary, might want something. He also has a grown daughter in New Mexico—nobody has spoken to her in years. Anyway, I really didn't have time to dispose of all his belongings. I had to get back to work. I just had the stuff put into a storage unit and paid for a year. Sooner or later I'll have to get rid of it, I guess."

"I'll make a deal with you," I said. "I'd like to go through his files to see if there's anything related to my case. If you let me do that, I'll also look for anything that might shed some light on Jack's death. If I find anything, I'll share it with you and the police."

She hesitated. "You said you're a federal prosecutor?"

"Right," I lied. "I can give you a couple of references if you'd like."

"I don't know." She spent a few more minutes asking questions about me and my background. Finally she said, "The files are all closed. No real downside in having you go through them, I guess. But maybe you'll find something. Give me your email address. I'll send you the information you need, and I'll fax the paperwork to the storage place to let you get in."

"Great. Would you happen to have a phone number and address for Lynda Parrish?"

"Somewhere here. Hang on."

She was back in a minute with the information. I thanked her and clicked off. Then, after signaling for my check, I called Lynda.

The woman who answered sounded wary and even a bit fearful. "Yes?"

I explained who I was and that I wanted to talk about Jack.

"I don't think I can help you," she said.

"Why not?"

"I just—I really can't."

"Lynda, it could be important."

"Please don't call me again," she said and disconnected.

Chapter 22

The storage facility was located in an industrial neighborhood in the Midway area of St. Paul, north of University Avenue, near the border with Minneapolis. It was early evening when I arrived, with nightfall closing in. I used an entry code provided by Catherine Dahlen and then showed my ID and picked up a key from the manager, who warned me that the office would be closing shortly.

I found Schott's unit in a narrow lane between two long buildings lined with overhead garage doors. The facility didn't have a lot of light, and I couldn't see any other customers as I drove down the lane to the unit. I got out, looked around, and unlocked the door. Then I struggled with the overhead door but managed to raise it enough to get in and get the faint light on. I surveyed the unit's contents: a couch, a couple of easy chairs, a table, folding chairs, and about a dozen cardboard boxes. Three of the latter appeared to be file boxes.

The boxes were heavy. I got the first one down fairly easily and maneuvered it onto one of the dusty end tables. Then, squinting in the sickly light, I started going through the contents. The files were alphabetical by client, starting with K and ending with S. I spent close to half an hour going through the folders one by one, finding nothing of interest. The files contained the work of a typical small private investigator: surveillance on disability claimants, background checks, investigations of faithless spouses. Each case, it appeared, had been closed for some time.

It took more effort to get the second box down. It contained, in addition to the files from A through K, a couple dozen old-style eight-millimeter videotapes. I matched up the label on each cartridge and confirmed that it corresponded to a closed case in one of the files. The files in this box contained two cases that had been open at the time of Schott's death, but they were no different from the types of cases that had been closed. One client was the same insurance company that accounted for much of his caseload. I couldn't see anything interesting about any of it, and I closed it up.

The third box was a problem. It was up higher than the other two, and I couldn't reach it at all. I brought out my telescoping pointer, but it was too flimsy to move the heavy box. I found a table lamp, moved it over, and tried to use it to push the box close to the edge of the pile. I thought maybe I could get it to fall into my lap. It was more likely that I'd have the folders and their contents scattered all over the floor.

"Let me help you with that."

I jerked around, startled. A figure stood at the door. Tony McCort. I backed up. McCort reached past me, took the file box off the pile, and set it down on the end table. Then he turned around and went back to the door.

He pulled it shut, with both of us inside. Too late, I reached for my purse and the cell phone inside it, but he grabbed the purse out of my hands and tossed it on the couch, out of my reach.

"What do you want?" I asked.

"Just to chat a little."

"How did you get in here? You have to have an access code."

"That's electronic." He pulled out an electronic device about the size of a cigar box, with a little screen and a tiny keyboard. "Anything electronic can be hacked."

"Why did you trap me in the elevator at your building?"

He smiled. "I just let Ivan have a little fun with you. He predicted you'd crack. I didn't think you would. You cost me twenty bucks." He jammed his hands into his pockets and studied me.

"We wanted to see what you were made of. Not much, it turned out."

I felt the heat flooding my face. "Are you going to lock me in here, too?"

"Don't know. I might, if I feel like it. Depends on the answers you give me." He gave me a pitiless once-over. "I'll bet you were hot when you were younger. When you could walk."

Despite the rage I felt at the offensive comment, I found myself, as women are conditioned to do, involuntarily considering his words. Not only was I not so young and unable to walk, but I sported spindly, atrophied legs, permanent calluses on my hands, and shoulders like a linebacker's from propelling myself in a wheelchair.

No, I wasn't hot anymore.

I tried to stuff my rage and shame and focus on the immediate threat. "What do you want?" I asked again.

"We put a tracker on your vehicle," he said. "You took it. That was my property."

He seemed to expect me to respond. I didn't.

"You're from California," he said. I couldn't see what that had to do with anything, but he went on. "I warned you against interfering." He walked across the little room, hands in pockets, looking down. "Specifically, I warned you against trying to pin Lofton's murder on me."

"I thought you had an alibi."

He stared at me, quiet menace in his eyes. "I really, really hate it when someone insults my intelligence. When the police did it—when they questioned me and sent somebody to Arizona to confirm I was there the night of the murder—I didn't mind. They were going through the motions. They have to do that. But you . . ." He leaned closer. "Do I look like an idiot? Somebody too poor or too incompetent to hire out a murder? To hire the best?"

He stood up, and the anger seemed to leave him. "Nobody you've talked to has even suggested that possibility, am I right?"

"You're right."

"I will be governor, and I will get there cleanly and easily, without murder allegations inconveniencing me."

"So what's going on? Everybody just thinks you're a swell guy who would never do anything illegal?"

He laughed. Then he shook his head. "Who's the most obvious suspect in Blake Lofton's murder, Pen? Forget the evidence — who has the most to gain?"

"You."

"Of course. Yet nobody even hints at that possibility. Why not? Because they're fair-minded people who want to give me an even break?" He paused for dramatic effect. "No one has tried to implicate me for one simple reason: I don't want them to. They know there would be serious consequences. Very serious. I thought you understood that, too. But you're from California."

I didn't know what to say.

"The police have left me alone," he continued, "because they know I'm their friend. How about your pal Lexi Candiotti? Fearless and incorruptible, right? Has she suggested that I was involved? Just the opposite, I'll bet. And the prosecutors and reporters? They may not be so sure what would happen to them. But they know there would be something bad. Something that would end their careers . . . or their lives. Or the lives of their families."

He let it sink in. "Ellie Ostlund knows better," he said. "She has a big mouth, but she's wisely decided to keep it shut when it comes to anything personal. She sticks to talking about education policy. A couple of left-wing bloggers didn't understand who I am. They were naive, in over their heads. Let's just say it didn't end well for them. The mayor doesn't care for me, but I own his police supporters. Palmer is looking for a way out, but in the end, he'll have to just shut up and take his medicine."

And now I understood what must have happened to Blake Lofton, the only man with the power and willingness to take on this monster.

He walked over, leaned down, and put his face directly in mine. "I own this state. Soon I'll own it in name as well as in practice. And then people who might be inclined to oppose me, looters and moochers and whiners and parasites, will be encouraged to leave. Very strongly encouraged."

He stood up straight. "So here's a little reality check for you. Andre is going down for murder. Get used to it. Get over it. If you give me any trouble, that nice-looking stepdaughter of his will vanish from this earth. And that hacker nephew of yours? He's very good. He has the capacity and willingness to be a productive citizen, so we'd let him live. But he'd have to spend a couple of years in prison for hacking—just his own reality check. And, of course, when these things happen, you won't be around to see them. Are we communicating here?"

I fought off the need to vomit. When I didn't answer, he said, "I own you. I own your life. You move about this earth and draw breath because I allow it. Now, for that to continue, you need to assure me you're with the program. Are you, Pen?"

"Yes," I whispered.

"Louder."

"Yes," I said, louder.

He walked over, put his foot on my wheelchair, and give it a hard shove. I slammed against the wall behind me, hitting my head on the concrete block. Then he reached down, tore open the front of my shirt, and felt me up with ice cold hands. "I *own* you," he hissed. "Every miserable, crippled square inch of you."

My head spun and my arms seemed to flop helplessly, unable to fight back. I gasped but couldn't scream.

"Nice," he said. "Maybe you've got potential after all." He stood up. "We've put another tracker on your van. You're not going to do a thing to interfere with it. You won't use any other vehicle, either. You'll drive the one you've got, tracker and all, and you'll do it with a fucking smile on your face. You owe me three hundred dollars for the last tracker, the one you stole. But you don't need to pay me now. I've already reimbursed myself from your bank account." He lifted the garage door, then gestured toward the file boxes. "We've been through all this shit. Waste of time." He left.

I don't know how long I sat there in the weak light, alone, outraged, violated, incredulous, and terrified. The door was open now, but there was only darkness and silence outside. Part of me wanted to leave and get as far away as possible, as fast as possible. But I was afraid to leave. Afraid to move. Finally, after a few minutes of breathing deeply and pulling myself together, I pulled my shirt closed and left, pumping my arms, moving my chair as fast as it would go, leaving the door open and the light on.

Chapter 23

I've never actually been thrown from a horse. But, like all parents, my father had always insisted that the thing to do after a mishap was to climb right back up into the saddle. The morning after my confrontation with Tony McCort, I lay in bed, wondering what the hell I was going to do. My father's advice may have been sound, but what if the horse was the wildest, nastiest ride you'd ever been on, an animal that seemed to live only for throwing you violently and then trampling you underfoot for good measure? To successfully remount, I knew I'd need to hold onto this wild steed called life with all the strength I had.

I barely remembered making my way back to the guest house the previous night. I'd wanted to take a long, hot shower, but it would have been a hassle in the guest house's less-than-fully-accessible facilities. More than that, I'd seen *Psycho*, and last night just wasn't the time.

I had woken up several times during the night but was somehow able to get back to sleep each time. The lights in the bedroom, and the rest of the house, were still on. I fought to get the image of Tony McCort out of my mind, but I knew that would take a while. I wished Andre hadn't dismissed so cavalierly the need for security cameras outside the house. But the storage facility had probably had them, and what good had it done?

I looked at my phone; it was ten-thirty. I stared at the ceiling for a couple of minutes, took a long, deep breath, exhaled, and got up. I forced myself through my morning routine. After a shower, a bagel, and some coffee, I felt halfway human again and able to get the fear under control. I called Lexi and arranged to meet her early in the evening. Then, at the crack of noon, I collected my purse and coat and got back up onto the horse.

I didn't see anybody following me as I drove back toward the city, but of course I had to assume McCort was telling the truth about replacing the tracker I'd removed. And I couldn't take it off by myself. Now that the fear had receded a little, I could think about why McCort had assaulted me last night. The easy answer was that he wanted me off the case. He had definitely wanted to keep me from pursuing anything linking him to the murder. But he hadn't actually asked me to withdraw — not last night, and not the previous time I'd seen him. To the contrary, by putting a tracker on my vehicle, he'd seemed to assume I would continue my efforts. So what was going on?

The answer seemed to have something to do with Jack Schott, who had been asking questions about McCort in the candidate's old neighborhood. McCort told me he had already gone through all of Schott's files in the storage unit. And now he was tracking me as I tried to find out who had hired Schott and what, if anything, the detective had found out about McCort. A couple of tentative conclusions seemed in order.

First, it was likely Blake Lofton who had hired Schott to investigate McCort.

Second, Schott had probably found something significant, enough to reward Isaac Woodruff with a new vehicle and convince Lofton that he now possessed an "October surprise" that could ensure his victory over McCort.

Third, this damaging information was still in the wind. Lofton hadn't had a chance to use it, and McCort was still very interested in finding it. If he'd had Lofton killed, the missing evidence hadn't been recovered after the murder.

Fourth, the information seemed to relate to McCort's distant past, perhaps to something that had happened in his old neighborhood.

These hypotheses seemed solid enough to proceed on for now. Still, it was a big leap to suggest that McCort had hired a hitman to kill his opponent, even though everybody thought—and I now agreed—that he was more than capable of doing just that.

But, suspiciously, nobody seemed to think he had actually done so.

I called Kenny. "One more thing I'd like you to check out," I said. "There are two left-wing bloggers who were critical of Tony McCort. They reportedly ran into trouble—may have been injured or killed or had other bad things happen to them. Could you do a quick check for that?"

"Sure. I'll have that other stuff for you shortly."

"Fine."

Now that I was back up on the horse, I returned to the storage facility. Taking a deep breath, I entered, apologized to the manager for leaving the unit open last night, and returned to the scene of the crime. With frequent glances out the open door, I went through the third box of Schott's files, which Tony McCort had thoughtfully taken down off the stack for me. As McCort had predicted, I found nothing of interest in the carton. I put everything away and closed up the unit.

My next task seemed even more problematic. I needed to take another crack at contacting Lynda Parrish, Schott's girlfriend. When I did, McCort would know about it. Would he approve or not? I hated the thought of being monitored and of a creep like McCort deciding what I could and couldn't do. Even worse, it might put Lynda in danger. But McCort had almost certainly talked to her already. And right now, I couldn't see another way. I left the storage facility and began driving north.

Parrish's apartment was in a three-story building, consisting of about forty units, in Roseville, a suburb north of St. Paul. It was close to four-thirty when I rolled into the entrance, only to be confronted by a security door. The button for Parrish's unit, 204, was just out of my reach. I waited for a couple of minutes until an older woman came along. She smiled at me as she produced her own key and turned the lock. "Do you need help?" she asked.

"Hi," I said. "I can't quite reach the button for Lynda in 204. I tried calling her, but I think she's on her phone."

"She may be driving," the woman said. "She probably isn't quite home yet."

"Fine. I'll just wait." One problem with that was that I didn't know what Lynda looked like.

She didn't offer to let me in, even though most people seem to think I look pretty harmless. "She shouldn't be long at all," the woman said and went through the door.

The door closed slowly, which enabled me to unobtrusively shove a credit card into the door jamb when the woman's back was turned. I saw her push the elevator button for the third floor and get onto the elevator a minute later. When the elevator reached the third floor, I pulled the door open, went through, and took the elevator to the second floor, where I waited a couple of doors down from 204.

Waiting gave me a chance to think about Tony McCort and the things he'd told me last night. I couldn't swallow his claims to "own" all of Minnesota's major politicians and institutions. Still, his influence seemed to reach both broadly and deeply across the state, to places and people I didn't want to think about.

How about your pal Lexi Candiotti?

Lynda appeared less than fifteen minutes later, a plump woman in her early fifties with a heavy, weary step. She took her key out, and I rolled forward. "Lynda?"

"Yes?"

"I'm Pen Wilkinson. I called yesterday."

"About Jack."

"Yes."

Her expression, panicky at first, resolved itself into unmistakable fear. "I don't have anything to say." She quickly tried to jam her key into the lock, fumbling with it.

"It'll only take a minute."

"No, no."

After a couple of vain attempts to fit the key into the lock with a trembling hand, she looked up, tears of frustration and fear in her eyes.

I rolled closer and took her unresisting hand. "What did they do to you?" I whispered.

"Nothing. They—they . . ." She broke down.

A minute later we were sitting in her small living room while she dried her tears. Finally, she blew her nose. "I can't say anything," she said. "They'll kill me."

"Who are 'they'?"

"I don't know."

"If they've already questioned you, and you can't identify them, you're probably not in any danger."

She considered that. "Maybe."

"What did they do?"

She took a breath and exhaled. "There was one man. He wore a mask."

"When did this happen?"

"During the summer. Shortly after Jack . . . shortly after he died."

"What happened?"

"He said he was a cop. He flashed ID, but I couldn't really read the name on it. When I opened the door, he shoved me into a chair, tied me up, and started asking me questions. He asked about any files or information hidden by Jack. He asked about other residences or rental properties or storage units Jack might have owned. I told him about the cabin, but I didn't know of anything else. Then he asked if Jack was involved in any cases concerning politics or politicians. I said I didn't know anything about his cases."

"What happened next?"

"He hit me . . . oh, God, he hit me. He threatened to kill me. But I didn't know. I just didn't . . ." She sobbed, and I took her hand. Eventually she calmed down. "He kept me tied up and searched the apartment for over an hour. He tore everything apart. But he never found what he was looking for."

"Did he ask anything else, Lynda? Think hard."

"He asked about close friends or family members Jack might have confided in. I couldn't tell them much of anything. He has one daughter, who lives in New Mexico. He hasn't seen her in years, and they rarely talk. His ex-wife died a couple of years ago — they'd been divorced for fifteen years. He hardly ever sees his mother, Mary. She lives up in Wisconsin somewhere." She hesitated.

"Is there something else you want to tell me about Mary?"

"She's crazy."

"What did you do when the masked man left?"

"I managed to free myself. Then I just stayed here for a couple of days. I was too afraid to leave. Too scared to call the police."

She'd been a little slower to get back up onto the horse than I had, I thought. But she had done it. "Is there anything else you can remember about what happened that night?"

"No. If there was, I'm not sure I'd tell you. But I guess it feels good to have told somebody about it. I can't see how any of it helps Andre Woodruff."

I couldn't, either.

"They might know I've met with you," she said. "Is he going to come back?"

"I doubt it. No guarantee, but I'm sure he's satisfied he got everything from you."

She nodded. "Who is he?"

I just shrugged. I didn't want to tell her he probably worked for the next governor.

I started back to Lake Minnetonka, frustrated and apprehensive. McCort hadn't gotten what he had sought from Lynda Parrish. Where had he looked next? And where should I look next?

I drove back toward Minneapolis on I-35W, then exited the freeway on Stinson Boulevard. I turned onto a side street and immediately noticed a dark sedan following me. I made a couple of turns on side streets. The sedan followed. I returned to the freeway frontage road, pulling in at a McDonald's. I backed into a parking spot at the rear of the restaurant and shut the engine off. The dark sedan that had followed me parked across the aisle. Lexi Candiotti got out, walked over, and got into the passenger seat. She produced an electronic device the size of a cigar box and switched it on.

"I borrowed this from the tech people," she said. "If they've bugged the van, this will thwart them."

"Nobody following?" I asked.

"No. You were clean. They're relying on the tracker. Do you want me to take it off?"

I swallowed hard. "Yes."

She was back with it a few minutes later. "Same type as before," she said. "It has its own power source, so it will keep running until you take the battery out."

"Thanks."

"So, you apparently had another chat with Tony McCort?"

"Yes."

"Want to tell me about it?"

I decided to skip the nastier details. "He's trying to manipulate me, to get me to find something that Jack Schott left behind. But he also seemed concerned that I not try to pin the Lofton murder on him."

"But he's in the clear on that."

"Yes, he is. Could we talk about that a little?"

A wary look passed over her face. "He has an alibi. So does his buddy, Bolger."

"What if he hired somebody else to do it?"

Her response was measured. "That possibility was investigated, of course. It was rejected for two reasons. First of all, we checked with all the state and FBI sources and snitches. There was absolutely no hint anywhere on the streets, in wiretaps, or elsewhere about a professional hit in Minnesota."

"Okay."

"Second, there were aspects of the crime itself that didn't appear professional. There was the use of a knife, which is messy. Not unheard of, but unusual. And the knife wasn't used in an efficient, professional fashion. It took several thrusts, not well aimed. More than that, there were several thrusts more than necessary, indicating possible overkill."

"Personal," I said.

"Looks that way."

"All of that makes sense. So then, why did McCort taunt me?"

"Taunt?"

"He bragged that he owned the police and media, and that nobody was even mentioning the possibility that he was involved."

"I don't know why he'd say that."

I gave her a few more seconds, but she obviously wasn't going to say anything further, and this wasn't the time to confront her about McCort's boast that she would never go after him.

I nodded and squeezed her hand.

After Lexi left, I looked out at the drive-through and the parking lot and the Big Macs for a long time. Of course I should stop. I should never have started. Every instinct told me not only to go home, but to call James and tell him I was ready to quit doing this kind of thing. But I felt myself being pulled, as always, toward the darkness, into the black hole of uncertainty and messiness and, yes, of evil.

Traffic slowed to a crawl as I drove west on I-94 near downtown. I could see numerous flashing lights from police cars up ahead. Eventually the police directed us up an exit ramp and onto a makeshift detour. It must have been a huge accident, I thought.

When I got back to the guest house, Alicia came over with a pizza, and we sat in the kitchen, eating, saying little. I wanted to tell her I was making progress, that there was hope for Andre. But I couldn't.

Anita came over about half an hour after Alicia left.

"Hi," I said.

She nodded and sank heavily into an easy chair, looking exhausted and stressed out. "Tell me something good," she said.

"I wish I could report a lot of new information, but I can't. I'm following the only real lead I've found so far." I described my efforts to reconstruct Jack Schott's activities and find any information he might have left behind.

Anita didn't say anything.

"I know, it's not much," I said.

She didn't contradict me. "Where is Tony McCort in all this?" she asked.

"I think he's trying to manipulate me, to use me to locate what Schott found." I didn't tell her about McCort's assaulting me in the storage unit. I was afraid to even bring it up, not to mention ashamed and humiliated.

Anita didn't talk for a long time. Finally she said, "What do you hear about Blake Lofton?"

"I'm having trouble finding anybody who genuinely disliked the guy," I said. "For all his insensitivity, there seemed to be a genuineness about him that appealed to a lot of people."

She nodded. "He was unique. He was from an old, wealthy family, a corporate CEO, but he was a liberal. Not a wild liberal, but progressive. That's not totally unprecedented, but it's a little unusual. The real difference was marrying a black woman. Having black kids. He was our best hope for real healing in this state."

That might be true, I thought, but Lofton wouldn't have seen it that way. In his mind, he was simply having things the way he wanted them.

"Tell me," Anita said, "what do you hear about Andre?"

"Nothing bad."

"Of course not. He's a low-key, go-along, uncomplaining kind of guy, right? A loyal servant, doing Blake's bidding for decades. Yes, Blake. No, Blake. Right away, Blake."

She sat up straighter. "Let me tell you something, Pen. Andre is the strongest man I've ever known. A very proud man. He did what he did, going along with Blake for all those years, for his family, not himself. And I know it sounds crazy, but he did it for Blake. For his friend. It took superhuman control to act the way he did, to stuff all the anger and resentment at playing second fiddle." She paused. "And he did it for his people, absorbing all the condescension and shit, making himself acceptable to the white power structure, like his father did. It was a conscious decision he made, to be the adult in the room—quiet, dignified, competent, in control. Tony Dungy or Barack Obama. It's what James could never pull off. He just didn't have that kind of control. Few people do."

I nodded. James hadn't been a good fit for the corporate world, a place where he couldn't be his brash, aggressive self. He'd needed to run his own business.

Neither of us spoke for a long minute. Finally Anita said, "You think Andre did it."

"What I think doesn't matter."

"It not only matters," she snapped, "it's the whole ball game. Our only hope is to find somebody who believes in his

136

innocence, who's willing to look at alternatives." She sat back and seemed to shrink into the chair. "I can't lose him. Alicia will still have James. I won't."

Anita left, and I got ready for bed. I turned on the news, which led with the story of a massive demonstration organized by Rights for People of Color. And now I realized that the traffic jam on I-94 hadn't been caused by an accident; RPC had blocked the freeway.

The scene shifted. Darkness had fallen, and police were forcibly removing the demonstrators from the freeway. Dozens of officers were picking up seated figures and dragging them to paddy wagons.

A third scene materialized on the TV screen, also showing arrests being made at the freeway protest. But in this scene, the demonstrators weren't going quietly, and an officer was beating one of them with a baton. Other protestors tried to intervene, and soon more batons were swinging, the police shouting the name of Duke Sorrel as they roughed up the demonstrators. The camera shots turned jerky and there was blood, screaming and shouting.

Horrified, I watched the screen, a window to a world going dark, where despairing rays of hope succumbed to the nightfall. As the violence continued, the cameras recorded our descent into a dystopia where all the features of a civilized society—rationality, principle, rule of law and, ultimately, truth itself—gave way, reverting to the brutal, primal reality of the tribe. I shut the television off and stared at the blank, black screen. And then, for Alicia, for James, for the world we lived in, but mostly for myself, I cried.

Chapter 24

June 8, 1989

Andre waited until his father had left for a meeting of church elders, then went downstairs to the dining room, where Simone was doing her homework at the table. He sat down across from her.

She looked up. "Hey."

"Hey," Andre said. "When are we going to talk about what's going on around here?"

Simone put her pencil down. "What do you mean?"

"Come on, Sim. Don't play dumb. Did you know that you and I are not on scholarship at Talmadge? That Dad pays everything out of his pocket?"

She looked surprised, but not shocked. "I didn't think he had that kind of money."

"He doesn't. Any idea where it comes from?"

"No. Did you ask him?"

"I did. He lied. Said we had insurance money and wealthy benefactors from the church. We don't."

"Have you asked Isaac?"

It was a reasonable question, Andre thought. Of the three siblings, Isaac was closest to their father. Andre didn't answer. Instead he asked, "Have you ever met Isaac's friend Aaron who comes to services every Wednesday night? Has a nice car with Illinois plates?"

"I've seen him," she said. "I've never talked to him."

"What is Isaac up to?"

"What do you mean?"

138

"Come on. Do you really believe this Aaron works at the hospital?"

"Why wouldn't he?"

Andre sighed and clasped his hands together on the table. "Sim, something's not right here. Dad and Isaac have been bull-shitting us. They're up to something."

"You're being overly dramatic."

"I'm just the dramatic type, right? Come on, things just don't add up. Why does that creep Tony hang around here and at the church?"

She looked defensive. "He doesn't have much of a family, Andre. Dad feels sorry for him. And I—I guess I do, too."

"It doesn't make sense. This neighborhood has gotten dangerous for a white kid. Dangerous in general. Why would he brave the crack and the gangs?"

"Drugs are everywhere. Crack in our neighborhoods, powder out in the suburbs."

"He'd be safer in the suburbs, or a white neighborhood in the city." Andre paused. "Of course, he has the world's biggest crush on you."

She smiled. "Maybe a little."

"Damnit, you think this is a joke? Something is seriously wrong here."

She sighed, looked away, and turned back to Andre. "So there are some things that don't quite make sense. What do you want me to do about it?"

"You're pretty friendly with a cop."

"You mean Officer Dave? I guess I know him a little bit."

"A little?"

"A little," she said firmly. "He responded when I called him about that vandalism at the church. After that, I interviewed him for a school project. I guess I've run into him a couple of times since then."

"Totally by accident?"

She gave him an exasperated look. "Yes, big brother. By accident."

"Okay, okay. Do you trust him? I mean, really trust him?"

"I think I do."

"Maybe you need to talk to him now."

"I'll think about it."

Chapter 25

It took a ton of effort, but I mounted the horse again the next morning. Before leaving the guest house, I called Mary Schott, Jack Schott's mother. She didn't answer, so I left a detailed message, explaining who I was and asking to talk about her son. I assumed McCort had already attempted to speak with her and presumably hadn't learned anything. I couldn't expect much, either, but it was the only lead I had left.

After making the call, I drove into the city and met Kenny for breakfast. I asked him to come to a different restaurant downtown, instead of in the university area. There was no reason to make it any easier for McCort to know whom I was meeting with. Kenny had said he didn't have much to tell me and could probably tell me over the phone, but I figured I at least owed him some more pancakes for his efforts. The GPS tracker sat on the seat beside me. I'd keep it there, working, until I saw a serious need to go off McCort's grid.

My nephew was already seated at the diner when I arrived. "Hey, Aunt Pen."

"Have you ordered your pancakes yet?"

He grinned. "Absolutely."

I ordered a bagel, yogurt and coffee. "What did your discreet snooping tell you?" I asked.

"This guy—Schott—didn't have much of an online presence. He didn't have a lot of money and was usually slow in paying his bills. Early in the year, he'd gotten pretty seriously behind and was carrying some decent-sized credit card balances."

"Did he have any money coming in?"

141

"Yes, but not enough, apparently. He got fairly regular payments from two insurance companies."

"His largest clients."

Our food arrived, and Kenny dug in. "Then he came into some money," he said with his mouth full. "In June, he got a payment of over $50,000. That was bigger than anything he'd ever received."

"What was the source of the money?"

"I couldn't tell. It came from an offshore corporation, and I couldn't find out who was behind it. If you gave me some more time I could probably dig it out, but I didn't want to set off any alarm bells."

"Good thinking," I said. I was reasonably sure the money had come from Blake Lofton.

"Anyway," Kenny continued, "Schott pretty much used the money to get current on his bills."

"Could you find any files stored online?" I asked.

"No. Like I said, he didn't seem to do much online. But here's the interesting thing: Somebody else has been looking. Seriously. They're good, but I was still able to pick up their tracks. Some of the searching occurred after Schott's death."

"But in your judgment, they didn't find anything?"

"Nope. No more than I did."

"Anything else on Schott?"

"Not that I could find."

"What about Isaac Woodruff?"

"He has a chronic case of the shorts, but nothing too serious. Owns his house outright. Bought it in . . ." He consulted notes on his phone.

"Two thousand three," I said.

"Right. He gets a regular monthly income, which is enough to pay most of his bills, but with basically nothing left over. No luxuries."

"Where does the income come from?"

"Weird again, Aunt Pen. Another untraceable offshore corporation."

I hadn't expected that. "Not the same—"

"No, a different outfit from the one that paid Schott."

I mulled that over. I'd assumed that Isaac had been receiving money regularly, but I figured it had probably come from Andre or Simone, or both. But apparently it hadn't, nor was it likely to have come from Lofton, assuming it was he who had paid Schott.

"Isaac took title to a new SUV four months ago," Kenny said. "It's not clear where the money for that came from."

I nodded. I'd have to give it all some more thought.

"I looked for those left-wing bloggers," Kenny said. "I think I found them."

I sucked in a breath. "Go ahead."

"One of them was named Jane Hyser. She wrote a respected blog on state politics and was one of Tony McCort's biggest critics. A little over a year ago, she was found dead in her apartment. The coroner ruled her death to be from natural causes, but they never isolated the actual cause. The other blogger was a guy named Brad Van Ness. He was a badass—very snarky, and I have to say, he really tore McCort apart, just ridiculed the hell out of him."

"What happened to him?" I asked, feeling sick.

"Last year—just a couple of weeks after Hyser died—he vanished. Just flat-out disappeared without a trace. The FBI and St. Paul police have been looking for him, and they've had a few tips, but nothing solid."

"Given they were both critics of McCort, these cases sound like fertile ground for conspiracy theorists on the Internet."

"You'd think so, but nobody has suggested anything sinister about McCort, at least not that I saw."

"I guess I wouldn't, either."

"Hyser and Van Ness wrote about a lot of stuff besides McCort. And there are other bloggers who attack him all the time."

"Interesting," I said.

"It sure is." He turned serious. "Aunt Pen, has McCort threatened you?"

"No, no."

"Good." *Bullshit*, his expression said. "Do they have good security at that place you're staying at out on the lake?"

"They have an alarm system."

"With all the publicity about Andre Woodruff, they need more than that. Cameras and motion sensors for sure."

"I'm just a guest there, Kenny. It will be fine."

He gave me another reluctant nod. "Well, be careful."

"Of course. In the meantime, stay handy."

Kenny left. I checked my phone and noticed that a message had come in during breakfast. It was from Mary Schott, Jack Schott's mother. I called her back, and a clipped, brittle female voice answered.

"You have questions about my son?"

"That's right."

"Explain who you are, please."

I repeated my pitch.

"You are not the first person to inquire. An employee of the Minnesota Bureau of Criminal Apprehension contacted me after Jack's death. And then there was another man."

"Bolger?" I guessed.

"Yes."

"Did you talk to him?"

"No. He came up here, but I did not speak to him of any matters of substance."

"Why not?"

"I would prefer not to discuss that with you without meeting you in person."

"I only have a few questions," I said. "It wouldn't take long."

"You may visit if you like."

I jotted down directions to her house, which was located on a lake in western Wisconsin.

"You may visit this afternoon," she said.

"I'm leaving now."

Chapter 26

Mary Schott's home was a couple of hours north and east of Minneapolis, across the St. Croix River in Wisconsin. I felt my tension easing a bit as my route took me around lakes and through forests. I had left the GPS tracker in Minneapolis. I couldn't really articulate a reason for doing it beyond gut instinct, nor did I want to think about McCort's reaction to the removal. I had little hope that Jack Schott's mother would be able to tell me anything useful; I felt as though I was going through the motions in pursuing my sole, fading lead.

*　　*　　*

"You're going where?" Tony McCort said into the phone.

"Amery, Wisconsin," Bolger replied. "Where Jack Schott's mother lives. I'm on my way there now."

"I thought you already talked to her."

"I did. I got jackshit out of her."

"You were convinced she didn't know anything?"

"Yes, I was convinced. The old biddy is batshit crazy. But just in case, I paid a professional busybody who lives down the road to let me know if anybody interesting ever visits the Schott place. Guess what she told me today?"

"Maybe that a white handicapped van showed up?"

"Bingo. I jumped in the car as soon as I heard."

"The tracker still shows her back at Lake Minnetonka. She took it off, the bitch."

"Apparently."

"She's really going to regret that," McCort said.

"I still doubt the mother knows anything. But we can't be a hundred percent sure, and who knows? Maybe Pen is a whiz at extracting information from senile old women."

"So what will you do?"

"I'm not sure. Just play it by ear for now."

"Good luck."

*　　　*　　　*

I followed a quarter-mile winding driveway through dense, color-splashed woods. The Schott home, though modest, was a house, not a cabin. I parked in front of a single-story frame structure which looked uncommonly neat and well-kept. I transferred and descended the ramp to the gravel yard. I rolled up to the house, wondering how I would get up the three steps to the front door. We could talk outside, as I often did when visiting people in inaccessible places, but it was uncomfortably cold on this overcast October day.

The door was opened by a small but formidable-looking woman with dyed brown hair, small, severe eyes, and half-glasses on a chain around her neck. She looked me up and down. "You are Ms. Wilkinson. You didn't advise me of your handicap."

I shrugged. "You didn't advise me of yours, either."

She gave me a startled look.

"You wear glasses," I said. "Your eyesight is defective. That is irrelevant to your mental and social capabilities. So is my handicap."

Her face scrunched up in thought. "You're correct. You may come in."

Before I could react, she had grabbed the handles of my chair and turned me around. "Wait," I said. "You don't have to—"

"Quite all right. I used to be a nurse. I am capable."

147

Showing amazing strength for a small woman who looked to be in her seventies, she pulled me up the three steps and into the house. Startled, I found myself inside a room that was spotless, tidy, and smelled of disinfectant. She closed the door behind me.

"Thanks for making time for me, Mrs. Schott," I said and held out my hand. She regarded me with a stony glare, and after an awkward moment, I withdrew the hand. I followed her into the room, scanning walls and shelves in vain for personal photographs or mementos.

"Would you like coffee?" she asked, sounding as though I didn't have much choice.

"That would be nice, thank you."

Mrs. Schott disappeared, and I could hear the sound of running water for several minutes as I scanned the room again. The walls were bare except for a crucifix and two statues of the Virgin Mary.

She returned with a tray, which held a coffee pot, two cups, and containers of cream and sugar. As she poured coffee for me, I noticed that her hands were red and raw. I spooned sugar into my cup.

"When did Mr. Bolger contact you?" I began, noticing that she was wiping off the sugar spoon I had used with a tissue.

"It was approximately fourteen weeks ago. I will provide you with the exact date when we've finished our coffee."

"No need for that," I said, taking a sip of the coffee. It was strong enough to keep a moose awake for three days.

"No trouble at all. I like to be exact."

"What did Bolger want?"

"He asked questions about my son. I didn't tell him anything."

"Why not?"

"He told me he worked for a Mr. McCort, who is a political candidate. I distrust politicians. He also said he used to be a police officer. I do not care to deal with police officials. They treated my son abominably. They destroyed his life, forcing him out of his employment with the St. Paul police department. But worst of all, Mr. Bolger acknowledged to me that he is not a God-fearing man. Are you a God-fearing woman, Ms. Wilkinson?"

"I don't know how to answer that. I'm not much of a churchgoer now. My father took us regularly to a Methodist church when I was young."

"Methodist," she said doubtfully, apparently placing that somewhere in between Scientology and the Jehovah's Witnesses. "Do you believe in God?"

"Yes." I'd had some fairly serious doubts at times, but I wasn't about to share them with Mrs. Schott.

She stared at me for a full minute, appraising, deciding. "Very well. I believe you are a God-fearing woman. I will share with you what Mr. Bolger said."

"What is that?"

"He asked if my son could have left sensitive material with me, or hidden it on these premises, before his death."

"What did you tell him?"

"We had the aforementioned discussion about his religious beliefs, and I resolved not to speak further with him."

I managed to finish the rest of my coffee. "How did he react to that?"

"He behaved in a manner that confirmed my suspicions about him. He offered me money for the information. When I refused, he threatened me with physical harm."

"My God—are you all right?"

"Oh, yes. I was not intimidated." She reached into a narrow vertical case beside her chair and withdrew a shotgun. I gasped and flinched.

"I ordered him to leave the premises," she said. "I followed him out the door and shot out his windshield. I said that I had seen a firearm under his coat and that he should place it carefully on the ground, which he did. I then stated that if he didn't leave at once, I would kill him. He left, and I have not seen him since."

I suppressed an astonished smile. "That's quite a story, Mrs. Schott."

"It is unfortunate that a widow living alone finds it necessary to arm herself. But I am confronted from time to time by solicitors and officials of the government. I have treated them similarly."

Suddenly I didn't feel quite so comfortable in her presence. "You apparently didn't answer Bolger's question. What would you have told him?"

"I would have replied that my son did not hide any sensitive materials with me or on these premises."

I nodded. "Well, thank you, Mrs. Sch—"

"However, I believe that Jack may well have done so in another place."

My pulse rate doubled. "Go on."

"Jack visited me approximately two weeks before his death. I'll provide you with the exact date."

"That's not nec—"

"Follow me, please." She stood up and headed down a short hallway. I followed her to a little alcove next to a back door. A small table sat next to a bookcase containing dozens of identical green notebooks, carefully numbered but otherwise unmarked. Mrs. Schott took a loose-leaf notebook from the top of the shelf and flipped through plastic-covered sheets. Glancing across the table, I could see page after page of painstakingly handwritten indexes containing names, subjects, page numbers, and dates.

"Yes, here it is." She replaced the index, took the book numbered fifty-six, and leafed through it. "Here it is," she repeated. "June fourth. Jack visited and stayed for one hour, twenty-two minutes."

She consulted the index again, then opened a page in the same volume. "Mr. Bolger visited on July eleventh. He stayed for seventeen minutes."

"Your diaries are . . . very detailed," I said.

"I try to be complete and exact."

"If you don't mind my asking, what are those numbers next to each day?"

"My investment numbers. I advance my number by one for each date."

"Your investment numbers?"

"Yes," she said patiently. "It took me a long time to derive the system, but I know it's the proper one. It consists of the partial combined birthdates of myself, Jack's father, and Jack, divided by three—the Holy Trinity is a constant, you know—multiplied by a number representing each day's date, which advances by one. It took me a lot of experimentation, and a lot of thought and prayer, but I know it's right. Of course, the return is not yet complete. Only the Lord knows when the bulk of the return will occur."

"Your investments are lottery tickets," I said.

"It's the only way of putting my investments in the Lord's hands, to be determined by fate, by the laws of God, rather than the laws of men. Stocks and bonds—those markets are controlled by wicked men who lend at usury. I'm a widow, of course, and I don't have a great deal of money to invest, since Jack's father was not a good provider. But I've learned my lesson about money. It's in the Lord's hands, along with the rest of my affairs."

I felt cold seepage along the upper part of my spine. "Your husband is deceased?"

"Yes. Robert died four years, twenty-six days ago. He was, God rest his soul, a weak man. He was steady and never hurt anyone, but he was spineless and lacked ambition. He worked for the same insurance company as a bookkeeper for thirty years."

I had a sudden desire to get out of there as quickly as possible. "Mrs. Schott, you said there was a place your son might have hidden sensitive material."

She returned volume fifty-six to the shelf, went back to her seat, and clasped her hands together on the table. "I believe that Jack could have hidden something at his father's lake cabin. I have not looked for it, since it would not have concerned me."

"His father's cabin. Not his, or yours?"

"Correct. Robert's family and mine each had cabins in this area. That is how we met each other, in fact. Jack's sister, Catherine, will inherit my family's property, which includes this house. Jack inherited the cabin belonging to Robert's family. For some reason, he never sold it. I do not know whether the title was ever transferred to his name after Robert's death."

I would have bet that it hadn't been, and that the failure to transfer title had been the reason McCort and Bolger hadn't found it. Or maybe they hadn't thought to search in a rural Wisconsin county at all. Catherine apparently hadn't thought of it, either, in winding up Schott's affairs. "Jack had his own cabin in Minnesota," I said. "Did he ever use his father's property here in Wisconsin?"

"Rarely. He preferred his own."

"How far away is your husband's cabin?"

"Six point seven miles."

"Mrs. Schott, would it be possible to take a look at your husband's cabin to find whatever Jack may have hidden there?"

She stood up. "Yes. We can go there now."

Chapter 27

I followed Mary Schott's precisely-articulated directions as she sat in my van's passenger seat. It took us about fifteen minutes to reach her late husband's family cabin. I carefully negotiated the long, rutted gravel driveway, with branches brushing against the van on both sides. I parked in a small clearing next to the dilapidated structure, which was far smaller and more rustic than the house Mary now lived in. Dusk was setting in, and nightfall wouldn't be far behind.

"Please remain here," Mary said. "I believe it would be more efficient for me to conduct the search."

"Do you have someplace in mind to look?"

"I do. There is a space behind a board by the fireplace where Jack used to hide toys from his sister."

"Okay."

"He persisted in doing so even after I imposed severe disciplinary measures." She got out and walked briskly up the two rickety wooden steps to the door, letting herself in with a key. A light went on inside. I opened my window, letting in cold, quiet air, pungent with the smell of leaves. I hoped Mary Schott would find what we were looking for. And then I hoped I could leave this woman, who gave me a serious case of the creeps, as quickly as possible. Idly, I pulled out my phone. Zero bars. My discomfort level ratcheted up another notch.

Mary was back in two minutes, apparently empty-handed. She locked up and then came over and got into the van.

"Any luck?" I asked.

"Yes." She pulled a memory stick from her pocket.

I took it with a shaking hand. "I don't suppose you have a—"

"No, I don't have a computer, and I have no idea what information might be contained on this device."

She directed me back to the house, where I thanked her profusely. "Some dangerous people are looking for this," I added. "I'd keep that shotgun handy."

"Would that be Mr. Bolger?"

"Yes."

"I am not afraid of him."

A little more fear might be a good idea, I thought. She'd surprised Bolger last time; he'd be ready if he returned.

It was dark when I left Mary's house, trying to retrace my route using my memory and Mary's directions in reverse. I wanted badly to find out what was on the flash drive, but without a computer or electronic tablet, there was no way to check. The information had to be important; Schott had gone to a lot of work to hide it.

I'd gone about two miles when the headlights appeared in my mirror. I didn't want to drive any faster on a dark, winding gravel road. I did anyway. I couldn't see how Bolger could have tracked me here, but there was no reason to take any chances.

The headlights were closing fast—way too fast. I increased my speed a little more, but I was already driving faster than I wanted to. It was no use; the headlights came right up behind me. And then they swerved to the left.

I sped up some more as the vehicle moved up beside me. It appeared to be an SUV, but I couldn't get a good look at it, since it was dark and I had to pay attention to the road. Up ahead, the road came to an end at a T intersection. I pushed hard on the hand brake, skidding on the gravel. The SUV was forced to drop back. I took a right turn, which would eventually lead back to a county road.

The SUV was on my bumper almost immediately. The driver flashed his brights, signaling to me to pull over. I pushed the hand accelerator, but the pursuer stayed on my tail. Once again, he began to move around to overtake me. And once again he was forced to back off when we reached a sharp bend in the road. When we'd rounded the curve, the SUV tried a new tactic. He nudged my van with his bumper. I screamed as metal hit metal and the van jerked forward. Was he toying with me?

Bang. I was thrown back against my seat as the SUV hit my bumper again. Up ahead, the road narrowed as it went over a little bridge spanning a creek. Instinctively, I slowed down. But then I realized that the bridge was probably too narrow for two vehicles side-by-side, so I shot forward. My pursuer dropped back a little as we both crossed the bridge.

Bolger was on me immediately after we crossed the bridge. I didn't know for sure it was him, of course, but who else would it be? The road curved to the left as he came up beside me. As he did, I slammed on the brake, hard. The SUV shot forward, fishtailed, and went partway into the ditch. I fishtailed myself, fighting to stay in control on the gravel road, and within seconds I was also partway in the ditch, with two wheels off the road. I saw the SUV just ahead of me, spinning its wheels, spraying gravel.

I stopped myself, took a deep breath, and ever so slowly inched forward, finally succeeding at getting the passenger side front wheel onto the road. And then I got the hell out of there, leaving the SUV spinning its wheels. Within thirty seconds, however, I could see the headlights in my mirror again. I slowed down abruptly as I reached the asphalt county road. I was supposed to turn left. But maybe I should turn right to throw off Bolger, or whoever he was. Then I noticed that the gravel road I was on actually continued on the other side. With only slight hesitation, I drove forward.

I crossed the road and pressed the accelerator. After going a couple hundred feet, I shut off my lights and slowed way down. In my mirror, I saw the headlights appear at the intersection. After a long pause, they turned left, the way I'd originally planned to go. After a few seconds, I turned my lights back on and kept going down the gravel road. I didn't want to be on the county road, where the SUV's driver might see my headlights.

For a good half hour, I continued on an aimless course through the countryside on gravel roads, now thoroughly lost, putting as much distance as I could between myself and the county road. Finally I pulled over to the side of the road and sat for several minutes, willing my heartbeat to slow down, wiping off sweat and fighting off nausea. I checked my phone again: still no signal, which rendered my navigation app useless. I looked up in the sky; the moon had been in front of me when I had left Mary Schott's place, traveling west. I figured if I drove toward the moon I'd be headed in a general westerly direction, toward Minnesota. It wasn't much of a plan, but I couldn't think of anything else.

So I drove on toward the moon, stopping every few minutes to check my cell reception. After about fifteen minutes, I came to a major highway. I turned left, and within a few minutes a sign identified the road as state highway 35, the main north-south route along the Wisconsin side of the St. Croix. After a few more minutes I had a cell signal, and my navigation app duly directed me across the river at Osceola and into Minnesota. After a few more minutes, I pulled over again and called Mary Schott, warning her that Bolger had probably tried to run me off the road and that he might come back to confront her again. She still didn't sound concerned.

Next, I took the burner cell phone Lexi Candiotti had given me and used it to place an anonymous call to the Polk County Sheriff's Department, warning them of an imminent threat to Mary Schott. I figured there was no point in reporting my altercation with the SUV, involving a vehicle and driver I couldn't identify, doing things I couldn't prove. I couldn't even say for sure where the attacks had occurred.

Finally, I called Anita Woodruff and warned her that Bolger was after me and might well try to find me at their house. She said the family would spend the night elsewhere. That done, I resumed the trip to Minneapolis. It was all I could do.

Chapter 28

I woke up at eight the next morning at James Carter's condo downtown. I hadn't wanted to go back to Lake Minnetonka, and safety trumped pride. I got dressed and called Lexi Candiotti, describing how I'd gotten the memory stick from Schott's mother and how I'd been chased by the mystery SUV in rural Wisconsin.

For once, she sounded impressed rather than skeptical. "I'll be damned, Pen. You've got a live one. I never would have thought the Schott angle would amount to anything. But how does it find us another suspect in the Lofton murder?"

"I don't know. That depends on what's on the jump drive. I need to retrieve my computer from the Woodruffs' house in order to read it."

"And you think Bolger might be watching the place?"

"It's the logical place to pick up my trail."

"You could find another computer somewhere."

"I know. I need some clean clothes."

Silence. She wasn't impressed.

"I also need to get my stuff."

More silence.

"You know. Paraplegic supplies."

"Oh, right." A lot of people were uncomfortable with, and nearly always uninterested in, the clinical details of a paraplegic's day-to-day existence of catheters, infections, and complications.

Lexi said, "I'll see if I can get the local police to watch the place this morning."

"I told the Woodruffs to leave last night. They'd like to go home."

"Let's evaluate after you make your visit. If there appears to be any threat, we'll deal with it. Have you kept the tracker in the van?"

"No, I left it at the Woodruffs'."

A pause. "You know, there's probably nothing we can do about the SUV that came after you last night."

"I know."

"Let me know what's on the memory stick."

"You know I will, if I can."

My next call was to Anita. I told her there should be some protection at the house this morning, but that I couldn't make any commitment beyond that. She didn't sound pleased, and I couldn't blame her. "We stayed at Simone's," she said. "I hope this was necessary, Pen. Andre is supposed to be home every night while he's on monitoring. Hankinson had to wake up a judge and get permission. What's going on?"

"I'll know more when I read the jump drive."

I retrieved my van from the condo's underground garage and took the now-familiar route west on Highway 7. When I reached the gate, I doubled back for a couple of miles, making sure I hadn't missed any lookouts and that no one was following me.

When I reached the house, a Deephaven police department patrol car sat on the road outside. I sighed with relief and gratitude; Lexi had successfully called in a marker, and I could now feel safe in retrieving my items. I let myself in the gate, waving to the cop in the police car. Then I went inside.

I panicked when I saw a figure sitting in the living room. But it was Andre.

I rolled over to him. "You owe me some explanations," he said. "You told Anita there's a threat to my family. I want the details."

I brought him up to date, detailing my conversations with Isaac, Sam Wigginton, Catherine Dahlen, Lynda Parrish, and Mary Schott, omitting any mention of my dealings with Lexi Candiotti, the mayor, and Kenny.

"We asked you not to talk to Isaac," he said.

"Not exactly. You discouraged me."

"All right, now I'm asking you explicitly. No, I'm ordering you. Don't talk to Isaac."

"Why not?"

"I have my reasons."

"Are they the same as Simone's reasons?"

"I suppose they are. And I give you my word that they have nothing to do with the Blake Lofton murder."

"I need to be the judge of that."

"No, you don't. You work for me, and I'm telling you, don't do it."

"You'll fire me if I insist?"

He rolled his eyes and stood up. "What is it with you? Why can't you just accept this?"

"What if Hankinson proposed to talk to Isaac? Would you fire him?"

"He wouldn't ask."

"That's why you hired me, to find out things that might not fit with Hankinson's story. To find the truth."

Andre walked over to the picture window and gazed out at the lake. "You don't understand how surreal all this is to me," he said. "That I'm charged with killing Blake Lofton. My friend for thirty years. My brother-in-law. My boss."

"To me, the most surreal part of it is the racial aspect."

He nodded. "Nobody's quite sure how to approach this one. People with sympathy for minorities would be inclined to support me. But they'd be inclined to support the guy I'm accused of killing, too."

"Because he had a black wife?"

160

"More than that. He had black children." He turned back to me. "Blake was a moderate liberal. For years, he'd been cautious in calling for increased police accountability. And then one day, about four years ago, his son Tyler was pulled over and hassled by the Minneapolis police. Blake was so steamed, he called up Ed Stinson, the head of the police union, and gave him twenty-four hours to apologize. Stinson and the officer showed up at Blake's house the next day and apologized. But relations between Blake and the police have been strained ever since. Blake got a lot more strident about accountability, and the police began to genuinely dislike him."

Andre returned to his chair. "What's on that jump drive?" he asked.

"I don't know."

"So put it in the computer and let's see what's on it."

"I don't want you to know, at least not yet."

"Why the hell not?"

"You may have to testify. You may be better off not knowing. We just don't know what it might say."

"Anybody ever tell you you're infuriating?"

I didn't respond. *All the time* probably wasn't the answer he wanted to hear.

After studying me for a long moment, Andre stood up. "Don't talk to Isaac," he said.

"I'll take your request under advisement."

He walked slowly from the room, muttering to himself. "Request . . . Under advisement."

*   *   *

Back at the condo downtown, I showered, changed, and sat down at the kitchen table with my laptop. I plugged in the memory stick and found several documents, which appeared to have been photographed with a cell phone. I studied the documents for a long time; they consisted of court records and social services reports and were more than thirty years old. Now I could see what all the fuss was about; the documents showed that Tony McCort had pleaded guilty in juvenile court to a charge of simple assault for beating up another teenager in a neighborhood several miles from his home. The report made reference to other, unspecified charges that had been dropped as part of the plea agreement, but the documentation for those other charges seemed to be missing. The other offenses might involve drugs or a gun, I thought, but that was just speculation. Reading on, I saw that McCort had served less than six months in a juvenile correctional facility.

The documents raised several questions. First of all, how had Schott managed to find the records and get them unsealed? He had most likely used his connections in the police and court systems and spread some of Blake Lofton's money around. Second, how had he known to look for them? Third, who else knew about the offense? Since the entire Woodruff family had known McCort in those days, it was possible that at least some of them had known, or at least suspected, that McCort had been in trouble with the law.

The most interesting questions, and the most difficult for me to answer, related to politics. I knew little about politics in general, and even less about the Minnesota variety. What impact would public disclosure of these facts have on the race for governor? My instincts told me it wouldn't be a big deal; McCort had been a kid, coming from an impoverished background. The offense was more than thirty years old, a youthful indiscretion. He'd been on the straight and narrow ever since, at least as far as people knew. On the other hand, in the final days of a very close race, would the words "teenage thug," however dated and misleading, create just enough doubt to throw the election to Ellie Ostlund?

It seemed safe to assume that McCort wouldn't have wanted the information to become public, although it was unclear just how concerned he would have been. And I was unsure where the entire situation left me. Apparently, McCort badly wanted to retrieve these records and had been relying on me to search for them. So I'd need to watch my back even more carefully. But it was far from clear what implications, if any, the search for dirt and these results had for the murder of Blake Lofton. My best shot at finding out seemed to be to retrace the steps taken by a now-dead private detective.

Chapter 29

The new Nissan SUV was parked in the driveway at Isaac's house, but there was no answer at his door. He was probably just avoiding me. But I wasn't going to be put off easily. I was about to go next door to get help from June when she appeared from around the corner. "Hi," she said. "No answer?"

"Right. I'm not sure if he's home."

"Oh, he's in there. He never leaves without his car."

"I'd really like to talk to him."

June walked over, stood on tiptoes, and peered into the window. "Uh-oh," she said.

"What?"

She walked over and tried the door, which was locked.

"June? What's going on?"

She walked around the back of the house and was back two minutes later, coming out the front door. "The back door was open. He says not to call an ambulance."

"What in—"

But she had disappeared again.

She was back a minute later with her grandson, who pulled me up the steps into Isaac's house. Isaac lay on the floor, conscious but injured, his face bruised and bloody. "No ambulance," he croaked.

He lay partially on his side. "Can you turn over?" I asked.

"No!" Which meant, I thought, that he might have broken ribs or internal injuries.

"Call an ambulance," I told June.

"No ambulance," he said again.

"Do it anyway," I said. June pulled out her cell phone and went into the next room.

"Isaac," I said, "who did this to you?"

"I fell down the stairs."

"Was it Bolger?"

"I fell."

"I want some answers."

He shook his head.

"Here's the deal," I said. "You tell me what's going on, and you can give the EMTs any story you want. You hold out on me, and I'm reporting everything to the cops, and there will be an investigation. McCort will find out about it."

"No!"

"Then start talking. We only have a few minutes. What did Schott want to know when he first came here, and what did you tell him? And 'I'd rather not go into that' doesn't cut it anymore."

Isaac drew a painful breath, closed his eyes, and opened them. "He wanted to know about any problems Tony had when he was young, or any bad shit he did. Schott said he'd pay."

"What did you tell him?"

"You got to understand. I didn't want to tell nothing about Tony, but I needed the money."

"Go on."

"I told him Tony had problems with the law, but it was a long time ago, and it was juvy. Schott said he still wanted to know; he might be able to get the records anyway. I told him Tony was busted for beating up a guy."

"Did Andre or Simone know about it?"

"No."

I was far from sure he was telling the truth about that, or about anything else, but I pressed on. "Did you tell McCort about your conversation with Schott?"

"I had to."

"Why?"

He took another painful breath. "It's been going on for a long time."

I waited.

"Tony came to me—it must have been sixteen, seventeen years ago."

"Two thousand three?" It was when Isaac had bought this house.

"Right. He came to me, and his business was going good. He had money. He said he was going into politics, and he did. He ran for state house a couple of years later. He said I needed to keep quiet about what he did when he was a kid."

"The assault charge?"

"Yeah. He told me, 'You keep quiet and I'll take care of you. You talk and I'll kill you.'"

Considering the length of time that had passed, and his age at the time, it seemed an overreaction, even for McCort. "Go on," I said.

"He said if anybody come around asking about me, you keep your mouth shut and you call me. He set me up in this house to keep an eye on the old neighborhood, to be here in case anybody come nosing around."

"Has he supported you?"

"Yeah, but it's not really enough to live on. I need more."

"What happened after you talked to Schott?" I asked.

"I told Tony that Schott come around, but I said I didn't tell him nothing."

"And McCort believed that?"

"I doubt it."

"How did you explain the SUV?"

"Told Tony I got it with a workers' comp settlement."

"A new SUV seems pretty generous for what little you gave Schott. There was no proof, and Schott had to dig out the actual records himself."

I heard a vehicle outside and the slamming of doors.

"They're here," June said.

"Isaac, you have to tell me. Why did Schott give you the SUV?"

"You got to understand. I needed wheels."

"What did you tell him?"

"I had to give him something more for the car."

The paramedics came into the room. "Move aside, please," one of them said.

"Isaac, *what did you tell him?*"

Another long, agonizing breath. "I told him Dad's death didn't happen like everybody thinks."

*   *   *

Ivan Bolger slipped into the secure conference room in the intel center and carefully shut the door behind him. Tony McCort waited with the dreaded blank expression on his face. "You're convinced that's all she has?" he asked.

Bolger, tired from a long night of chasing Pen Wilkinson around rural Wisconsin, sat down at the table. "Yes, I'm satisfied. If she knew more, she would have gone to the cops, and we'd know about it. And I'm satisfied Isaac was telling me the truth."

His boss nodded.

"We should have whacked him, Tony."

McCort waved off the protest. "I'm just a hopeless sentimentalist, that's all. Now do you understand why we needed to keep track of Pen?"

"Sure. She's a savant at getting information out of the mentally ill."

"She's still on the trail. What will be her next move?"

"Isaac. After that, she'll want to find out what happened to the old man."

"Agreed," McCort said. "That means talking to the cop. I don't know why he'd talk, but Pen seems to have the knack. And this time, we let her do it."

"I'll be waiting."

"And you're working on our . . . other project?"

"I'm researching it now."

McCort stood up. "All right, let it play out. And this time, see if you can find out what we need to know without beating it the hell out of somebody."

Bolger smiled. "But if I need to?"

Chapter 30

The Reverend Carl Woodruff sat at the table in the little alcove off the dining room, which he used for a study. It was Friday night, and he sat with a yellow pad, making notes for Sunday's sermon. He looked up, removing his reading glasses, when Andre appeared at the entrance.

"What's happening?" Carl said.

"Got a minute?"

"Sure."

Andre, feeling shaky, sat down.

"What's the matter?" Carl asked.

"We need to talk about what's happening around here."

"What do you mean?"

Andre couldn't look him in the eye. "Dad, I know you and Isaac are . . . doing something illegal."

"Now wait a minute—"

"I know. There's no reason to pretend. Please be honest with me."

Carl leaned back slowly, toying with his glasses. "Is your sister at home?"

"No, she's still at the movies."

Andre watched as his father stared off into the distance, continuing to play with his glasses. Pondering, considering. "What do you think is going on, Dre?"

Andre marshalled all the questions and arguments he had prepared and rehearsed, but his response came out as pure anguish. "Dad, how could you *do* this?"

"Do what?"

Anguish turned to anger. "I told you, I *know*. I know this guy Aaron brings the product up from Chicago and gives it to Isaac at the church on Wednesday nights. I watched the whole thing—and I saw Isaac pay him. And then the next night, I saw Isaac slip the stuff to Tony at that community meeting you always go to. You're a part of this, Dad. You're in charge. You would never let Isaac do these things on his own. And we've got money coming in, for private schools. For tennis and music lessons."

"I don't know what you're—"

"Don't lie to me! I told you, I *know*!"

This time it took Carl longer to respond. He leaned forward. "Are you sure you really want to know? You'd be much, much better off not knowing."

"Come on, treat me with some damn respect."

"Your sister can't know."

"You think Simone is an idiot, too? She'll be in here asking these same questions soon enough."

"So you're a mature adult, are you? You know it all? Then you should already know full well why this happened."

"Because you want money."

"Because we *deserve* money. But we're denied legitimate ways to earn it."

This would be the depressing part, Andre knew. The excuses, the rationalizations. "With crack and gangs tearing the community apart, you're dealing *drugs*?"

"Not in our community. Not in our neighborhood. And not crack."

Now Andre understood the role of Tony McCort. The white kid, able to sell a white product to white people in a white neighborhood. "What, then?" he demanded. "Powder? Why is that any different?"

Carl stood up. "Of course it's different. Rich whites, they're going to get their stuff. Why shouldn't we benefit from their degeneracy?"

"By responding with your own degeneracy?"

"By doing what we need to do. Why should you and Simone go to the crappy, dangerous public schools in this neighborhood? Why? Because you made the mistake of being born into the wrong family? Because your father is the son of an illiterate Arkansas sharecropper? Because your parents never got the chance to get a real education?" He leaned forward, hands on the table. "Because you were born with the wrong skin color?"

Now it was Andre's turn to be silent. Finally he said, "So what are we going to do?"

"Do?"

"We can't go on like this."

Carl leaned against the wall. "Oh, now don't get all righteous and foolish on me. We aren't going to *do* anything."

"You can't keep this up. If nothing else, you'll get caught."

"We won't get caught. And what are we supposed to do, pull Simone out of Talmadge? Send her to Minneapolis North?"

"But it's dirty money."

"It's productive money. Look around you. Look at all the punks and hoodlums making enormous sums off crack and then squandering it. We don't live in a fancy house, Dre. We drive old cars. We don't take vacations. We are using our modest proceeds, from our small sales, for this family, for education and advancement, so that we can carry on the fight, for our people."

"Come on, Dad. Don't try to make something noble of this. It's wrong. It's illegal."

"Really? You don't seem to have much problem accepting the benefits of it. After all, you have your diploma from Talmadge. Now you're moving on to an exclusive private college."

Andre said nothing.

Carl came around the table and put his arm around his son. "You think I like this, Andre? You think I like being marginalized? That I enjoy being used by the white power structure, by the big shots who expect me to keep our people in line and out of their hair? I've sheltered you from the worst effects of being black, and I wouldn't have it any other way. But being sheltered has made you naive. You don't understand how the world works. Isaac—he wasn't born with your gifts, or Simone's. I haven't been able to shelter him. And for that reason, he understands, believe me."

Carl leaned down and looked directly into his son's face. "Legal doesn't matter to these white hypocrites, Andre. Ethical doesn't matter. Power is what matters. That's the world we live in, that we've always lived in. And unless we take matters into our own hands, to do what we need to do to advance ourselves, that's the way it will always be."

Andre looked up at a man he now realized he didn't know very well. Carl Woodruff projected the public image of a non-threatening, magnanimous person. A healing, soothing, reassuring establishment civil rights figure. But underneath it all, he was a very angry man.

Chapter 31

After an hour of research on my laptop, followed by a couple of phone calls, I was on the road again. My destination was Mansfield, Minnesota, a town of twelve hundred people near St. Cloud, north and west of Minneapolis. The town was home to Dave Pawloski, a retired Minneapolis police officer. In a previous life, he had shot and killed Carl Woodruff during a routine traffic stop. And now, for reasons not entirely clear, it seemed critical to learn what had really happened on that August day thirty years ago. I honestly had no idea what had been secret for so long, but whatever it was, it had been worth a brand-new SUV for Isaac Woodruff.

My research had unearthed surprisingly little detail on the long-ago shooting. Pawloski, an eight-year veteran of the police force who had served in Vietnam, had stopped Woodruff for a broken taillight. When the preacher had gotten out of the car, Pawloski said he thought Carl was reaching for a gun, but no gun was found after the shooting. During the altercation, eighteen-year-old Andre had been sitting in the passenger seat and hadn't witnessed the actual shooting.

The shooting had been the cause of outrage and mass demonstrations, especially in north Minneapolis. A grand jury had declined to indict Officer Pawloski, but the city had paid a large settlement to the Woodruff family. The city had failed in its efforts to fire Pawloski, but the officer had nonetheless resigned and moved to Mansfield, where he'd become the town police officer, remaining on the job for twenty-five years before he retired. His wife had divorced him after the shooting, moving with their two children to Arizona.

As I drove west on I-94 across a country covered by flat, mostly-harvested farmland, I wondered what it could have meant that Carl Woodruff's death "didn't happen the way that people thought it did." Had Carl struggled with the officer? Could his death be shown not to have been a racially motivated quasi-execution by a trigger-happy cop, as outraged critics, then and now, alleged? Whatever had happened, it appeared likely that the martyred civil rights icon wouldn't come off looking especially good. Yet it seemed undisputed that Officer Dave Pawloski had killed the unarmed preacher. And in the back of my mind, I carried the suspicion—and maybe the hope—that Tony McCort was in some way involved.

I had called Anita and asked her about the killing. "Andre never talks about that day," she'd reported. "I've never taken that to mean he's willfully withholding information. It was just traumatic, and he didn't want it brought up again." I'd thanked her and we had ended the call, but not before she had added a most intriguing fact: Pawloski had known the Woodruff family personally—not Andre, but Simone and Carl himself. This was something I hadn't seen in news reports.

When I had talked to Pawloski, who surprisingly had a listed phone number, he had readily agreed to talk to me and had almost seemed to be expecting my call. He hadn't gone into any specifics, but I sensed that he had something to tell me. I just hoped it would lead me to Blake Lofton's killer.

Mansfield was a dying little town with empty storefronts on Main Street and sad-looking houses on the side streets. I drove along the main drag to the west end of town, past a farm implement dealer, a grain elevator, and a Dairy Queen. Dave Pawloski's house sat on a large, nearly treeless lot about three blocks north of the highway. Given the spacing of the houses, the lots must have been two or three acres. The house was a neatly-kept twenty-year-old rambler with a double garage. A pickup truck with a topper sat in the driveway, but there was room for me to pull the van in and get out.

I wheeled up to the front door, where I was confronted by two formidable steps. Before I could take out my retracting pointer to ring the doorbell, the door opened, revealing a man in his late sixties with a grey crewcut, walking painfully with a cane.

"Hi," I said. "I'm Pen."

The man scrutinized me with cop eyes. He saw the impracticality of a handshake and settled for a little wave. "Dave Pawloski. If you don't mind, maybe we could just talk in the garage. It's heated."

"Sure."

"Just go over to the door—I'll meet you there."

The overhead door to the attached garage was ascending as I approached, and I wheeled inside. Pawloski, standing at the front of the garage, pressed a button to lower the door again. The garage wasn't just heated; it was flat-out nice. Everything was spotless—cleaner than my apartment, probably—with benches and tools lined up neatly along the walls. A smaller door with a window in it provided access to the outside.

Pawloski descended two steps from the inside door to the house and took a cane chair with a well-worn cushion. I rolled over to him. "Thanks for making the time, Officer."

"Dave, please."

"Sure."

"I'd offer coffee or something, but I'm afraid I'm soloing today, and as you can see, I'm not moving around too well. My lady friend, Tina, is in St. Cloud." He smiled. "Thank God for Tina. I never remarried when Donna left me after the shooting. Who would have thought that thirty years later I'd find true love?"

"I'm sorry to bug you about this after so many years."

"I've always expected this day to come. In fact, earlier this year I thought it might have arrived."

"You got a visit from Jack Schott," I guessed.

He lifted an eyebrow. "That's right."

"Did you know he's dead?" The retired cop shook his head, and I described the circumstances of Schott's death.

"What do you think?" he asked. "Was his death an accident?"

"I have my doubts."

Pawloski nodded. "This whole thing sounds questionable. When Schott showed up here and gave me his pitch, I didn't feel comfortable with him. Practically the first thing he did was offer me money for the inside, untold story of the Carl Woodruff shooting, and he didn't seem to have a great reason for needing to know it. He wouldn't tell me who he was working for. He said he'd heard a rumor that it might not have happened the way it was reported."

"He heard it from Isaac Woodruff."

Another lifted eyebrow. "More than just a rumor, then."

"I guess you'd like to know my reason for wanting to know about the shooting," I said. "Unfortunately it's a little speculative." I told him about my conversation with Isaac, his receipt of money from Schott, and Schott's subsequent death, along with my conclusion that Blake Lofton was behind Schott's investigation.

Pawloski thought for a long moment, rocking slightly in his chair. "Andre's freedom is at stake," he said. "To be honest, I'm not sure what Carl's shooting might have to do with Blake Lofton's murder. But that decision should be made by Andre's attorneys, not by Andre himself."

"You mean Andre already knows what you're going to tell me?"

"Yes, he does. I can imagine his reasons for not telling you, and there's a good chance he might not want me to reveal it. But

I think thirty years is long enough. It's time to put the story out there and let the chips fall where they may."

Chapter 32

August 13, 1989

Simone watched from her bedroom window as her father went out the back door and walked toward his Honda. Andre had confirmed that Isaac, as usual, had taken delivery of a package from his friend Aaron last night, at the Wednesday prayer meeting at the church. And tonight Carl would be attending a weekly community meeting at another church about, ironically, combatting the crack epidemic in north Minneapolis. And at that meeting, Isaac would slip the cocaine to Tony McCort, who would sell it in the suburbs, while delivering the proceeds of the past week's sales to Carl.

She had resisted the truth when Andre had told her, but at some subconscious level, she had always realized what was happening. Even after they had both accepted the facts, they couldn't decide what should be done about it. Both agreed that the drug operation couldn't go on; they couldn't have their education financed by drug money. But they couldn't think of a way to stop it without destroying their father, with all he had built up in his church and in the community, not to mention permanently tearing their family to shreds. And so the summer had gone on, with everyone politely ignoring the huge secret that threatened to consume all of them. Carl seemed confident that his children would never put their own futures in jeopardy by torpedoing the operation.

Andre had mentioned Officer Dave during their first conversation about the problem. Simone's acquaintance with Pawloski was closer than she had let on; closer, in fact, than it should have been. The officer was in his thirties and married, albeit unhappily. And Simone was sixteen. The cop was perhaps a little too friendly with her, maybe even a little bit in love with her. She wanted to avoid taking advantage of his fondness for her. But not as badly as she wanted to save her family. She wanted Andre to be clear of what would happen, so she had waited to act until tonight, a full two months after his conversation with Carl. And she had told him nothing of what would happen tonight. He would be as surprised as Carl.

She watched Carl get into the driver's seat of the Honda. She couldn't see the passenger, but she assumed it was Isaac, who normally went with his father to the Thursday night meetings. An hour earlier, she had gone down to the driveway, made sure no one was looking, and smashed one of the Honda's taillights with a hammer.

The car pulled out of the driveway, and Simone went to call Officer Dave.

*   *   *

Carl Woodruff buckled his seat belt as he and Andre pulled out of the driveway. In an effort to change things up, to avoid being too predictable, he had sent Isaac separately in his own car, a Chevy Impala, and asked Andre to come with him. He needed to get Andre out more, to show off his clean-cut, highly-educated son, to have him serve as an example to young people in the community. His confrontation with Andre about the cocaine had gone about as he had anticipated. He hadn't expected his son to stay blind to the operation forever. But Andre had, as he had hoped, put aside his initial shock and outrage. Carl knew he wouldn't do anything to endanger his family, or to besmirch his own reputation.

For all the street smarts and worldliness that came with growing up black in north Minneapolis, Carl acknowledged that his children—at least the two younger ones—were naive. They had gone to a wealthy white school and had mostly been treated well. They hadn't acquired the gut-level knowledge of how life worked, which had come from staring down the barrel of Mr. Jim Crow in rural Arkansas in the forties and fifties. And that experience now told Carl not to be too trusting or too predictable, thus the last-minute switch, taking Andre with him and sending Isaac separately. He fingered the gun in his jacket pocket.

You could never be too prepared.

There might be a problem if Simone found out. She was guileless, totally devoid of cynicism or worldliness, and Carl loved her for it. But if she learned the truth, the shock might make her act unpredictably. It was especially important to keep Tony McCort away from her. Tony had done a good job, serving Carl loyally, and he'd been compensated well. He'd slipped up once and had to serve a short stretch in juvy. But he hadn't talked, and the incarceration had served only to strengthen his street cred. Carl had had to tell him to stay away from Simone, but Tony was hardly the only red-blooded male who'd had to be warned off her. And the fact that his daughter seemed unaware of her mesmerizing effect on men only made her more appealing. Now she seemed to be running into that white cop quite often; Carl would have to have a chat with him before long.

*   *   *

Andre was mad. He resented being used for window dressing by his father, trotted out to community groups as a fine example to other young people in the community. And he resented the cavalier way his father took his silence—even his complicity —in the drug operation for granted. But, despite turning it over in his mind for the past two months, he couldn't think of a way out. Simone seemed in no hurry to do anything about it; she was still in denial, as far as Andre could tell. And it was no use confronting Isaac; he and Carl wouldn't be pried apart on this.

Isaac was, unfortunately, a loser. He hadn't received the high-priced education his siblings had, but he hadn't shown the potential for it. Andre liked his brother, who was good-natured, with a great sense of humor. But he feared that as a low-level drug dealer, Isaac might have reached his highest potential in life.

They were driving east on Olson Highway when he saw Carl take a long look in his rearview mirror. "Damn." He slowed down.

"What's going on?" Andre said, looking back.

"Cop."

"How fast were you going?"

"I wasn't speeding." Carl pulled off the highway onto a side street and stopped at the curb.

They both watched as Officer Dave Pawloski got out of the squad, which he apparently occupied by himself. He walked slowly toward the Honda.

"*Shit.* Simone," Carl muttered under his breath.

Carl rolled down his window. Pawloski looked down. "Good evening, Reverend."

"Officer." He produced his license and registration, which the cop waved off.

Pawloski stepped back. "Would you step out of the car, please?"

"What's the problem, Officer?"

"Just get out of the vehicle, please."

"I'd like to know why you stopped me."

"You have a broken taillight, sir."

Andre saw fury in his father's eyes as he got out of the car. "Just stay here, son." And then Andre saw the bulge in Carl's jacket pocket.

Oh, God.

Pawloski said, "Would you step around to the rear of the car, Reverend?"

"Why?"

"I'd like you to open the trunk, please."

Andre thought he might faint. Had Simone really tipped off this cop? Why oh why hadn't she told him? To protect him, of course. And Pawloski would find the cocaine in the trunk. And Carl would go to jail.

No, he wouldn't. Pawloski had no probable cause or warrant for searching the trunk. The search would be disallowed, and there would be no case against his father. But he'd be arrested, and his reputation would be destroyed. He couldn't believe Simone had set this up. Was Pawloski freelancing?

Andre turned in his seat, straining to see what was happening at the rear of the car. His father was arguing with the officer. Andre wanted to get out of the car, but his father had told him to stay put.

The argument was getting louder.

Andre got out of the car. Pawloski gestured toward the trunk and said he would unlatch it himself. He started toward the driver's door, but Carl stepped in front of him. The cop tried to shove him out of the way. The two men tussled. Andre watched in horror as Pawloski drew his gun. Woodruff lunged for it, knocking the weapon to the ground. The officer pushed the minister, sending him reeling two steps backward.

Then Carl drew his own gun.

Pawloski stepped backward, holding his hands up. "Drop the gun, Reverend. Don't make this worse."

"Make it worse?" Carl screamed. "You're screwing Simone! What could be worse than that?"

The cop retreated another step. "No, no. You've got it wrong!"

"You think I'm an idiot? You stand there with a badge and a gun and treat me like a fool and screw my daughter—well, you can eat this!"

The gun fired. Pawloski flinched, then tripped, falling to the ground. The shot had apparently missed. Carl moved forward, aiming carefully. "You're going to pay!"

Andre, without realizing it, had picked up the cop's gun. "Dad, no!"

Carl leaned down, aiming his pistol at point-blank range at the helpless cop.

A gun fired.

Carl Woodruff dropped to the ground. Pawloski looked up, looked at Andre, who was still holding the gun. The cop scrambled to his feet and rushed over to Carl, who was bleeding profusely from a chest wound. "Cover the wound!" he shouted to Andre. "Press on it!" Andre pulled off his shirt and pressed it onto his father's chest. The shirt was soaked with blood almost immediately.

Pawloski ran for his car to call for help. A minute later he was back with a first aid kit, pulling out a large bandage. But it was too late. Andre stepped aside as Pawloski applied more first aid, trying to revive the minister, to no avail.

Dave Pawloski slowly stood up and leaned forward, hands on thighs. Then he studied Andre for a long moment. He had expected Isaac, Andre now realized.

Finally the cop straightened up, looked around, and then stared hard at Andre. "Andre, listen to me carefully. Are you listening?"

Andre nodded.

"You have to do as I say. It's critical, for Simone, and for you. Your entire future is at stake. Do you understand?"

Andre gave him a questioning look.

"You never got out of the car until you heard two shots in quick succession. When you got out of the car, your father had already been shot. Do you have that?"

"But—"

"*Do you have that?*"

"Yes," Andre heard himself say.

"Your father did not have a gun. Do you have that?"

Andre nodded.

"Say it."

"My father didn't have a gun."

A siren began shrieking. It sounded very close.

Pawloski picked up Carl Woodruff's pistol and stuffed it under his shirt, in the small of his back. Then he picked up his own gun and fired it into the air.

The siren was deafening.

Pawloski walked over to the driver's side of the Honda, reached down, and released the trunk latch. He and Andre peered inside.

The trunk was empty.

Chapter 33

The garage was quiet when Pawloski finished. I tried to slow my brain as I struggled to absorb the incredible story. "Isaac switched the drugs?" I asked.

"Yes. He misunderstood. Carl just wanted him to take his own car. He didn't want him to take the cocaine with him." He shook his head. "Poor Isaac. Always kind of a screw-up."

"So Carl could have let you open the trunk. He had nothing to fear."

"He actually didn't have a lot to fear, anyway," Pawloski said. "You see, I was never going to bust him. I was never even going to tell anybody. My deal with Simone was that I would catch him red-handed, confiscate the drugs, warn him to knock it off, and then let him go."

"It was all just . . . theatre."

"That's exactly what it was. It was a farce that turned into a tragedy."

I was silent for another long moment. "So can I ask the obvious question?"

"Why?"

I nodded.

"Why did I take the blame? Because I *was* to blame. Andre was a kid who acted out of reflex—no way can you blame him. But me? How many rules did I break leading up to Carl Woodruff's death? I made a stop with no real probable cause. I attempted to make an illegal search. I would have let a drug dealer walk without so much as a traffic ticket, if I'd gotten the chance. I let myself be disarmed. I let a suspect draw on me. It goes on and on. We had one man dead, a prominent community leader, a man of the cloth. There was no reason to compound the whole thing by destroying two more lives."

"You did it for Simone."

"And Andre. But you're right, mostly Simone. Carl was wrong, by the way—I wasn't screwing her. Plenty of unchaste thoughts ran through my mind, but that's one huge mistake I managed not to make. What would her life have been like if everybody knew she'd tried to set her father up on a drug bust and gotten him killed? It's bad enough that she's spent all these years consumed by guilt, with nobody she can share it with except Andre."

"Andre—my God, he killed his own father. And he hasn't told anybody."

"Killing his father was awful enough. He felt incredibly ashamed and guilty, even though it was a split-second reflex action. But Andre is also ashamed because he didn't step up and assume responsibility for it. There's no reason for him to feel that way about it, but he does. If anything, he should be proud for saving a life. *My* life. I couldn't see ruining that young man's future, at least any more than it was already wrecked by losing his father. He had great potential, which he's proven by being a huge success in the business world. What was my future? I was just a cop, a cop who'd blown it."

"The aftermath wasn't pretty for you," I said.

Dave Pawloski shook his head, emitting a weak chuckle. "Yeah, you could say that. The traffic stop was weak to begin with. Broken taillight—classic DWB stop. And then I told the investigators that I thought Carl was pulling a gun. People all but laughed in my face at that. A prominent, respected, peacemaking community leader and a minister, no less. Little did they know. I was worried they'd find the slug from that shot he fired, but they never did. He missed pretty badly. He wouldn't have missed again, though. Andre stuck to his story, and I stuck to mine."

"It was polarizing," I said. "There were protests."

"Sure. And hate mail and threatening phone calls. Even so, I'd say Carl Woodruff's shooting is almost a bigger deal today than it was at the time. It's become the stuff of legend."

"But you couldn't stay in your job."

"I had to quit. But you know what? It was okay. I ended up a lot more comfortable and effective as a cop here in a small town. I got out of a marriage that wasn't working. And eventually, I even found true love, with Tina." He smiled. "I'm due for a hip replacement in a couple of months, but I'm still going strong."

We looked at each other. He'd told me the truth. Andre and Simone hadn't told me, but could I blame them, really? The inevitable letdown began to set in; I'd come all this way, dug out an immense secret from thirty years ago. And it wouldn't do my client any good that I could see. In fact, I could see how it might hurt Andre. Suppose Blake Lofton had learned the secret somehow, probably from Simone? I could easily imagine Lofton using the secret against Andre—to force him to stay at AgriMinn, for example. Wouldn't that create a motive for murder?

My thoughts were interrupted by movement in my peripheral vision. The side door to the garage was opening. And there stood Ivan Bolger, holding a gun.

"Who the hell are you?" Pawloski demanded.

"I'm just a friend of Pen's."

"His name is Bolger," I said. "He's security director for Tony McCort."

This did nothing to clear things up for Pawloski, who continued to look angry and confused. Bolger walked over to me. "You have something that belongs to us. Hand it over."

"It doesn't belong to you."

Bolger pointed the gun directly in my face. Pawloski began to get up, but Bolger swung the gun over and pointed it at him. "Just stay put, old-timer." To me: "Let's have it, Pen."

I pulled the memory stick from my purse and handed it to him "What's on here?" he demanded.

"The juvy conviction."

"Nothing after that?"

I shook my head. He pocketed the memory stick, his expression neutral.

"There's more, isn't there?" I said. "This isn't what you've been looking for."

"More? No, this is all we're worried about."

I studied his expression, harder than I'd ever studied a face before. I couldn't tell for sure. But I thought he was lying. If he was, I hadn't given up Andre's secret for nothing. "Schott tried to sell it back to you," I guessed.

"At the same time he was giving it to Lofton. Tony and I weren't going to stand for that."

"So you killed Schott."

"We weren't going to be held up. He was drunk that night, anyway. All I had to do was walk up behind him and give him a whack on the head." He shook his head. "I was so sure I'd find the goods in his cabin."

"But you didn't. So you terrorized Lynda Parrish."

Bolger shrugged. "She didn't have it, either. Good thing you got it from the crazy old biddy."

"So now what?" I asked. "Are you going to kill us, too?"

"I don't think so. I don't think you're going to give us any trouble at all." He pulled out a second memory stick from his pocket. "This contains the entire conversation you've been having here. I picked it up with a parabolic microphone from a van a couple of doors down. This will destroy Andre's defense. It will destroy him as a person. He'll be exposed as a man who killed his own father and covered it up for thirty years. So, if you expose those juvy convictions—you almost certainly made a copy of these records—we'll release this recording. Oh, and Simone will be destroyed, too. She cooked up a scheme with a white cop that got her father killed, with Andre pulling the trigger. And she covered that up, too. So let's be good, Pen."

"You're going to kill Isaac."

"I should have done it yesterday, but we don't need the complication now. So I settled for . . . a discussion. We'll take care of him after the election."

"So who killed Blake Lofton?"

He shook his head. "Poor Pen. Are you really the only person in Minnesota who doesn't get it? Blake Lofton was killed by your client." He pocketed both memory sticks, walked over to the door, and paused. "Keep spinning your wheels if you want," he said, "but what Tony said at the beginning still stands. If you try to pin anything on us, we won't just release the recording. We'll kill you." He left.

Pawloski and I just looked at each other for a long time. "What do we do now?" he asked.

"I'm afraid the answer is 'nothing.'"

He nodded. "We've got no proof that he broke in here or held us up. Just our word against his."

"And," I added, "he's probably got plenty of reliable people who will provide him with an alibi." In truth, there was a lot bigger reason not to report Bolger's intrusion and theft. I'd have to answer a lot of awkward questions about why I'd been visiting Pawloski and why Bolger had burst in on us. The result would be that the world would learn the truth about Carl Woodruff's shooting.

"I only wanted to help Andre," Pawloski said. "Now it looks like I've sealed his fate."

I didn't answer.

"You think he was serious about killing you?"

"Yeah, I think so."

He fingered the handle of his cane. "So do I."

Chapter 34

I drove back to Minneapolis, seething, letting the dimensions of the disaster sink in. Ivan Bolger had casually admitted to murdering Jack Schott. He'd dismissed his home invasion, interrogation, and beating of Lynda Parrish with a shrug. He'd beaten and severely injured Isaac Woodruff. The whole crime wave had, at least according to Bolger, been designed to retrieve McCort's juvenile records, but it hadn't been necessary. I had, as McCort had hoped, found the records for him. I'd traipsed right into the smug bastard's trap.

The process had taken an unexpected turn, focusing on what had happened during a traffic stop thirty years ago. But it turned out that Tony McCort had not killed Carl Woodruff. Worse, unearthing the facts now exposed Andre and Simone to blackmail, which could destroy their reputations and cripple Andre's defense.

To top it all off, Andre now looked really good for the Lofton murder. Being passed over for promotion might have provided a plausible motive for him to kill Lofton. But if Schott, in Lofton's employ, had learned that Andre had killed his own father, Andre's desire to bury that fact provided a motive that was more than plausible: it was compelling. It wasn't lost on me that Anita, not Andre, had hired me to dig out the facts. Now I tried to imagine how I would tell Alicia her stepfather was a murderer after all.

And yet, there still might be a chance of salvaging some hope from the entire episode, disastrous though it was. I couldn't forget that brief expression on Ivan Bolger's face when I'd asked him if there was more. Had it betrayed a lie?

It was a little after nine when I pulled in at the Lake Minnetonka guest house. I shut the engine off and sat, staring silently
into the darkness. I had, at least in part, created this mess. I had to
step up and own it. But more than that, I had to figure a way out.

I stashed my belongings, then went over to the main house.
Andre answered the door. "What's wrong?" he asked.

I'd never make a living playing poker. "We need to talk.
Why don't you come over to the guest house?" We could talk
privately there, without running into Anita or Alicia.

Andre followed me over to the smaller house. He sat down
in a leather club chair and waited.

I figured I might as well get it all out. "I saw Officer Dave
Pawloski today."

"I see."

"He told me about what happened when your father was
killed."

He shifted in his chair with what might have been a small
shrug. Now, here was a poker player.

"When Pawloski told me this, Bolger eavesdropped on us.
He knows everything."

Finally, Andre's composure gave way. His face lost color as
he sank back into his chair. "My God, what have you done?"
His head sank into his hands.

"The flip side of that is, I've got proof that McCort had a
juvenile assault conviction."

He looked up, studied me, and pondered this. Then he understood. "The memory stick. That's what Schott found." So
Anita had told him about Schott.

"Yes."

"So, are we at a standoff? We sit on our information and he
sits on his?"

"I'd say so, although we don't have an explicit deal."

"Why did you go to see Pawloski?" Before I could respond,
he waved off my answer. "Isaac. Now you know why I didn't

want you talking to him. He's remained silent for a long time, but he never has quite enough money. Goddamnit, Pen."

I pressed on, telling him about the attack on Isaac and about his brother's disclosure that the accepted version of Carl Woodruff's murder was false. Then I gave him a complete account of my meeting with Pawloski, including Bolger's admission that he had killed Schott.

"I can see why Anita hired you," he said without enthusiasm. "You have a knack for digging out the facts, whether we want them dug up or not." He got slowly to his feet. "Do you want a drink?"

"Desperately."

Andre went into the kitchen, returning a couple of minutes later with a highball for himself and wine for me. He remained standing. "I was actually starting to think I'd pulled it off. Thirty years. I never told anybody, and neither did Simone—not even Blake. But when the protests started during the past year, with people invoking my father's name, I started to wonder."

I sipped my wine.

"I know how it looks," he said. "I'd have a strong motive to kill Blake if he found out. But I've seen no indication that Schott actually found out what happened, much less that he told Blake."

He had a point, I thought. Pawloski hadn't told the PI anything.

"I killed my father," he said. "Why? Why should he die, and not some white cop with a crush on Simone? Do you know how much time I had to make that decision? None. It wasn't even a decision; it was pure reflex. I shot a figure, trying to stop a murder. I didn't know what the hell I was doing, and I'd give anything on earth to take it back. There was no time to decide whether my father lived or died. Whether he committed a murder or I did. Whether the community continued to have a powerful voice and a respected leader, or whether his rinky-dink drug operation would be thwarted, undoubtedly soon to be replaced by some other small-time dealer. He loved us so much that he turned to crime. And he kept nothing for himself. He invested it all in his children's future." He paused. "What difference does it make? I did what I did. I killed my father. And I can tell you I never intended to do it."

I had no idea how to respond.

"It was harder on Simone. She'd really tried to do the right thing. And it wasn't a bad plan. Man, it was a scheme that would have made Machiavelli blush. It could have worked out nicely, stopping the drug dealing without leaving any fingerprints. It was nice of Pawloski to take the rap. But of course, he sort of owed me, too, since I saved his life and all."

"We still don't know who killed Blake Lofton," I said. "And we're running out of suspects."

"I didn't do it."

Call me a fool, but I believed him.

"McCort needs to get through the election," he said. "I need to get through the trial. I guess we each just hold our breath."

"Did you know about McCort's juvenile record?"

"No, but I'm not surprised. He was young and got into fights. And then I found out he was dealing for my father. It's not exactly a shock that he got busted."

Andre retrieved the wine bottle from the kitchen, refilling my glass and bringing a fresh drink for himself. He sat down across from me. "Do you think McCort is in the clear on Blake's death?"

"Even if he had Schott killed in order to retrieve those juvenile records, it's hard to see any reason for him to have killed Lofton."

"Wouldn't he have had to assume Schott had given Blake the documents?"

"If he'd already delivered them to Lofton, there would have been no reason to hide them away at the cabin. Remember, he was playing a double game, also trying to sell them to McCort."

"So does McCort have any motive for the murder at all? You'd think there would have been better ways to assure he'd win the election than killing his opponent."

"Here's what's going on," I said. "Blake had something more on McCort, something different from the juvenile conviction, and more damaging."

"Bolger told you they'd found what they were looking for."

"He was lying."

His features contracted in skepticism. "You're saying McCort could have killed Blake in an effort to retrieve this other information?"

"Right. According to Ellie Ostlund, Blake seemed confident of winning, more confident than the polls warranted. He'd been prepared to spring an 'October surprise' on McCort if necessary."

"That would be this still-missing damaging information about McCort?"

"Presumably, yes. And of course, there's the most telling indication of all: they didn't shut me down. McCort wants me to keep looking."

"What could Blake have on him?"

"You tell me."

Andre's face wrinkled in thought. "I have to imagine McCort has been investigated thoroughly for shady business dealings or brushes with the law—things like that."

"According to Ellie, that's true."

"McCort's story is pretty well known. Of course, he had to stop dealing when my father was killed, and that's where his Horatio Alger story begins. He got his GED, worked as a towel boy at a health club, and eventually saved and borrowed enough money to buy his first club, with a partner named Mark Tomlinson. Tony proved to be a whiz at business. He borrowed tons of money and expanded aggressively. It paid off—he's supposedly worth two hundred million."

"What happened to Tomlinson?"

"Tony bought him out within a few years. I believe he died about a year ago." He drained his glass. "Pen, we don't have a lot of time. Your theory is speculative to begin with. Where do you even begin looking for this mysterious blackmail material?"

I set my own glass down on a side table. "With a couple of unfortunate bloggers."

Chapter 35

Via Snapchat

*A^{lic_Carter: has added you*}

Alic_Carter:	Hey.
Ken.Sellars:	Hey. How are you?
Alic_Carter:	I'm OK. Did you know Pen is in town?
Ken.Sellars:	Yeah. That's why I asked you to add me.
Alic_Carter:	Pen says you're cool.
Ken.Sellars:	Pen is cool.
Alic_Carter:	For sure. Are you really a genius?
Ken.Sellars:	LOL I'm getting a D in english comp. Pen says you're really nice.
Alic_Carter:	Hope so cause I'm sure not a genius.
Ken.Sellars:	Really sorry about your stepdad.
Alic_Carter:	Thanks.
Ken.Sellars:	Are things OK at school?
Alic_Carter:	Not great. Some kids are hassling me about Andre. They say he's a murderer.
Ken.Sellars:	Does your mom know?
Alic_Carter:	Yeah. I didn't tell her but she heard about it.
Ken.Sellars:	Pen will figure it out.
Alic_Carter:	I hope so. But I'm scared. About Andre and about Pen too.
Ken.Sellars:	She's into some dangerous stuff.
Alic_Carter:	I think so too.
Ken.Sellars:	She's staying with you, right?
Alic_Carter:	Right.

Ken.Sellars:	Is your place secure?
Alic_Carter:	IDK we have a security system.
Ken.Sellars:	Is it gated or fenced?
Alic_Carter:	Yeah but the fence is easy to climb over. I do it all the time. All these TV people are hanging around looking through the fence.
Ken.Sellars:	She's looking at this guy McCort. He sounds creepy.
Alic_Carter:	Yes scary.
Ken.Sellars:	Can you keep an eye on Pen?
Alic_Carter:	I can try. I'm gone a lot and I don't always know when she's coming here.
Ken.Sellars:	Let me think about that.
Alic_Carter:	K
Ken.Sellars:	How is Pen doing?
Alic_Carter:	My dad says not so great. She has nightmares. Drinks a lot too. They broke up.
Ken.Sellars:	I heard. Does she drink too much?
Alic_Carter:	Maybe IDK.
Ken.Sellars:	Can I snap you again tonight?
Alic_Carter:	K should be home by 9.
Ken.Sellars:	Cool.

Chapter 36

In starting work the next morning, the first order of business was paranoia. Kenny had taught me to anonymize my web surfing using something called a Tor browser, which was a nearly foolproof way to avoid leaving electronic tracks on the Internet. Given Tony McCort's apparently advanced hacking capabilities, I figured it was only prudent to keep my research confidential. I also couldn't be sure how secure the Woodruffs' wifi system was. So I used Tor, which slowed down my surfing somewhat but gave me a little peace of mind.

I booted up my laptop and found the political blogs written by Jane Hyser and Brad Van Ness that Kenny had located for me. I bookmarked the blogs, then spent an hour looking for other bloggers who mentioned Tony McCort with any frequency. Using Google searches, I ultimately found seven of them. Then I began the laborious process of going through all the McCort references in all of the blogs and listing controversial topics that might have been sore spots for the candidate. I had to sort through all the listings, and the titles often didn't give a good idea what the posts were about, so I had to actually scan the text. Some of the posts went back a long time, since McCort had served in the state senate for a dozen years and was politically active before that.

It was mid-afternoon by the time I'd completed my listing of subjects for the seven blogs. After a break for lunch, thoughtfully brought over by Cristina, I went back to the Hyser and Van Ness blogs and started making similar lists. Jane Hyser had, before her mysterious death, been a respected longtime reporter for the Minneapolis newspaper before being laid off. Her posts were mostly serious and wonkish, but as McCort had become a viable candidate for statewide office, she had started to raise questions about his character. Brad Van Ness, as Kenny had noted, had been very snarky, personal, and addicted to controversy. He had attacked McCort's character for years. And then he had disappeared.

By dinnertime, my lists were completed. I hoped I hadn't overlooked anything. Notably, there had been no posts suggesting any involvement by McCort in the Blake Lofton murder. Most of the articles had addressed his controversial policy positions. Some posts combined the political and the personal, noting, for example, McCort's lack of support for public education, as well as his own modest education. In final form, my list of personal, potentially sensitive topics included:

- Speculation on McCort's sexuality;
- Speculation on the source of startup financing of his business empire;
- Speculation that McCort might have bugged or wiretapped political opponents;
- Reports that McCort had been accused of sexual harassment by female employees of Together Fitness;
- A report that McCort had been involved in a fistfight in a local bar;
- A report commenting on McCort's hardscrabble childhood and questioning why he hadn't tried to exploit it for political gain;
- Rumors of ties between McCort and white supremacist groups;
- An unsubstantiated report alleging that McCort had fathered a child, who now lived with her mother in Florida;
- Rumors that McCort had been involved in a hit and run accident while drunk, after which he had paid off the victim and witnesses to bury the incident;

- A story about a lawsuit filed by the Minnesota attorney general, and later settled without admission of guilt, which alleged that Together Fitness engaged in deceptive high-pressure sales tactics at its clubs; and
- Charges that McCort had bribed local officials in Colorado to obtain the necessary permits to build one of his clubs.

It was a formidable list. McCort was no doubt capable of any of these misdeeds. But it seemed unlikely that even he had done all of them; the list undoubtedly included a healthy measure of gossip, rumor, and fake news. The trick would be isolating the allegations that might have set off his concern. So I set to work, cross-referencing the allegations with the bloggers. After an hour and a half of painstaking work, my attention began to focus on one topic. Jane Hyser had written, on August 20th of last year:

"McCort has displayed a notable lack of transparency and detail when it comes to explaining how his health club chain, Together Fitness, was financed at its inception. Accounts of his company's history tend to begin when the firm went public. But that occurred eight years after it was officially founded. McCort has said simply that he relied on "bank loans" and "investors" to start the company, without identifying either the banks or the investors. Apologists for McCort might question the relevance of events occurring more than twenty-five years ago, but when it comes to financial matters, McCort has the obligation to provide full disclosure."

Brad Van Ness, while less cautious and civil, had made the same point on September 8th:

"So Tony McCort, the poor but hardworking and self-reliant inner-city kid, built his business empire by pulling himself up by his bootstraps. But who provided the boot? Tony's a little sketchy on the details, which for Tony isn't exactly unprecedented. He first claimed Together Fitness was initially financed by "his savings." Yeah, he was a frugal guy, I'm sure, taking his lunch in a brown bag and passing up those fancy lattes at Starbucks. But eventually the Fitness King realized he'd have to cough up a little more detail than that. *Very* little, I'd have to say. When pressed, he now says that he relied on unnamed banks and investors for startup and expansion capital. Right. And what about his former partner, Mark Tomlinson, whom McCort bought out many years ago? The word on Tomlinson is that he wasn't in any financial position to finance a huge health club, either. But since he died last year, we can't exactly ask him about it, can we?"

This must be it, I thought. This subject was the only one that had been addressed by both Van Ness and Hyser, and only by them. And each had written about it only once, in each case shortly before they had died or disappeared. It was a huge leap, assuming that McCort had caused the death of Hyser and the disappearance of Van Ness because he didn't want any attention called to the initial financing of his business empire. True, he had tried to intimidate me by hinting that he had been responsible for the bloggers' fates. But he may not have expected me to figure out what the forbidden topic was; both writers had been critical of McCort on many topics. Or he may have simply assumed that even if I figured out the forbidden topic, I was powerless to do anything with the knowledge.

So where did I go from here? How could I investigate McCort's financial transactions from twenty-five years ago, when two experienced journalists had done the same and met with tragic endings? One option closed to me was talking to the man who seemed likeliest to know the facts: his former partner, Mark Tomlinson, who was now dead. I made a note to follow up on his death. The only other option seemed to be to follow the same course taken by Van Ness and Hyser, the course that had caused them to vanish and die, respectively. Foolish? Probably. But I couldn't help myself.

I'd have to be careful.

I first accessed stories about Hyser's death. Most had taken pains to emphasize that there had been no evidence of foul play. In scouring the few articles written in the weeks that followed, I found no indication that foul play had been ruled out, either. Hyser's death was still unexplained. She was survived by her parents and by an ex-husband who lived in Virginia. In several of the articles her father, Bernard, who lived in St. Paul, had given quotes to the media in which he'd lauded his daughter's virtues and demanded a full investigation into her death.

I found an online listing for Bernard Hyser, which included a phone number, and glanced at my phone; it was 9:45 PM. A little late, but I decided to give it a try. I punched in the number.

"Bernie Hyser speaking." The voice was gruff and wary.

I introduced myself and started explaining my connection to his daughter. It didn't go well. "You work for *Andre Woodruff?*" he said.

"Right. Now, I'm interested in finding out—"

"You think Jane knew something about the Lofton murder? It happened after she died."

"I know that, but—"

"Look, Jane was a journalist. She was respected, mainstream. She had no time for fake news or rumors or gossip or conspiracy theories. She stuck to the facts."

I gave him a few seconds to calm down. Then I switched to a less incendiary topic. "Tell me about your daughter, Mr. Hyser."

"About Jane? She was . . . She was . . . Oh, God." He began to sob. I waited patiently while he pulled himself together. "I'm sorry," he said quietly.

"Perfectly all right," I assured him.

"She was—well, her life wasn't going great when she died. She'd been engaged to be married again and then broke it off. And of course she never made much money doing blogs and podcasts and freelancing—not like when she was with the newspaper. It was a damn shame, how they let an award-winning journalist go."

"Were you satisfied with the police investigation?" I asked, inching back toward more sensitive territory.

"Well, it wasn't much of an investigation. There was no evidence of foul play. They did a thorough autopsy and a tox screen and couldn't find any poison or drugs. Just one of those things, they said. Her heart stopped. Natural causes, no real explanation."

"Had she received any threats?"

"There you go with conspiracy theories again."

"Then let's try some facts. Fact: She questioned how Tony McCort could have financed his business. Fact: She died mysteriously shortly thereafter."

"Come on. She also ate sushi for the first time several weeks before her death. You think maybe there was a connection?"

"Mr. Hy—"

"Look, I just don't want to hear it, okay? She was a good person. She was my daughter. She died. I just don't need the crap."

"But—"

"Goodbye."

And on that encouraging note, Bernard Hyser hung up. I couldn't say I blamed a grieving father for rejecting sinister explanations for his daughter's death. But he didn't know all the facts I knew. And he didn't know Tony McCort the way I did.

Chapter 37

Neil Nyquist walked through his garage to the door leading to the house. He opened the door and hollered something. The overhead garage door was open, and Nyquist had pulled his truck out into the driveway. In the garage, Nyquist had cleared a space on his workbench next to two large pumpkins and pulled down a retractable work light from the ceiling. A minute or so later, two young boys, aged five and seven, came out of the house. Talking loudly, each boy began drawing a face on one of the pumpkins.

Nyquist lived in a suburb called Maple Grove, northwest of Minneapolis. He and his wife had bought this split-level house four years ago, and Nyquist had done the finishing work on the basement himself. His wife's parents, who lived nearby, reveled in the role of doting grandparents.

From a van parked a block over, through a telescope hidden in a phony air vent in the top, Ivan Bolger observed the activity in the garage. He had watched the house and its occupants off and on for several weeks, just as he had surveilled Duke Sorrel. He knew what time Nyquist left for work and what time he returned and had noted his wife's departure and arrival times as well.

Since the Sorrel killing, Minneapolis police officers had all been warned to be on their guard. But the Nyquists hadn't seemed to take the warnings very seriously. Perhaps Officer Nyquist had exercised additional vigilance and caution while on the job. But here at home, the Nyquists' routines remained, well, routine.

In the garage, the boys had finished drawing on the pumpkins. The face drawn by the younger brother, Michael, had irregular features, resembling a Picasso portrait. Now the mother, Hannah, came out of the house to inspect the ongoing work, offering praise and making suggestions. Nyquist cut holes in the tops of the pumpkins and pulled out handfuls of sloppy seeds, placing them in a trash can held by Hannah. Now the carving began, with the Nyquists guiding their sons' hands as they used the sharp instruments.

Bolger knew what time the school bus picked up the two boys, who attended an elementary school nearby, and what time it brought them to a neighbor's house in the afternoon, where they waited until the father returned home from work. Bolger knew that the older brother, Trevor, had a congenital defect in his right hip, which would require expensive surgery. Fortunately, the health insurance provided by the Minneapolis police department was comprehensive and would cover everything at little out-of-pocket cost.

The Nyquists were living the good life, a young family full of love, with a promising future. But it was a future that was soon to change, to be marred by tragedy. Bolger began to pack up his surveillance equipment; he knew all he needed to know. But then he went back to take one more look at the family, and in particular at the person who somehow expected, even with all that had happened, to be safe at home.

Officer Hannah Nyquist.

Chapter 38

I got an early start the next morning. The murder of Officer Duke Sorrel still dominated news reports, but the police reported no progress in solving the cold-blooded killing. At the state capitol, RPC demonstrators remained in their makeshift camp, but counter-protesters were planning a large march in support of the police for this evening. The authorities, fearing violent clashes, were threatening to clear the encampment.

After breakfast, I resumed my research. Unlike Jane Hyser's father, who had a listed phone number, it proved trickier to track down the family of Brad Van Ness. News accounts said he had grown up in Idaho, but there was no indication whether he was married or otherwise attached, or whether he had any family in Minnesota. I knew if I asked Lexi for help, I'd have to bring her up to date. Truth be told, I was still troubled by Lexi's quick dismissal of any involvement by Tony McCort in the Lofton murder. But I had to trust somebody. I made the call and spent a few minutes updating her, leaving out any mention of Dave Pawloski or the killing of Carl Woodruff. She agreed without hesitation to see what she could find out; apparently my discovery of the jump drive had convinced her I was onto something.

While waiting for a response to my query, I set out to learn what I could about Mark Tomlinson, McCort's long lost and dead partner. There was surprisingly little information about him available online. I learned that he had co-founded Together Fitness with Tony McCort some twenty-five years ago and then left the company eight years later, McCort apparently having bought him out. He had then moved to Colorado and managed an investment portfolio of stocks and real estate. Tomlinson had died a year ago when his car had plunged off a cliff near Puerto Vallarta, Mexico, where he had maintained a vacation home. A brief obituary in the Denver newspaper noted that he had been preceded in death by his parents and by his wife, Heather, who had died only a few weeks earlier after a long fight with breast cancer.

I sat back and considered my options. Mark Tomlinson appeared, like Brad Van Ness, to have no easily accessible family members to question. Worse, he had lived in Colorado and died in Mexico a year ago. Lexi might not be of much immediate help in tracking anybody down in these faraway jurisdictions. The story of how Together Fitness had been financed more than a quarter century ago seemed to recede even further into the distant mist.

It was close to noon by the time Lexi got back to me. "I found Van Ness's fiancée," she reported. "Her name is Sadie Noll, and she lived with him in an apartment downtown." She recited the phone number and address.

"That's in Minneapolis," I said. "Your department must have investigated Van Ness's disappearance."

"I'm ahead of you on that. The detective was a guy named Tom Stoller. He caught the case just before he retired, and he now lives in Belize."

"Lexi . . ."

"Look, Pen. At some point you've got to let the conspiracy theories go. I know Stoller. He was the proper guy to handle the case. He'd planned his retirement to Belize for years, although I don't think it will last. He would have made a thorough effort to find Van Ness."

"I'm sure you're right," I said, although increasingly, I questioned whether I was being paranoid enough.

"So, Pen. Are you . . . doing okay?"

"Sure," I said, not knowing why on earth I had said it. Lexi didn't know much about my personal struggles, but there seemed no reason I couldn't confide to her my fears for my personal safety now. McCort had flat-out threatened to kill me if I did basically anything substantive, and I was now a hundred percent sure that he was a killer, though I wasn't certain about all the people he had killed. Lexi knew he had twice placed trackers on my vehicle, though she didn't know about McCort's assault on me at the storage facility.

Yes, I had gotten into one of those "things I do" again. But they were *my* things, and I needed to do them pretty much alone. If I didn't, I'd be playing into James's narrative: that I needed help, that I was afraid, that maybe I had lost the abilities and the independence—the entire inner impetus—that had made me a survivor. I hadn't let the love of my life go only to turn around and tell someone else I couldn't handle things on my own.

"I'm fine," I told Lexi. I thanked her and called the reporter's fiancée.

Talking to Sadie Noll was a starkly different experience from my attempt to reason with Bernie Hyser. She listened respectfully to my pitch, asking insightful questions. Part of the difference was undoubtedly due to the mystery of Van Ness's fate. Hyser had known that regardless of whether he cooperated with me, his daughter would still be dead. But Sadie Noll was a woman grasping at straws.

"I didn't pay particularly close attention to his work," she said, "but I do recall that he was interested in McCort."

"Did he have a file on McCort? Either electronic or paper?"

"I don't know. You don't think McCort had anything to do with Brad's disappearance, do you?"

"I think it's worth looking into."

She hesitated. "I'm not sure what I'd be searching for. Would you like to come and look through his stuff?"

"I'd be happy to." We made arrangements to meet at her apartment at four.

*   *   *

I left for downtown, hoping that McCort hadn't placed yet another transmitter in my van. But I had to assume he had. And this time, his interest in my destination wouldn't result from idle curiosity. If he really had caused Brad Van Ness to vanish, any show of interest in the blogger would set off a shrill alarm. I drove in a circuitous pattern through several residential neighborhoods, satisfying myself that nobody was following me. Then I went downtown and parked in the garage of James Carter's condo building. This was a place I'd been before and might be expected to go again. Once inside, I rode the elevator not up to the twenty-third floor, where the condo was located, but to the second floor, the skyway level.

Downtown Minneapolis is connected by an extensive skyway system, running above street level for almost its entire length and width. I began wheeling my way from building to building, block to block, dodging pedestrians. By the time I reached Sadie Noll's high-rise apartment building on the opposite end of downtown, I was breathing heavily. I took a few minutes to rest before calling upstairs.

Sadie buzzed me in, and I took the elevator to the nineteenth floor. Upstairs, she appeared in the hallway and motioned me down to their door. Sadie was tall, thirtyish, and athletic-looking, with her blonde hair tied in a ponytail.

"Hi," she said, extending her hand.

"I'm Pen." I showed her my attorney's license and handed her a business card. "You have a lovely place." The living room was furnished in teak and glass with modern art on the walls and featured a large window overlooking the Mississippi.

"Thanks." She sat down.

"What do you do for a living?"

"I work in merchandising at Target. I was the major bread-winner. I mean, Brad was—is—a great journalist, but writing blogs doesn't pay all that much." She sighed. "He's a combative guy, though—never backed down from a fight. I always wondered if he'd piss off the wrong person."

"So what happened when he disappeared?"

Sadie shrugged. "I just came home one night—about this time, I guess—and he wasn't here. He worked here at home—I'll show you his office in a minute. His car was still downstairs, and there was no trace of him. We'd planned on going out that night. There'd been no hint that anything was wrong."

"What did you do?"

"The first thing I did, of course, was to call his cell." She paused. "It rang in the next room. He'd left it here. That's when I knew something weird was going on. Why would he have left without his phone?"

"What happened next?"

"I waited. I made some calls to people he knew. Nobody had heard from him. He didn't come home that night. I didn't get much sleep. In the morning, I called the police. They refused to even take a report. It had been less than twenty-four hours, he was of legal age, and he wasn't a danger to himself or others."

I nodded. I'd gotten the same response when I'd come to Minneapolis to search for Kenny when he'd gone missing earlier in the year.

"I was worried sick all the next day," she continued. "I stayed home from work and kept making calls. I talked to the manager here at the building, who agreed to check out the surveillance cameras for me. They couldn't find any footage of his leaving, even though he obviously did."

I felt a chill. *Anything can be hacked.*

"I kept after the police," Sadie said, "and finally, after three days, they sent a guy over."

"That was Detective Stoller?"

"Right. He seemed pretty thorough. He asked tons of questions. I gave him a list of Brad's friends, relatives, and co-workers. He'd already checked Brad's cell phone records and bank accounts. Then he went into the office and looked through Brad's computer and files."

"What was he looking for?"

"He mostly seemed to be looking for personal problems—an affair, gambling debts—things like that."

"Nothing work-related?" I asked.

"He did ask if Brad's blogs could have angered someone. I said sure, they probably ticked off just about every leading political figure in the state, and a few nationally. So I imagine Stoller was looking for that kind of thing, too—threats, cranks, angry correspondence. As far as I know, he wasn't looking for anything about McCort specifically."

"Do you know if Brad had any interaction with McCort, or anybody working for him?"

"I don't know."

"Did Stoller find anything at all?"

"No. When he left, he said he would follow up on tips. I figured that meant he'd reached a dead end."

I followed her into the room that had functioned as Van Ness's office, a space furnished with a desk and chair, a laptop, a scanner, a few stacks of papers, and very little else. "Does Brad have any paper files?" I asked.

"No. He tried to be as paperless as possible."

"Can you get me onto his computer and phone?"

She sat down at the desk, booted up the laptop, and entered the password. Then she moved the chair aside so I could roll up to the desk. "This may take a while," I said.

"Fine." She continued to stand next to the desk. I could see she was torn between the awkwardness of looking over my shoulder and her unease at having a stranger paw through potentially intimate or embarrassing details of her partner's life. Finally, she came to a decision. "I'll be in the next room. Just let me know if there's anything I can help with."

I found the Documents window and saw a folder for Posts. He'd established a subfolder for every blog post he'd written over the years, labeled by the date of the post. I opened the folder for the first blog, which had been written nearly five years earlier. The folder contained a Word document containing the final text of the entry and a second document containing notes and drafts. There were also several articles Van Ness had used to research the entry. I randomly opened the subfolders for several other entries; all had similar contents. Finally, I opened the folder for September 8th, the date of the fateful post I believed had triggered McCort's concern, and possibly Van Ness's disappearance.

Unlike the other folders, this one contained only one Word document. The one containing the post's text looked identical to the online entry. But the other document, the one for notes and drafts, didn't exist. I glanced at the folder's contents again; there were no articles from other sources, as there frequently were for other posts. I spent a few minutes looking through other subfolders but couldn't find any others that contained no material besides the post itself; all had at least some notes, outlines, research, or other supporting material.

This was a little much. If September 8th had been just another post, why had all supporting material either never existed or, more likely, been wiped clean? I spent another hour searching through the computer for anything that might be related to the September 8th post, or anything McCort-related that I hadn't already seen. After coming up empty, I called Sadie in and explained what I hadn't found. "Do you think such a document could exist?" I asked.

"I just don't know."

"I think there may be relevant information that's been deleted from the hard drive," I said. "I'd like to try to recover it."

"You can do that? Even after it's been deleted?"

"Sometimes. Would you mind if I called in an expert to see if it can be retrieved?"

Again, a slight hesitation. Then she nodded. I put in a call to Kenny, who said he'd be right over. In the meantime, I started going through Van Ness's cell phone.

I was finishing up about half an hour later when Sadie showed my nephew into the office. I greeted him and held up the cell phone. "Nothing interesting on here. Let's see what we can find on the computer." I moved out of the way, and he pulled a chair up to the desk. Then he reached into a backpack and pulled out his own laptop, plugging it into Van Ness's machine.

"So you think he deleted a document titled '9/8 notes'?" Kenny asked.

"Yes."

"So, is this hard drive backed up?"

I groaned. "Why didn't I think of that? I didn't check."

I looked at Sadie, who had stayed in the room. "Probably," she said.

"Let's find out," Kenny said. He began rapid-fire typing, with windows and folders opening and closing and lines of code opening and scrolling. "Here it is," he said after a minute or so. "He uses an online backup service."

I waited anxiously as he pulled up a browser and went online to the backup site. "Don't you need his password?" I asked.

Kenny avoided rolling his eyes and simply said, "No," which I took to mean that he'd hacked into the site. He started navigating. "Slow Internet," he complained. After a couple more minutes he said, "It's not on the backup, and this site doesn't have a complete history. To confirm that the document ever existed, I'd need to—well, go deeper."

"You mean hack in deeper."

He shrugged.

"Let's save that for now," I said. "Why don't you go back to the hard drive and see if you can recover the deleted file."

Kenny exited the backup site and turned for the first time to his own laptop. He entered some commands, which I assume loaded recovery software onto Van Ness's machine. I settled in to wait.

"Here it is," Kenny said. My gaze jerked back to the screen. It had taken him less than a minute. "He deleted it about two weeks after it was created."

"Let's see it," I said.

He swiveled the screen in my direction. Sadie leaned in beside me. There were two pages of notes, including a rough outline of the post's main points. One item that caught my attention was a link to Mark Tomlinson's obituary in the Denver newspaper, which I'd already seen. There was another significant link: to the blog post on the same subject by Jane Hyser. At the bottom of the page was a note, separated by several lines from the main body of the text. It read: "Tomlin. add. 2dfid@iicom. Must del all ref."

"What's with that last line?" Kenny asked. "Does it mean anything to you?"

I nodded, concentrating hard. My right foot, which I can't actually feel, was doing a phantom fidget. "The 'Tomlin.' probably stands for 'Tomlinson,'" I said. "That's Tony McCort's old partner. The email address I think refers to 'second fiddle.'"

"So who does the address belong to?"

"I think it may be an old address for Mark Tomlinson himself. He might have played second fiddle to McCort when they were in business together. Maybe it's still in use by somebody he knew or was related to."

"If you gave me some time I might be able to find the IP address," Kenny said. "But it would be hard; ii.com is a major email provider. They have, like, millions of customers."

"I think I'll use the direct approach. Just send a message to it and see what happens. Van Ness might have made contact with somebody using that address. But after making the contact, he decided he needed to cover his tracks."

"Let's see how well he covered them." Kenny returned to the keyboard and continued searching for about ten minutes. Then he turned back to me. "I can't find anything else on the hard drive. Brad's email is web-based. That means I can't find out locally what messages he might have deleted, either received or sent." He left the statement hanging and looked at me quizzically, undoubtedly wondering if I wanted him to hack Van Ness's email service.

"I'll stick with the old-fashioned approach, at least for now," I said.

Kenny nodded and moved aside. I rolled up to the computer and composed a message:

"I am trying to reach family members or associates of Mark Tomlinson. I am following up on contact you may have had with Brad Van Ness. I am investigating a very serious situation concerning Tony McCort. Please respond ASAP. If this message has been misdirected, I apologize, and you may disregard."

I signed off with my name, email address, and cell phone number. Then I pressed *Send* and leaned back.

And immediately panicked. What if McCort was somehow receiving messages at that address? I tried to calm down; nothing to be done about it now.

"What do we do now?" Sadie Noll asked.

"We wait." And with that, I sent Kenny home and went back to Lake Minnetonka for the night.

Chapter 39

"Pen! Pen! Wake up!" I opened my eyes. Alicia was standing next to the bed, shaking me awake. I'd been in front of the open freezer door again.

"I'm okay," I told Alicia. "What time is it?"

"Eight."

This was a lot later than the nightmare usually occurred.

"I'm sorry to walk in on you, but I heard you shouting."

"It's okay."

We looked at each other for a long minute while I woke up and caught my breath. "Dad told me about the nightmares," she said. "But I never imagined how horrible they must be, what you must go through every time."

"I'm fine."

"No, you're not," she said with unexpected vehemence. "You need help."

"I'm working on it."

"You're making it worse."

"Could you reach those clothes for me?" I asked.

She watched, fascinated, as I placed my sweatpants, first on one leg, then on the other, and then, lying down on the bed, struggled into them. "Here, let me help you," she said, helping to pull my pants up. Then she pulled my chair up and helped to maneuver me into it. In truth, I probably could have completed the process more quickly on my own. But it was a surprisingly intimate moment.

"Give me a little while," I said. I completed my morning routine and then joined her in the living room, where we consumed the bagels and coffee she had brought. We said little. We had reached the same impasse her father and I had come to.

You need help.

James's words sounded so logical—even self-evident. I'd been through a series of intense events during the past two years. I had been threatened and nearly killed, more than once. These happenings had been traumatic—some downright horrific. Anybody would have had some problems coping.

You need help.

The concept of "help" sounded so simple, so appealing. But the prospect of erasing or dulling the impact of the traumatic events—and above all, of ceasing to do the type of thing that had caused them—had forced me to face an uncomfortable truth. I wasn't an adrenaline junkie. But the same endeavors that had created so much pain had also made me feel empowered, alive. If getting help meant taking away those feelings, I wasn't sure I could do it.

James meant well. So did those who echoed his advice, including my sister, Marsha, and my friends Pam and Cassandra. But when it came right down to it, none of them understood what it was like to be handicapped, to be a victim, to be dependent. To have a life worth living meant doing what I did and relying on myself.

"I came over to give you this," Alicia said, handing over a small package. "A courier brought it over a little while ago. I know this will probably lead to something dangerous. I just don't want you to . . . Oh, God." She burst into tears. "Can't you think of us, Pen? We don't want to lose you."

I gestured for her to come around the table, and I held her for a long time.

After Alicia left, I took the package, which bore no return address, and tore it open. Inside was a disposable cell phone, similar to the one Lexi had given me. I booted it up, and a notification appeared, indicating I had a message.

I made my way through the menu and accessed the voice-mail. The message was delivered in a jarring, synthesized voice: "We are responding to your email from last night. Drive to the supermarket parking lot at Highways 7 and 101 and await instructions." That was it. The message ended, and I was left to decide whether I would do what the respondent asked, or refuse because it might be a trap. I'd given them my name, an email address, and a phone number—was that enough to trace me here? It was for a professional—someone like Tony McCort.

I had asked this person, or persons, whoever it was, to contact me. They had complied. The proposed destination was a public place, which should be safe enough. On the other hand, they'd given me a secure phone; why couldn't they just call me? And even if the contact process was to begin in a public place, they were going to give me further instructions.

My decision process was a sham. There was never any doubt about my going. I made a mental note to carefully think through what I asked for next time. Actually receiving it could be a little unnerving.

The skies were gray and threatening when I went out to the van. As I waited for the ramp to extend, I heard a faint buzzing sound. I looked around but couldn't locate the source. But the buzzing was persistent, getting louder, and then more faint. Finally I looked up and soon located the source: a drone. It gave me the creeps, and I wondered who'd sent it to spy on me: the people who'd responded from the Tomlinson-related address, or McCort?

What if they were one and the same?

I got in and started driving. I glanced up every once in a while but couldn't tell if the drone was still following me. My mysterious hosts had shown extreme security consciousness by sending me the burner phone; I hoped they still knew what they were doing. The intersection the caller had directed me to was in a busy commercial district a few miles from the Woodruffs', toward the city. I pulled into a space in front of the supermarket and waited, trying not to act paranoid.

I suddenly realized I should have told somebody where I was going. I called Lexi, got her voicemail, and told her I was meeting someone who had known Mark Tomlinson. Then I gave her the time and place. Having left at least a bit of a trail, I sat back and waited some more, bemoaning my amateur status in a game for professionals.

I jumped when the burner phone rang. I picked it up and this time got a live voice, sounding like it belonged to a young man. "Please drive to the southeast corner of the lot and wait." The call disconnected.

I looked around and figured out which directions were south and east, then drove around to the side of the building away from the road, but still relatively open. I parked again, leaving the engine running. The phone rang again.

"Yes?"

"Hello," said the same voice. "Thank you for coming. We've determined that you were not physically followed here."

"So it was you that sent up—"

"The drone? Yes, that was us. Now, as I was saying, you weren't physically followed, but we need to be sure you weren't electronically followed, either. To that, we'll need to transport you to another location in our vehicle."

"Now, wait a minute—"

"And you'll need to be blindfolded."

"Come on. You can't expect me to go along with that." I looked around, trying to determine where the call was coming from.

"We realize you'll need some assurances," the man said. "Here's what we propose: My partner and I are employees of Redstone Security. We are a reputable international firm. My name is DJ Cerone, and my partner's name is Margaret Lanier. Please take a few minutes to check us out. Then I'll call you back."

He hung up. I switched to the Internet browser on my phone, and sure enough, Redstone Security was a far-flung, reputable outfit. I called the number for their Minneapolis office and asked for DJ Cerone. I got voicemail and heard the message. It was the same voice as the guy who'd called me.

Cerone called back. "Are you satisfied?" he asked.

"I guess so. But if you're operating openly, under your own names, why all the cloak and dagger?"

"Because our client doesn't want to be linked to you or your inquiries in any way at this time, and our client is a very cautious person."

"Who's your client?"

A short pause. "We don't know."

I took a deep breath, left Lexi another message, and went along. Margaret and DJ were very nice and professional, showing me multiple forms of ID, providing a comfortable blindfold, and handling me gently as they lifted me into the back of an SUV. They checked me over thoroughly with an electronic scanner and made me leave my phone in the van. I didn't like that at all, but they were insistent.

They didn't say anything during the ride, which took about half an hour through multiple abrupt turns. When they finally stopped and removed my blindfold, we were in an underground garage. They lifted me out and placed me in my wheelchair, which they'd folded up and brought along. I followed them to an elevator, which we took up to the fifth floor of an eleven-story building. We went through an unmarked door, which was secured by a retinal scanner, and into a room that was bare except for two chairs. Then Cerone, a tall young man with thinning, buzz-cut hair, opened up a second door after again looking into a scanner.

I followed them into the second room, which was equally bare except for a table, on top of which stood a computer and a large screen. Margaret Lanier, a woman with Asian features who was nearly as tall as Cerone, entered some commands on the computer keyboard, and the monitor flickered to life. The scene on it looked like somebody's living room, but there was a tall folding screen in the center of the room. Lanier and Cerone exited the room, and I was left staring at the living room with the screen.

"Ms. Wilkinson?" asked a voice, presumably coming remotely from the living room.

"Yes?"

"Thank you for coming. I apologize for all the rigmarole. I'm Mark Tomlinson."

Chapter 40

"You're—Tomlinson? But he's—"

"Dead. But, well—you know. Greatly exaggerated reports and all that."

"So what's going on?"

"First, some ground rules," the voice said. "I've researched you thoroughly, and I've decided to trust you. But my trust goes only so far. You will never receive any proof that I am alive, or that the voice talking to you is Mark Tomlinson. That's for my protection, of course, but for yours as well. I'm going to give you some information that could really only have come from me. But it's nothing recent; there's no proof that it came from a living person."

"Well, if you wanted to get my attention, you certainly have it," I said. "But I have no idea where you are or how to find you. Why can't I see your face?"

"Again, for your own protection. If closely questioned, you won't be able to say you saw me alive. All you will have heard is a voice claiming to be me."

"Then why should I believe it's really you?"

"You'll have to make your own judgment about that. But I'm sure that when we're through talking, you'll be satisfied that it's me."

"Okay, then. Amaze me."

He laughed. "What, all this cloak-and-dagger hasn't been enough to impress you? Well, let me tell you, Pen. I'd never heard of you until recently, when the latest Tony McCort drama began. When I checked you out, I was the one who became impressed. I need somebody to handle this situation for me, and I believe you're the one."

"I already have a client."

"I know, and I wouldn't ask you to cooperate with me unless I was convinced it served Andre Woodruff's interests."

"I'm listening."

"Good. Why don't we start by your describing to me everything you've found about Tony in the course of your investigation?"

"Please. You think I'm an idiot? For all I know, I could tell you everything, and then I'd see McCort walk out from behind that screen."

He laughed. "Very good. I had to make sure you were as intelligent as you appeared to be."

"Okay, so I'm a genius. I'm sort of waiting to find out why you brought me here."

"Of course. First, the obvious question: What happened when I 'died' in Mexico? It was a miracle I survived, really. My vehicle caught on a clump of trees and didn't go all the way down. But I was still badly injured. And having survived, I had no desire to tempt fate again."

"So you faked your death."

"It wasn't all that hard. I was tight with the local officials, and I had plenty of money to spread around. But I knew Tony would be looking hard for any materials I might have left behind, so I had to make my disappearance complete."

"McCort tried to kill you?"

"Oh yes. It was Tony."

"Why?"

"Because my wife died."

I recalled that Tomlinson's wife had died from cancer shortly before Mark's own "death."

"That doesn't make any sense," I said. "What did your wife's death have to do with it?"

223

"I guess we'd better go back to the beginning," said the voice.

"Please."

"In the early nineties, I was a guy with an accounting degree, a job as a bookkeeper at a health club, and a coke problem. Tony McCort was a very smart man who'd grown up poor, who read a lot of books and was very ambitious. The legend is true; he did in fact start as a towel boy at the club, although he was quickly promoted to assistant manager. We became friends. He had the thought that we should go into business together."

"So you started a health club?"

He snorted. "Hardly. Not then, anyway. We had no money, and no prospect of raising the funds necessary for that kind of investment. The first step was, Tony told me to kick the coke habit. Amazingly, I did. That took about three months. After that, we began our fundraising."

"I thought you said—"

"We had no prospect of raising the money, right? I forgot to add one word: 'legally.'"

"What does *that* mean?"

"Tony and I were both smart young guys, it was true. But we had something else in common: a background in drugs. We both had contacts, and we started dealing seriously out of the club we worked at. Within a year, we were the leading suppliers of coke for the western suburbs of Minneapolis. I'll tell you, we were good. We made tons of money. And Tony was really, really careful. He'd served a stretch in juvy, so he knew the pitfalls. Anyway, within a couple of years, we'd made enough to leverage into our first club."

"So you kept dealing?"

"No, we didn't. And that's really the remarkable thing. We knew when to quit. So even though we were making a killing— more than we'd ever make in the health club business—we knew it couldn't go on forever. So we did the impossible: We went straight. We hung it up and poured all of our energies into our new club. Pretty soon we were expanding like crazy. Everything was going well."

"Until . . ."

"Until a few years later. One day Tony walked into my office. He said, 'Mark, it's time.' I knew what he meant, of course. It was time for me to go. He tossed a check for fifteen million dollars onto the desk and said 'Be gone by five today.'"

"What did you do?"

"You've had a couple of encounters with Tony McCort, right? What do you think I did?"

"You went. By five."

"Damn right I did. I'd always known the day would come, of course. Tony had become the dominant partner, while I was the number two guy."

"The second fiddle," I said, recalling the enigmatic email address.

"Exactly. Now, fifteen million was a fair price at the time. All the increase in value that came after that—that was due to Tony. I was no slouch, either. I took that fifteen million and moved to Colorado and invested aggressively. I parlayed it into many times that amount within a pretty short time. In truth, I was relieved to be free of Tony."

"So he told you to keep quiet about the drug dealing?"

"He didn't have to. I'd have been implicating myself if I told anybody. But as the years went on and all the statutes of limitations had expired, I had to start paying attention. Tony was starting his political career. But he knew he could count on my silence as long as Heather was alive."

"He threatened your wife?"

"He didn't need to do that, either. I just knew. It was implicit. And when she died, and he didn't have that hold over me, I was just another loose end."

"So then he tried to kill you," I said.

"He did, but before that, I started thinking about an insurance policy."

"Brad Van Ness."

"Brad actually contacted me first. I resisted talking to him, but he said, 'Look, McCort is going to be elected, and he's scary as hell.' He didn't have to tell me Tony was scary, but I wasn't up on the political situation. Keep in mind, this was a year ago. I said, 'You're sure he's going to win?' And Brad said, 'He's not going to lose.'"

It was, I recalled, almost exactly how Isaac Woodruff had put it. "Did Van Ness know how you'd financed the clubs?"

"He'd suspected it, and I pretty much confirmed it over the phone. I told him to erase any traces of his contact with me. And then we were going to meet, and I was going to give him the proof. But of course, we never got the chance to meet—Brad vanished shortly after our conversation. When Brad disappeared, I realized that Tony had been monitoring him electronically."

I stared at the unmoving screen in the generic living room. "So what happened to the proof you were going to give him?"

"It was a pretty complete package—accounting records, bank accounts, laundering techniques, names, dates—everything. I wasn't sure what to do with it when Brad vanished. I didn't want to just put it on the Internet—that would make it much easier for people to claim it was fake. I wasn't sure how to use the information politically—when to release it or how to spin it, to make sure it would have the maximum effect against Tony."

"So what did you do?"

"I flew to Minneapolis and put the package in the hands of Blake Lofton personally."

I paused to think as several key facts sorted themselves out and dropped into the proper slots. The package was Lofton's "October surprise." But presumably, the package had also gotten him killed. "So what happened next?" I asked.

"I figured they'd be coming for me. I suppose I should have just gone into hiding then and there. But I settled for setting up a second insurance policy by leaving a copy of the material with my attorney in Puerto Vallarta. But it didn't work."

Silence. He wasn't waiting for me to say anything; he was steeling himself to go on. "He came a couple of weeks later, a stocky guy with dead eyes and a heavy New York accent."

Bolger, I realized.

"It was . . ." His voice quavered. "I knew intellectually that such people existed, who were willing to do things like that to their fellow human beings, but . . . that someone would actually seem to *enjoy* it. He was waiting for me in my living room; he'd broken into the house. He pounced on me and broke my left leg with a steel pry bar, which immobilized me. Then . . . It went on for over two hours. I lost track of time. I passed out a few times. I never knew it was possible to feel pain like that. He kept at me with the pry bar. He broke my arms, my legs . . ."

I waited for him to compose himself.

"They'd gotten to my attorney and bribed him to give up the stuff. So they knew what I had, and they were obviously concerned about other copies being out there. That's why they questioned me. I told this guy some lies but ended up admitting I'd given it to Lofton. I don't know whether he believed me or not. I told him where to find a copy I'd hidden online. But I never told him about a second online copy."

I was astonished. "You held out after all *that*?"

"I knew I was going to die anyway. I knew the pain wouldn't stop, no matter what I said. Anyway, after the guy finished, he put me in my car and rolled it off a cliff. When I survived the crash—that was so farfetched that I'm sure Tony never had any doubt that I was dead. There are days when I wish I'd been killed."

"So you think McCort had Lofton killed in an attempt to retrieve the package?"

"That's the obvious scenario. But I still don't understand why they'd just kill him. How did he know Blake hadn't just done what I did? Stashed the information with lawyers, to be released in the event of his death?"

"Maybe Blake was like a lot of other people. He just underestimated how evil McCort is. He didn't seriously believe he'd be killed."

And, I reflected, Tomlinson had done exactly the same thing himself, and how had that worked out? But then why hadn't McCort tortured the location of the file out of Lofton instead of simply killing him? I could think of a couple of reasons why he wouldn't have wanted to take the risk, but the reasons didn't seem compelling.

"You're probably right about Lofton, even though I tried to warn him."

"So what happened to the package?" I asked.

"You tell me. You're investigating Lofton's murder."

"I have no idea. But presumably you have a copy of the materials."

"Sure. Scanned and hidden in that second online location."

"Why not just put it out on the Internet? The election is only three weeks away. There isn't a lot of time for political subtleties."

He hesitated. "Pen, you're investigating Lofton's death."

"So?"

"If the material surfaces now, Tony will probably assume you're responsible."

I exhaled. "You're probably right."

"Look, this has to be bound up with the murder somehow. Whoever Tony hired to kill Lofton was probably sent into that house with the idea of retrieving the package." He talked as though McCort's culpability in the murder was a given.

"That makes sense."

"The murder has to be solved, Pen. Tony has to be put behind bars. If he isn't, he's going to come after you, or Ellie Ostlund, or whoever he blames, when the materials are released. He'll still be free to create all kinds of havoc. And don't assume the package will be enough to lose the election for him, either. It probably will, but you never know. He'll attack it as fake news."

"How convincing is it?"

"To any reasonable person, it's conclusive. But a lot of Tony's supporters aren't reasonable. They'll believe what they want to believe."

To me, that analysis was staggering. Conclusive proof that McCort was a drug dealer might not be enough to keep him from being elected governor. More than that, anybody he suspected of releasing the proof could probably expect to die. "Good God, Mark. Where does that leave us?"

"I don't know, Pen. But now you can see why I think you're the only one who can handle this. To really make use of the proof, you have to put Tony McCort away for murder. He has to be stopped."

By now, I wasn't paying much attention to the monitor, since nothing had moved on it during our entire conversation. But now I sensed movement behind the screen in the remote living room. Tomlinson said, "I knew right away I wanted to help you, Pen. And now I'll show you why." I watched as a man in a powered wheelchair emerged from behind the screen. I looked at him and gasped. He was horribly disfigured, his face pieced together at strange angles, his left eye reduced to a slit, his mouth stretched over to one side.

"Won't win many beauty contests, will I?" he said. "I'm afraid that plunge off the cliff, and the fire that it caused in the car, didn't do much for my looks. Sorry to shock you like this. But you can see why I usually hide behind this screen when I communicate with those few people I trust enough to talk to." He looked up into the camera. "You and I have the wheelchair experience in common. Neither of us will walk again. But I can see your face. That was the real reason for all these convoluted security procedures, by the way—to take your measure, face to face. You're still beautiful, Pen. Don't take that for granted."

I was stunned, speechless.

"After all that's happened," he said, "my hopes and plans for this life are mostly gone. But I'm convinced that I survived for a reason. I need to put right what I started all those years ago. I need to stop Tony McCort, and by putting it in your hands, I'm giving that my best shot. But I do have one dream left. When this election is over, I'd like Tony McCort to be rejected by the voters and in jail. And then . . ." He hesitated, and I thought I saw a tear slide from the slit of his eye down his ravaged face. "And then, I'd like to come home."

Chapter 41

A t eight the next morning, it was Lexi Candiotti's turn to make the trip through the crowded downtown skyways in an effort to lose any would-be followers. Meeting me in person still entailed significant political and career risk for Lexi, but it was obviously a chance she and the mayor were now willing to take. The folks at Redstone Security had been very thorough and had spotted no signs of surveillance on me, but things could have changed since yesterday. I was afraid McCort might have penetrated James Carter's condo, so I had rented a guest unit in the same building, where Lexi was joining me for breakfast.

After making my way back to Lake Minnetonka yesterday, I had simply sat in the guest house for the rest of the day, making notes and outlines, and thinking. Mark Tomlinson had ratcheted up the pressure on me considerably, but he had also focused my thinking. Tony McCort's motive for killing Blake Lofton had just gotten a lot stronger. McCort had reason to kill Lofton not just to eliminate him as an opponent in the election, but to retrieve the package of incriminating information provided by Tomlinson. I'd developed some tentative thoughts, but I needed to discuss them with someone I could trust, and Lexi, despite my uneasiness about her, was still my best bet.

She appeared a little after eight, bringing bagels, yogurt, orange juice, bananas, and instant oatmeal. I supplied the coffee.

We sat down at the kitchen table. Lexi sipped from her glass. "So, things have gotten interesting."

"Yes. In a good way and in a bad way."

"I'm really waiting to hear the good way, Pen. Because if the facts are starting to point to McCort, that's bad. But, as always, it is what it is, so let's hear what you've got."

I understood. It would be nice to find a suspect other than Andre for the Lofton murder. But if McCort was implicated, life would get sticky for the mayor, given McCort's strong support among rank-and-file police. I told her Lofton had received evidence that McCort had been a drug dealer and had used the proceeds to finance his business empire.

"And you can prove that?"

"If necessary, I think I can. Eventually, we can get a copy of the evidence itself."

"I don't suppose you want to tell me how you found this out, or where the proof came from."

"Not without permission from my source. And my source, with good reason, doesn't want to go public unless and until McCort is behind bars."

"I suppose not. It didn't come from Schott?"

"No, a different source. This is later, separate, and a hell of a lot more serious."

"Just as you thought," Lexi said. "There was something more." She got up and boiled water in the microwave, then poured it into a bowl of instant oatmeal, bringing it back to the table. "Without the proof in hand—that makes it harder," she said.

"Maybe a bit. But if we just proceed on that premise, without requiring proof right now, it shouldn't make much difference."

She sliced banana into her oatmeal. "Maybe not. So let's say this material exists. Where does that leave us? How did the murder happen?"

"The most likely explanation is that Lofton was killed in an effort to physically retrieve the package, and failing that, to prevent him from using it."

Her face scrunched up in skepticism as she paused with a spoonful of oatmeal. "Wouldn't a man like Lofton just give it to his attorneys and tell them to release it if anything happened to him?"

"Guys like Lofton don't think like that. They can't imagine themselves being in any physical danger. You don't just murder or attack a corporate CEO and candidate for governor."

She ate more oatmeal. "Makes sense. But you're thinking they didn't find the material when they killed him."

"Correct. And that sort of explains everything McCort has done since then."

"So if we assume McCort was behind it, and he's got a solid alibi, we need to find out who he sent to do the deed."

"Exactly."

"Who knew Blake was staying in the city that night?"

"Simone. The volunteer driver—whom we cleared, by the way. Obviously Andre found out somehow—probably Simone."

"What calls did Blake make that evening?"

"Other than to the driver and Simone, nobody. I'm not sure what any of this tells us, Pen. McCort was probably watching him."

"That makes sense."

"I still see no indication that he hired a pro," Lexi said.

"I agree. Whoever it was had to talk their way in through that back door in the middle of the night. That points to somebody Lofton knew."

"He could have known Ivan Bolger."

"He of the four-cop alibi."

"Right."

"You know those four officers, Lexi. In your heart of hearts, would they conspire to give Bolger an alibi for murder, even of a politician they strongly disliked?"

She took a long time answering, eating a spoonful of oatmeal and washing it down with some juice. "No. No, I don't think so.

I don't like any of the Friday Night Group. They're mostly racist, and two of them are flat-out pigs. But I can't see it. Not murder."

"We'd also have to assume that Bolger could talk his way into the house," I said. "That's possible, but I think it was some-body Lofton trusted. Someone he could have confided in, who might have been able to learn from him where the material was—in a hidden safe or something."

"That narrows it down."

"Right. A family member or close friend or associate."

Lexi finished her orange juice. "Homicide looked at every-body."

"Not the way they looked at Andre. I know they were thor-ough, but . . ."

"Who are we talking about?" she asked.

"Feel free to add to the list, but I can see only three possibil-ities: Simone, Ellie Ostlund, and Lauren Jorgensen."

Lexi was already shaking her head. "I just can't see Simone."

"She has no alibi, and Blake didn't always treat her very well." I didn't add that she'd been keeping a very large secret about her father's murder, one that her husband might have learned and threatened to use.

"It's true that we focused on Andre at an early stage," Lexi said. "But Simone was not neglected. She went under the micro-scope, guaranteed. You always look at the spouse. Always."

That was hard to argue with, I supposed. Lexi should know; she was a former homicide commander. And it was consistent with what Simone herself had told me. But, microscope or no, Simone simply didn't have an alibi. "How about Ellie?" I said. "Her alibi is shaky. She had a good motive, and Blake's death has worked out nicely for her. And it's not as though she's the meek type."

"True, as far as the motive and alibi. But her personal-ity—I think you're arguing against yourself. If she had a lot of murderous outrage about being defeated in the primary by

Lofton, she's kept it under wraps. Hell, she went to work for him."

I'd been thinking the same thing. She had seemed resentful but resigned, recognizing if not accepting that maleness and wealth were always advantageous to a candidate. But if it wasn't her, that left somebody even less likely. Lauren Jorgensen was just difficult to take seriously as a suspect. Not only did she have a solid alibi, but she appeared to have no motive at all.

"I'll go back and talk to the investigators," Lexi said.

"Thanks. There has to be something. And we're running out of time."

Lexi got up. "Have to run." She leaned down. "For God's sake, be careful."

She left. I felt mildly irritated that she hadn't shown more concern for my safety. But I hadn't told her about McCort's assault on me. She knew about the trackers on my van, of course, and she knew about McCort's having stuck me in an elevator for a few minutes. Nothing to get alarmed about.

I looked up and screamed. Tony McCort was standing in front of me. Now walking toward me, now threatening me. Now tearing open my shirt, putting his hands on me . . . I screamed and screamed. And then he was gone.

I gripped the table, forcing myself to breathe, resisting the urge to search the rest of the apartment, to re-lock the door. I reached into the refrigerator for a bottle of wine. But my hands were shaking too badly to handle the bottle. I went back to gripping the table. After a few minutes I was able to pour out the wine, which I gulped down. Then I poured more and drank it.

I don't know how long I sat there. Time had disappeared. Space had disappeared. Objects had lost their permanence. I was losing my mind.

Eventually, with the help of the wine, my rational mind kicked in, telling me I had experienced a full-blown, wide-awake flashback. PTSD. What had triggered it? I didn't know.

I'd had one once before, when I'd relived my body-in-the-freezer scene. I hadn't told anybody. I wanted to tell somebody about the one I'd just had. But who?

I calmed down some more. As terrifying as these episodes were, I knew they weren't nearly as serious as those experienced by some people. There were soldiers, cops, abuse victims, and any number of others who lived in constant, paralyzing fear, while I was able to function fairly normally in between them, and I expected they would subside on their own before long. In fact, it would be embarrassing to complain. As always, I needed to rely on myself.

I sat in the kitchen for a long time, now sipping rather than gulping the wine, trying to rid my mind of Tony McCort. Other thoughts began to drift randomly through my mind. Thoughts about Blake Lofton and Andre. Then thoughts of my meetings at the campaign headquarters. Ellie Ostlund—abrasive, direct, and busy. Lauren Jorgensen—friendly, cooperative, and . . . not busy.

I sat up, placing my wine glass carefully on the table. *Not busy.* In a bustling, hectic political campaign headquarters, she'd been reading quietly at a clean desk. No ringing phone, no one running in and out of her office. She'd been home by four o'clock. She'd been relatively new to her job, but that should have meant even longer hours than usual, trying to get up to speed. It was the final push to Election Day, with all hands on deck. But she hadn't been busy.

"It was Lauren," I said out loud.

Chapter 42

I managed to shove the flashback aside and push ahead, thinking through my realization about Lauren. After a few minutes, I called Lexi and asked if she could find out who Lauren had used as an alibi for the night of the murder, recalling that it had been a friend who was a police officer.

"I can do that," she replied. Then, "Pen, are you okay?"

I must have sounded a little shaky. "Never better," I replied. Next, I called Kenny and asked if he was free to come downtown for a little while.

"I do have class in a few minutes," he said.

"That's all right—"

"But I'll skip it."

Before I could object, he hung up.

I thought again about Lauren Jorgenson's job. She had only recently been promoted to a position in the campaign after serving as Blake Lofton's personal assistant. But the promotion was a sham; she didn't have any work to do. So what had been Lofton's purpose in promoting her? It could have been a reward for excellent service as an assistant. But there might have been a dark side to it. The reward might have been rank personal favoritism, not for a good job done, but . . . for what? Services of a more personal nature? Her silence about something damaging? Or the promotion might have been a way of removing Lauren from Blake's daily presence. And that could have resulted from— what? An affair gone bad? Personal annoyance? I recalled that unlike Ellie, Lauren had seemed genuinely distraught about Lofton's death.

There were two people I could think of who might know: Simone and Ellie. But they were my other two suspects, and I didn't want to alert them. Either or both of them might have a close friendship with Lauren and be disinclined to tell me the truth, or worse, inclined to warn Lauren that she was under suspicion. At the very least, they might begin to act awkwardly around Lauren. I couldn't take the chance.

Lexi called. "Lauren's alibi was a Stillwater patrol cop named Jenna Martin. They've been friends since high school. Jenna says they had dinner at Lauren's house that evening and then she stayed with Lauren all night."

"Why would she do that?"

"Stillwater is a bit of a drive. It's a suburb, but it's to the east of St. Paul, on the St. Croix. It's not unreasonable that somebody would stay over in the city, especially if they've been drinking."

"What did the cell phone check show?"

"Lauren's was at her house all night."

"And Jenna's?"

"They didn't check it, as far as I could see."

"Why not?"

"I don't know. I'm not sure I would have if I was running the investigation. Maybe I would have if she wasn't a cop."

I would have been surprised if Lexi hadn't tracked that alibi down to the end. But I was never surprised at the way cops stuck up for one another.

"Do you have Jenna's contact information?" I said.

"Pen—"

"I won't actually contact her without getting your okay. I just want it handy."

"All right." I could tell she didn't believe me, but she read me the cell phone number.

"Thanks."

"Pen," she said, "what is this about? Why the focus on Lauren?"

"Just a hunch," I said. I didn't want to sound like an idiot by giving her the laughably weak observation that Lauren hadn't been busy at the campaign office.

Kenny arrived. I'd had an ethical decision to make. It was one thing to poke around in the affairs of a deceased person like Schott. It was quite another to invade the privacy, with no judicial process, of someone like Lauren Jorgensen, who was not only very much alive but entitled to a presumption of innocence. But that had to be weighed against the risk of sending an innocent man to prison for life, causing an explosion of racial violence, and letting a monster take political power in Minnesota. And mostly, there was my conviction, arrogant though it was, that I was right. I *knew* I was onto something.

Kenny had brought his computer and was ready for action. He sat down with me at the kitchen table and set everything up.

"Your mom would kill me," I said.

He grinned, showing beautiful teeth.

"And this is a little questionable."

"I trust you, Aunt Pen. Whatever it is you want me to do, I know there's a good reason for it."

I had already decided to skip my lecture on how my request might get him into trouble or put him into danger. It would be fruitless, I knew. But more than that, I knew that on some level, Kenny needed this, much as I needed my own "things."

"How are you on cell phone location records?" I asked. I handed him a slip with Officer Jenna Martin's cell number.

He shrugged. "It's doable. Trickier than call history."

"How would you do it?"

"Let's try the easy way first and hope there are location records on the phone. How could we get this person to access a web link on her phone? Maybe a text from somebody she trusts?"

"Let me think . . . She's a cop. She'll be suspicious about phishing schemes. Can you send her a text from Lauren?"

"It will look that way, yes." Kenny opened a notepad on his screen and moved aside. I typed:

"You should read this article about our problem."

Kenny moved back to the keyboard. "What should we use for the link?"

"Just find an article about the Lofton murder."

He quickly found an article. "I'm slipping a little something extra into the link," Kenny said. "If she clicks on it, we're in. What's the number you want it to come from?"

I gave him Lauren's number, and he sent the text. "Now we wait," he said. "If we're lucky, she'll access it right away."

We chatted for a few minutes until his computer gave a little beep. "Got it," he said, looking at the screen. "I'm into her phone. And here's the location log. That's good—she kept the GPS locator on."

I asked him to check the location of Jenna's phone on the night of Lofton's murder.

As he typed, I rationalized that I wasn't using Jenna's number to *contact* Jenna, which I'd promised Lexi I wouldn't do. But of course, this was something more serious.

Finally Kenny said, "The phone was at an address in Stillwater from four in the afternoon until eight the next morning."

"Are you sure?"

"Yep. It didn't move. And that address is the same as the billing address on the account."

"Jenna left her phone at home," I said. "Why would she do that, especially if she was planning to drive to Minneapolis and spend the night? And if she'd planned on providing an alibi for Lauren, she would have brought her phone."

Kenny didn't answer, and of course I hadn't expected him to. But I could see a pretty obvious answer: Jenna wasn't actually at Lauren's house. More than that, she didn't want her real location tracked during that time.

"All right," I said. "Let's see if we can check Lauren's location." Kenny repeated the process with Lauren, sending her a phony text that appeared to be from Jenna's phone, containing identical language, an identical link, and identical hidden software. The police had already checked, but I wanted to see for myself.

"They'll figure out these texts are phony," I pointed out.

"Sure, they'll know somebody is messing with them. But they won't understand what's happening or know who's responsible."

It took a little longer this time. While we waited, Kenny was hard at work at the keyboard. I wasn't sure what he was doing and wasn't sure I wanted to know. After about twenty minutes he looked up. "I've been fooling around a little and came across something interesting."

"Okay."

"I checked out county real estate records. Justin Jorgensen owns six properties in his own name. Two of them were underwater and set for foreclosure until a couple of weeks ago, when he redeemed both of them. It would have taken about two hundred thousand dollars to do that."

"Where did the money come from?"

"I don't know, and I suspect it would be really hard to find out."

"Ka-ching," I said. "Lauren got paid to do it."

A chime went off, indicating that Lauren had accessed the link, causing her phone to surreptitiously download Kenny's special program. Within minutes, Kenny had confirmed Lexi's information that Lauren's phone had been at home all night. "Can you look at her caller log?" I asked. This was something the police had also undoubtedly done.

Kenny pulled up the log, and I moved closer to the table to look at the screen. I scanned the numbers for a couple of days on each side of the murder. I don't know what I expected to see, but there was nothing that jumped out at me. I was about to tell him to close it down but then said, "Let's go back a couple of weeks."

Kenny obliged. I looked at the list again, and this time the pattern sprang off the screen. There were dozens of calls to the same number. The pattern went on for several days. The calls were short—usually too short to even leave a message.

"I'll be damned," I said. "I wonder if the police checked this." *Maybe not*, I thought. There had really been no reason to. Even with all my suspicion, I almost hadn't done it myself, and the police would have had to get a warrant and articulate a good reason to look, which they wouldn't have had.

"Who was she calling?" I asked Kenny.

"Already on it." After several minutes he looked up and said, "As best I can tell, her calls were made to a burner."

I sat back, pondering this.

Kenny pointed to a spot on the screen. "And after about four days, the calls just stopped."

I worked the pieces around in my mind, trying to nail down the sequence of events. The affair would have resulted from a lethal convergence of factors: a wealthy, powerful man with a somewhat distant marriage; an attractive younger woman; and daily, close proximity. But secrecy was essential; the man was not only married, but a corporate CEO and candidate for public office. Lauren was married as well, thus the burner phone. How long did it go on? We didn't know, although if necessary, we could trace Lauren's phone records back indefinitely.

Eventually, things went south. The affair fizzled. Lofton had reacted by engineering Lauren's "promotion," which got her out of his day-to-day presence. He probably also hoped she'd be mollified by receiving a job with higher pay and greater prestige. Who had initiated the breakup? That was easy—it was Lofton. And Lauren hadn't been happy about it. At all. She had called him repeatedly, obsessively, over a period of days.

And then, as Kenny had pointed out, the calls had stopped. They had to stop sometime, of course, but why had they stopped when they did, after about four days? To me, the answer to that one was pretty obvious, too: She had been contacted by Tony McCort.

Lauren was the perfect instrument for McCort's purposes. She met the "back door in the middle of the night" test, able to talk her way into the house. She was familiar with the house and might have had some ideas about where a cache of sensitive documents would be hidden. She'd been intimate with Lofton, which meant he might have given away information, perhaps inadvertently, about the package's whereabouts. After being dumped by Lofton, she'd really wanted him to die. Thus the overkill, typical of a crime of passion, that characterized the stabbing. If she got nabbed for Lofton's murder, she'd have a credible personal motive, a motive other than retrieving documents. She probably would have killed Lofton for free. That was useful for McCort. The problem was that Lauren hadn't been successful in finding Tomlinson's damaging information; McCort was still looking for it.

So that was the story. It was logical and fit all the facts. But all the story's elements had one thing in common: I couldn't prove any of them. I might never be able to.

As I explained the sequence of events to Kenny, something nagged at my subconscious, a feeling that I was missing something. I finished describing the events to Kenny and then went over all of them in my mind again. Then I realized what I'd neglected. I hadn't explained *why* Jenna had left her phone at home. Her alibi for Lauren was phony; if she had actually planned to provide Lauren with an alibi, she would have brought her phone along to make the alibi more convincing. So she hadn't actually been at Lauren's that night. Which now led me to ask, Where *had* she been? She had been somewhere else, the location of which she hadn't wanted known. Where? And why?

I was about to put that question onto the back burner when something occurred to me. "There's another phone we need to check," I said.

"Whose?"

"Justin's. But I don't have the number."

"Might as well try a public search," he said. Within a couple of minutes, he had admitted defeat on that front. "Hmm," he said. "You say they're a married couple?"

"Right."

He went back to his keyboard. Within half a minute he said, "Here it is. Justin Jorgensen."

"How did you find it?"

"Sometimes a husband and wife will go phone shopping together, and they'll be assigned consecutive numbers. That's what happened here."

"Great," I said. "But I'm not sure how to get this guy to open a link. I don't really know him."

Kenny gave me a small smile. "Just give me a couple of minutes." His fingers exploded across the keyboard. The computer screen was a kaleidoscope of shifting images, lines of code, and web sites. He finished, then leaned back, crossing his arms. "This may take a while. Maybe we should get something to eat."

"What did you do?"

"Uh—you're probably better off not knowing that."

"Kenny . . ."

He smiled. "It's okay. No blowback, I promise. Unfortunately, I've done things a lot sketchier than this." A little chirp sounded from his computer, and he turned back toward the screen. "Well, how about that? He bit right away. I guess this guy's not a genius."

"So you've got access to his phone?"

He nodded.

"Okay. Let's find out where he was on the night of the murder. Supposedly he was up north hunting somewhere."

Kenny typed furiously. "Okay, I've got multiple locations. For most of the day the phone was about a hundred miles north of here. Then, starting at about seven in the evening, he was on the move for about an hour and a half. A little after eight-thirty he was at this address in south Minneapolis. Looks like it's on Hiawatha Avenue."

"What's there?"

More typing. "Okay, here it is." He looked up at me. "It's a motel."

Chapter 43

"I need pictures of everybody," I said. "Jenna, Lauren, and Justin."

Kenny went to work, and within a couple of minutes had printed out the three images. Justin's had been the hardest to find, but Kenny had finally found a picture on a friend's Facebook page. I was relieved; he wouldn't have to hack into the state driver's license registry as he'd offered to do.

I took the pictures, folded them, and put them in my purse. "I should get going. I really appreciate all your help, Kenny."

"Wait," he said.

"For what?"

"I'm going with you."

"Kenny . . ."

"Look, Aunt Pen—it's not like I'm a tough guy or anything. But you need somebody with you. I know what happened to Brad Van Ness and Jane Hyser. And you say McCort hasn't threatened you, but I'm not so sure about that. I'm already uneasy enough about that house you're staying at. They need more security."

I knew I shouldn't let him come. His mother would be furious about my involving him further. But he was apparently going to pester me about it. And in truth, I wouldn't mind some company.

"I'll pick you up at eight," I said.

*   *   *

We waited until eight-thirty that night, which was about the time Justin Jorgensen would have gotten to the motel on the night of the murder. I hoped some of the same staff might be on duty. I picked up Kenny at his dorm at the University of Minnesota, and we drove southeast along Hiawatha Avenue, in the direction of the airport. It was a fairly dark stretch of road, with railroad tracks, grain elevators, and industrial properties on our left, and residential neighborhoods and a light-rail track on our right.

The Hi-46 Motel was a slightly dubious two-story place with about twenty units, laid out perpendicular to the road. I parked across the lot from the office, next to a No Vacancy sign.

"Wait here," I told Kenny.

"Are you sure?"

"Yes. You'll be able to see me through the window to the office."

He reluctantly agreed and helped me get into my wheelchair and down the ramp. There were only a couple of cars in the lot, but I noticed a smaller side lot, which appeared to be full. Guests exercising discretion, I figured.

The guy behind the desk was a huge man with bulging eyes, greasy brown hair, and a scraggly goatee. He stood up from his television program right away but made no move to help me as I struggled to get through the door. On my third try, I was finally able to yank the door open and roll myself through.

I took a moment to catch my breath, then tried my winning smile. "Hi," I said.

"We're full."

"Not a problem. I just have a question."

He was on full alert. He said nothing, as if in acknowledging my question he might somehow incriminate himself.

I pulled the folded picture of Justin out of my purse. I started to hold it up for him, but he held his hand up. "Wait a minute. Are you a cop? PI?"

"I'm an attorney."

"For who?"

"My client is a defendant in a criminal trial." I pulled out my attorney ID, which he also pushed away.

"No subpoena?" he said. "No court order?"

"Well, not yet, but—"

"Can't help you."

"Now, if you could just take a minute—"

"You hard of hearing? I said no." This time his tone was downright menacing. "Go back and get a court order."

"All right, I will," I lied. "You could save us all some time."

"Lady, I don't give a rat's ass about your time. You don't have a court order, take a fuckin' hike."

I was infuriated, but there was nothing I could do. "Fine," I said. "Meanwhile, you can take your vibrating beds, your hourly rates, and your charming personality and deposit them in a remote orifice where the sun never shines."

His face turned red. "You watch your mouth, lady." He stepped forward as if to come out from behind the counter, and I instantly regretted shooting my mouth off.

I struggled back through the door and out into the parking lot. The guy hadn't followed. Wiping sweat off my forehead, I rolled back to the van.

Where Kenny was nowhere to be seen.

I rolled right up to the van and looked again, but Kenny was gone. Panicky, I glanced around the parking lot, which was deserted. *Oh. God.* What was I going to tell Marsha? I pondered calling 911, but if Kenny had been taken, it was already too late. I decided to proceed cautiously down toward the side parking lot.

At home in California, I kept a knife in my van and a little canister of pepper spray on my key ring. But I hadn't been able to bring either of them on the plane to Minnesota. I settled for keeping my phone in one hand with 911 punched in.

"Aunt Pen?"

I jerked around; Kenny was approaching me from a side door, followed by another man. I exhaled and put my phone away. "Kenny, what on earth—"

"Sorry," he said. "But I saw Carlos here going over toward the Dumpster for a smoke break, and I thought I'd show him the picture."

I was too relieved to be mad at him. "Go on."

He held up Jenna's picture, displayed on his phone. "He told me he's seen her here."

"When?" I asked.

Kenny asked the man, a young guy with acne-scarred skin and a cigarette in his mouth, in Spanish. Carlos replied, and Kenny translated. "He says more than once. The most recent time was probably a couple of weeks ago."

The time frame fit, I thought. "How many times?" I asked.

Kenny asked him, and this time I understood the response. Carlos shrugged and said, "*Tres o quatro.*"

"Who was she with?"

Kenny asked, and this time the reply was longer. "He's sure she was with a man," Kenny reported. "But he really doesn't remember anything about the guy."

I held out the picture of Justin. Carlos nodded immediately. "*Sí.*"

"Can he be any more specific as to the date?" I said. "Maybe he could narrow it down to a day of the week?"

After a lengthy reply, Kenny translated. "He says it wouldn't have been a Monday or a Tuesday, since he doesn't work on those days. Other than that, he just doesn't know. He did notice that they didn't stay the entire night."

I'd run out of questions. Even if I could get my hands on the motel's register, it wouldn't help, assuming they'd used phony names. I thanked Carlos and pulled some money from my purse. The young man shook his head, refusing the payment.

"I hope I didn't get him in trouble with the manager," I said, glancing back toward the office. Kenny passed that along to Carlos, who shrugged, chuckled, and gave a short response.

"He says the manager's an asshole," Kenny reported.

I smiled and shook Carlos's hand.

"I didn't know you studied Spanish," I said as we returned to the van.

"I didn't study it, exactly. I sort of picked it up."

I shook my head, wondering what it must be like to be a genius.

We got ourselves buckled into the van. I looked over at Kenny, whose excitement was palpable. "Aunt Pen, you did it. You know who killed Lofton. You even know how it happened."

I exhaled. "What on earth do we do now?"

Chapter 44

"What's the latest?" Tony McCort demanded. He spoke over the scrambled phone connection from his office at Together Fitness.

"I found out where she's operating from," Bolger replied.

"Took you long enough," McCort snapped in a rare show of overt irritation. Usually the blank expression sufficed.

"She's at a condo building downtown on Nicollet Mall. There's a unit in the building owned by James Carter."

"So?"

"I'm still getting it set up."

This time McCort said nothing. He was pissed as hell, and Bolger knew it. What Bolger didn't tell his boss was that the unit had been entered and bugged two days ago. Eventually, from the total silence, Bolger had deduced that Pen was operating from somewhere else in the building. He'd learned that she had rented a guest unit, which he would enter and bug tonight if Pen stayed out at the Woodruffs'.

"Is there anything you *do* know?" McCort asked, now with exaggerated patience.

"Her nephew—the hacker—went into the building in mid-afternoon. A few hours later, the two of them went to a motel in south Minneapolis."

"A motel? Why the hell—"

"She tried to question the manager. Afterward, so did I. Turns out the guy's such an asshole, he blew her off and never even found out what she wanted."

"What do *you* think she wanted?"

Silence. Then, "I don't know."

"Do you think we need to find out?"

"I guess so. I mean, if we can't whack her—"

"No, we can't do that. Not yet. That's a bridge too far. After the election, she's a done deal. But in the meantime, she's a loose cannon. Who knows what she might stumble across?"

Chapter 45

"What on earth do we do now?"

My own words were repeated back to me by Lexi Candiotti, who had joined me back at the guest condo.

"Let me make sure I understand," she said. "You're saying McCort knew or guessed that Lofton had a package of information proving he was a drug dealer. He hired Lofton's assistant, Lauren, to retrieve it, and to kill Lofton."

"Yes," I said. "But I believe she wanted to kill him anyway, because they were having an affair and he dumped her."

"So Lauren goes to Blake's house, talks her way in through the door, kills Blake, but can't find the incriminating stuff."

"Correct. It's a little circumstantial."

"'Circumstantial' doesn't even begin to describe it. You say Lauren and Lofton had an affair. Where's the proof?"

"He promoted her to a job where she has no real work to do."

"I won't dignify that with a response."

I sighed. "Okay. Lauren made dozens of phone calls to him, obsessively, over a period of a few days, when I believe they broke up."

"And you know this how?"

I just stared at her. She knew damn well I'd gotten the phone records illegally. That made them inadmissible as evidence. If she'd known the calls were made to a burner phone, which couldn't actually be identified as belonging to Lofton, she would have been even more dismissive.

"Next item," Lexi said. "You say you can break Lauren's alibi."

"That's right. Jenna wasn't with her the night of the murder."

"Where was she?"

"At a motel, with Lauren's husband."

She lifted an eyebrow. "You can place them there the night of the murder?"

"Not exactly. But we have an eyewitness placing them there together several times."

"Not good enough."

"We can prove the husband was there the night of the murder."

"How?"

Once again, I simply looked at her. More illegal phone records.

"Did Lauren know her husband and her friend were getting it on?" she asked.

"I think she did know, or strongly suspected. At any rate, she didn't have any trouble getting Jenna to provide a phony alibi for her."

She threw her hands up in frustration. "What the hell am I supposed to do with all this, Pen? You're a prosecutor. If the cops came to you with this, what would you do with it?"

"There's at least enough to pull Lauren in and sweat her."

"You think she'll break?"

"Maybe."

"And if she doesn't, we are shit out of luck, Pen. We've blown our only shot at her. Your client will be toast, and so will the city."

I knew that, of course.

We sat for a long minute. Lexi stared at nothing, her jaw working back and forth. I had complicated her life immensely. Did she tell the investigators about my scenario, even though

254

she had no legal evidence to support it? I had tried to avoid compromising her; she didn't know for a fact that I'd done anything illegal. But that didn't make it any less awkward with the mayor or the police.

"I think Lauren is at least a little crazy," I ventured.

"If she did what you say she did, I'd have to agree. But where does that get us?"

"We have to get creative, Lexi. Maybe she has some buttons that can be pushed. Let's find out just how crazy she really is."

Chapter 46

"Things are coming to a head," Ivan Bolger reported over the secure connection to Tony McCort. "I can feel it."

"Specifics?"

"Our monitoring is picking up increased chatter everywhere. At the Loftons' and the Woodruffs'. Even at Ellie Ostlund's."

"And Pen?"

"She just left the condo, headed west. We've got a tracker on. But get this: Back at that condo building, we saw Lexi Candiotti going in through the skyway."

"Did you have it covered?"

"No. But we're ready to move. We've got it under control."

"If this is it, we need to be ready," McCort said. "We need to put everything to bed. With the other . . . thing we have planned for tonight, that will be it. We'll win going away."

McCort wouldn't say it over the phone, but everything was set for tonight's visit to Officer Hannah Nyquist.

Chapter 47

"Hello?"

"Hi, Lauren. It's Simone."

"Oh, hi, Simone. How are things going?"

"Actually, not so great. You see, since Blake was killed, I've had a chance to sit down and really think about what happened the night he died, and in the months before that."

Lauren didn't respond.

"And then," Simone continued, "I was going through Blake's things, and I found this cell phone. Not his regular phone, and not his work phone, but a cheap one, with a number I didn't recognize."

Simone paused for a response, but Lauren didn't bite, so she went on. "I looked through the call log. You know what I found? I found calls from you. Dozens of them. On a secret phone. What should I be thinking about that, Lauren?"

"I'm sure you're wrong," Lauren said, trying to sound soothing but coming off as shaky.

"No, no. It's your number. And then I thought to myself, 'Why would Lauren want to make dozens of hang-up calls to my husband on a secret phone?'"

Simone could swear she heard Lauren gulp at the other end of the line. "I'm not an idiot," Simone said. "Did you think I wouldn't figure it out?"

Again, Lauren refused to take the bait.

"But I was never seriously worried about it," Simone said. "Blake may have needed a change of pace once in a while. I got that. But I wasn't threatened. I mean, a low-class, lonely, slutty secretary . . ."

"You shut up!" Lauren's self-control finally gave way.

"It was only a matter of time until he dumped you. He decided to be nice about it—gave you a job with nothing to do. Given your skill set, that made sense."

"A *secretary*. I wasn't—"

"He treated you decently. You shouldn't have killed him, Lauren."

After a brief, stunned pause, Lauren said, "Now, wait a minute."

"You were always a logical suspect, of course—able to talk your way into the house at night, knowing the back door didn't have a camera. And you know what? I just found out the police don't know about your little fling with Blake. When I tell them, I think they'll be looking at you a whole lot harder, in a whole new light. Yes, I think you'll be auditioning for one of those 'Women Behind Bars' movies very shortly."

"You're playing a dangerous game, Simone."

"Really? I don't feel endangered at all. I feel good about finally nailing my husband's killer."

"But I have an—"

"Oh, right, there's that phony alibi you sold the police. Guess you forgot to mention your cop friend was getting it on with your loser husband that night. I can't blame the poor guy, I guess. But when the police check out their favorite love nest down on Hiawatha, I wonder what they'll find? Oops—no more alibi. And they'll get a subpoena for their phone records, too. Care to guess what that might show?"

"You *shut up*!" Lauren screamed. "You lying *bitch*!"

"Well, it's been nice talking to you, but I've got to run. I've got an appointment downtown with the police first thing tomorrow morning. And you know, that orange jumpsuit will set off your auburn hair very nicely."

Lauren hung up.

Simone clicked off her phone and looked up at Lexi and me. We were sitting at the kitchen table in the guest condo in James's building, which seemed a secure location for our purposes.

"That was one hell of a performance," I said.

"It wasn't a performance," said Simone, sounding genuinely wounded—even embittered. "I meant every word."

I turned to Lexi. "What do you think?"

"She didn't confess."

"We didn't really expect her to," I said. "It would be nice if we could actually find that burner phone."

"I'll keep looking," Simone said. "But I'd bet Blake tossed it into the river."

Lexi's cell phone rang. "Yes? I'd say you have about half an hour at the very least, but probably more than that . . . She'll want to make a plan of some kind . . . Okay, let me know when you're in place." She hung up. "They'll be in position within thirty minutes."

Lexi had positioned surveillance units at the Lofton residences in both Wayzata and Minneapolis. A police officer resembling Simone would be visible at each house.

"My money's on Wayzata," Simone said. "She knows that's where I usually am."

"Do you have a place to stay tonight?" Lexi asked.

"Yes, over in St. Paul. I'll be fine."

Lexi stood up. "I'm going to join the team in Wayzata," she said. "Let's hope it happens." She nodded to Simone and left.

I rode with Simone in the elevator down to the garage. "I'm sorry," I said. "Sorry for your loss. Sorry about what happened between Blake and Lauren."

She turned away and wiped her eyes. "At least I don't have to pretend anymore. Now everybody will know we weren't the perfect couple. I wasn't the perfect wife." She forced a smile. "Perfection was overrated, anyway."

"Thanks for helping," I said.

"Do you think she'll take the bait?"

"That depends on whether she's really crazy."

This time Simone's smile was spontaneous and genuine. "Oh, yes."

I was about halfway to the Woodruffs' when Lexi called. I clicked on my speaker. "Yes?"

"It looks like Wayzata. Lauren was last seen heading west on I-394. You called it, Pen."

"Good luck. Let me know how it turns out."

"Pen, it's better this way."

"Sure," I said and clicked off the phone. I had asked to be stationed with the police at the Wayzata stakeout. Lexi had vetoed my request as too dangerous, but I knew that wasn't the real reason. My presence might have raised awkward questions about my role in the operation and, worse, exposed my collaboration with Lexi and the mayor.

It was a little after six when I pulled into the Woodruffs' driveway and punched in the code for the gate. Andre and Anita were at Alicia's soccer match and would be attending a parents' dinner afterward.

I drove into the courtyard, shut off the engine, and rested my head on the steering wheel. I wished I had somebody to spend the evening with. I thought about James and how I'd felt when he was with me. Secure, peaceful. I thought about the good times we'd had, the amazing amount of sheer fun. "Fun" was a concept that hadn't been much in my life since the accident. I wanted to call him, just to hear his voice.

Out of the question, I decided.

I unhooked my wheelchair and unfolded it, then transferred and rolled down the ramp. I was digging in my purse for the key to the guest house when I heard a voice.

"Stop right there, Pen."

I wheeled around toward the house, where a figure, a person who'd been very much aware of the October surprise, walked out of the shadows, holding a gun.

Ellie Ostlund.

Chapter 48

Ellie pointed the pistol at me. "I don't have a lot of time, Pen. I want information, and I want it now."

"About what?" But I knew, of course. She was losing the race and becoming desperate.

"About the October surprise. Blake had something on McCort. I want it."

"I don't have it."

"I think you must have it, or at least know where it is. Roll over here, away from the van." She motioned with her gun. I complied.

"And throw your purse onto the ground."

Again, I obeyed, cursing myself for having revealed to her, in our first conversation, that I was staying with the Woodruffs.

"Why are you here?" I asked.

"I came here to save your ass, Pen. In case you haven't figured it out, Lauren is a little crazy. When she stormed out of the office and tore out of the parking lot, I figured she was going after you, that you'd learned about her affair with Blake and broken her alibi. I needed to get to you first. I need that package."

"Ellie, have you lost your mind? I know McCort is pulling ahead of you. But I don't have the information you're looking for, and I don't know where it is."

"Bullshit."

"You're obviously desperate to get the information," I said. "Did you kill Lofton to get it?"

She gave me a disgusted look. "What are you, the new president of the Tony McCort fan club?"

262

I felt foolish, and I remembered the words of the BCA guy. *Sometimes, things are just what they appear to be.* And Tony McCort appeared to be a killer.

"No, I didn't kill the bastard," Ellie said, "even though he deserved it. But I want the information. I'm tired of people cutting in line ahead of me."

"What is that supposed to mean?"

"You know very well what it means. After I'd been criss-crossing the state for two years, building up support for my campaign, Blake decides he's going to run. He slides right in, holds a fundraiser with his buddies at his country club, and instantly raises three times the money I had. He expected the governor's office to be handed to him, just like everything else in his life. And I was supposed to be just another servant, a hired hand. Then, just to rub my nose in it, he planted that bimbo of his in our office with nothing to do except keep an eye on me. I've had it. Tell me about the package, Pen."

"I don't know what you're talking about."

"What's the October surprise? Did McCort kill somebody, or deal drugs? Those are about the only things that would work for sure. Blake had that information, ready to pull out of his ass when the time was right. Not that he got it from his own genius or hard work. He undoubtedly got it the same way he got everything else: by buying it. Somebody has to stop McCort, or he'll just keep killing cops every time he needs a boost. That somebody is me, Pen. Hell, Lofton and McCort never seemed to have a problem with just taking what they want. It's my turn. Now where is the package?"

"I don't know."

I saw Ellie look past me. I followed her gaze and saw that a vehicle had appeared at the gate. Thank God, I thought.

But in the fading light, I could see it was a gray Audi SUV.

The gate opened, and the SUV drove through. The Woodruffs, I realized, had no idea how insecure their property really was. Ellie had gotten in, presumably by scaling the fence. And now Tony McCort was driving right in by hacking the electronic keypad at the gate using his magic little box, just as he had at the storage facility.

The gate closed, and the vehicle rolled to a halt. McCort got out of the passenger door and walked around toward us. Ellie swung her gun over to cover him. In doing so, she failed to see Ivan Bolger aim his gun through the open driver's window and shoot her. I screamed as she fell to the ground.

McCort walked over to me, drew a gun, and held it to my head. Meanwhile, Bolger got out of the car and walked over. Ellie lay on the ground, moaning. Bolger suddenly grabbed my right hand. As McCort held his weapon to my head, Bolger forced his pistol into my hand, pulled my index finger through the trigger guard, pointed my arm upward, and squeezed. The gun fired. I felt the recoil kick back down through my arm and shoulder. Bolger, using a gloved hand, tossed the pistol onto the ground.

"Thank you," Bolger said. A gunshot residue test, and fingerprints, would show that I'd fired the gun that had shot Ellie. McCort took his gun away from my head.

"You're going to frame me?" I said. "Who's going to believe I killed Ellie?"

"There won't be any other explanation," McCort said. "Of course, she'll kill you, too. It will probably drive them nuts, trying to figure out who shot first. But this will tie it up neatly from my standpoint."

"You were monitoring Ellie."

"Sure. When she came out here, we figured things must be coming to a head somehow." He looked around. "Andre should have taken his wife's advice. A little exterior security would come in handy now, wouldn't it?"

Good God, he'd bugged the Woodruffs' house. I began to hyperventilate.

"Now, take it easy," McCort said. "We have some talking to do."

Ellie moaned, blood flowing between the fingers she held to her stomach. "Help me," she gasped.

"For God's sake," I managed to say. "Let me call for help."

"We'll finish both of you off in a minute," McCort said. "First we need to talk about Mark Tomlinson's package."

"I don't have the material."

"You probably don't," he conceded. "But I suspect you have a pretty good idea where it might be."

"I don't know. Somewhere in Lofton's house, maybe."

He stood up straighter. "You disappoint me. I think you're lying. You haven't come this far, found out this much, to end up clueless like this."

"I don't know. Ellie didn't know, and I don't know. You're going to kill me anyway."

"You've known that all along, Pen. Removing obstacles is what I do. Tomlinson, Schott, Hyser, Van Ness."

"You killed Duke Sorrel, too," I said.

McCort smiled. "Forgot that one. Yeah, poor Duke. The latest polls have me ahead of Ellie, but you can't take anything for granted. And since she will have been murdered by a depressed, misguided cripple, I guess they'll have to find yet another opponent for me."

"Good Lord," I sobbed.

Ellie moaned again.

"Hyser took it like an adult," McCort said. "Ivan just gave her the injection and she slipped away. A neat, untraceable substance that never shows up in the tox screens. But Van Ness . . . he lost all his snark and snottiness in a hurry. Pleaded and blubbered, begging for his life. Ivan put him out of his misery."

McCort's cell phone buzzed. With a puzzled expression, he pulled the phone out, glanced at the screen, and answered. "Yes?"

As he listened, his face darkened. After a moment, he clicked the phone off and jammed it into his pocket. "The cops," he said. "How the hell . . . They don't have cameras. Are they tracking my phone?" He glanced over at Bolger. "They know we're here."

Just then, distant sirens began to wail.

"Shit," McCort hissed. "We've got Pen's prints on the gun. We'll have to just stay and tough it out."

Bolger looked uncertain, and I saw my opening. "Easy for him to say," I told Bolger. "The GSR test will show you fired the gun. Not him." Bolger tugged unconsciously at the glove on his hand. There was no time to dispose of it. I found myself mentally paraphrasing O.J. Simpson's attorney. *If it fits, you're in the shit.*

"For Christ's sake, don't listen to her," McCort said.

"Same with Tomlinson, Schott, and Sorrel," I said. "You were the trigger man. All the physical evidence will point to you. His hands look clean."

"Shut up," McCort said. But I was in prosecutor mode now. Inducing an underling to flip on his boss came as naturally to me as breathing.

"All of it was his doing," Bolger said, still looking uncertain. "He told me to do it."

"So you say. Where's the proof? Did he write you a memo saying 'Kill Duke Sorrel'?"

The sirens died. There were no engine sounds or signs of police vehicles. The cavalry wasn't going to show up after all.

"Why would I have done it without his telling me to?" Bolger said.

"That's easy. You knew it would please your boss. And it gave him deniability. Really inconvenient deniability, from your standpoint. You were just an overzealous subordinate." As I said the words, I realized, with terrifying clarity, that I was right. There was an excellent chance that Tony McCort would walk.

"The cops aren't coming," McCort said.

"They are," I said. "They're just running with the sirens off."

"They'll have to know Tony's behind it," Bolger said, sounding desperate now.

"Oh, sure. But with no real proof, it's your word against his. Staying to meet the cops and toughing it out—that might work out for him. I don't think so for you, Ivan."

"Son of a *bitch*," said Bolger. I flinched as he raised his gun and fired twice. McCort, his face registering shock, slumped to the ground. Now Bolger would be able to spin his own story, one that would blame the shooting on me.

I looked back toward Bolger. He was reaching down for Ellie's gun. After he shot me with her gun, he'd finish Ellie off with the one that had my fingerprints on it.

McCort, prone on the cobbled courtyard, tried to reach out with one hand. His mouth moved, and I rolled closer.

"Simone," he gasped. "Love . . . Simone." His eyes closed, and his hand dropped.

I found myself not surprised or even put off by this lifelong bachelor's Rosebud-type revelation. I had bigger things to worry about. Bolger began walking in my direction, his dead eyes boring into me.

I was next.

From the corner of my eye, I saw a split-second glint from behind the gate. With fierce concentration, I kept my eyes on Bolger. My van was parked between him and the gate. He couldn't see what I saw.

Or thought I saw.

I began retreating. He came closer and began to raise the gun, still shielded by the van. My response was an act of sheer, desperate instinct. I turned my back on him and rolled away from the van as fast as I could.

This annoyed the hell out of him. "*Shit.*" I could hear him walking after me.

I sped up, praying his route would take him clear of the van before he shot me.

He came closer, his shoes clacking on the cobbled court-yard. I changed directions suddenly, still facing away from him.

I could still hear him coming.

Then a female voice, from the direction of the gate. "Bolger, drop it!"

Then three shots.

I turned around.

Ivan Bolger lay on the ground. Lexi Candiotti held her pistol between the bars of the gate.

I yelled out the gate code to Lexi, and she opened it up. I saw her speak into her handheld, and half a minute later the first police vehicles rolled through the gate. The officers got out and crouched behind their car doors, guns drawn. Lexi yelled to me, asking whether there were any active shooters. When I answered in the negative, the officers moved cautiously out from cover and checked the prone figures of McCort, Bolger, and Ellie. Two more police cars arrived to secure the scene, followed closely by two ambulances.

After a few minutes, the ambulances took Ellie and McCort away while paramedics checked me over. Then the technicians moved in to check my hands for gunshot residue. An officer came over and asked me a few quick questions about what had happened. Crime scene tape was set up and photographs were taken.

Finally Lexi walked over. "Thanks," I said.

"I guess you know what happens next."

I nodded. Three gunshot victims and an officer-involved shooting. "We each answer about a million questions. Separately."

"Bingo. And none of yours get answered yet."

"Swell. See you tonight."

Chapter 49

Lexi arrived at the condo downtown at about nine-thirty. I was still going, on coffee and adrenaline. Through a supreme effort of will, I had avoided alcohol. My hands still shook, and my breathing was shallow.

Lexi sat down. "Hungry?"

"No."

"Drink?"

"I'd better not."

She hesitated, then nodded. "No ill effects?"

I closed my eyes. I knew I'd have nothing but ill effects, for months and maybe years to come. "I'm okay. How are the shooting victims?"

"McCort and Bolger are dead. Ellie might make it. She's out of surgery now."

"I was there, but I don't seem to know much about what happened."

"Lauren turned back when she was almost to Wayzata," Lexi said. "We've since picked her up. She admitted that she had a gun and was headed out to confront Simone, but she cooled down and thought better of it. I was still out in this area when I got the call."

"Call?"

As if on cue, my phone beeped, indicating a text. I pulled it up: Kenny. *I'm downstairs.*

As we waited for him to come up, I said, "I don't know what Kenny is doing here."

"I asked him to come."

Now I was really perplexed.

Kenny strode in, wearing a worried expression. "Are you okay, Aunt Pen?"

"Hanging in there," I said. He and Lexi sat down with me in the living room.

I looked at Lexi. "Enough," I said. "What the hell happened at the Woodruffs'?"

Lexi glanced at Kenny.

"I've been in touch with Alicia," he said.

I struggled to process that. "Okay."

"I told her I was worried about you, and she said she was, too. I saw what happened to Brad Van Ness and Jane Hyser. Alicia said they had a security system there, but no cameras. She said her bedroom window overlooked the courtyard, and she could see who came and went, but that she and her parents were gone a lot. I told her to put her laptop up to the window when she left, and to activate the camera on it and make sure the computer didn't go into sleep mode. I gave her an address for the feed and I said I'd try to check it once in a while. This morning she put the laptop up before school and texted me that she'd be home late tonight. So I looked in on the feed a few times. I was studying, half-looking at the screen, when I saw you drive up, and then I saw this woman step out from behind the building with a gun—that was Ellie Ostlund, right?"

"Right."

"Anyway, I kind of freaked when I saw that. I thought about just calling 911, but I wasn't sure what was going on or how long they'd take to get there. So I called Lieutenant Candiotti. I figured she'd know what to do."

Lexi took over the narration. "I was already in the car, headed back. I had Kenny give our people the internet address for the feed, and they pulled it up. McCort had gotten there in the meantime. They told me that Bolger had shot Ellie and put the gun in your hand. By then I was headed toward Deephaven, and I called in the troops. But I was afraid McCort or Bolger would shoot you before the cops got there. So I decided on the direct approach."

"You called McCort."

She shrugged. "What did I have to lose? I told him we were monitoring him and described what he'd done. Then we saw the three of you talking—let me guess: you got Bolger to turn on him."

"Yes. So you saw Bolger shoot McCort?"

"They played it for me later. Pretty damned cold-blooded. Anyway, I got the Deephaven cops to switch to a silent approach."

"Why?"

"It was a risk," she admitted. "There was a chance the bad guys would conclude the heat was off and go ahead and shoot you. It was a close thing."

"Um, yes."

"I wouldn't have gotten Bolger if you hadn't drawn him out from behind the van where I could get a shot. Turning your back on him was—well, that was genius."

"I didn't really have time to think about it," I said.

"But on some level you knew he wouldn't shoot you in the back. That would have made it harder to explain, screwed up his scenario of you and Ellie shooting each other."

"I guess. Well, thanks for saving my butt. Both of you."

"Our pleasure, Pen. The investigation may have had a lot of twists and turns and dead ends, but you pushed through all of them until you got to the finish line. There's only one person responsible for finding Blake Lofton's killer: you."

*   *   *

I couldn't sleep that night. It was the trauma, I told myself; the horror of the killings I'd witnessed and almost being killed myself. But was there something more? I should have been finished with the case. I knew there would be a long process of cleaning up details on all the murders, but there wasn't much reason for me to be involved.

Or was there?

I got up at seven. Still in my bathrobe, I pulled out the packet of materials and evidence I'd gotten from Lars Hankinson's office. I knew it was foolish, but I couldn't help myself. After an hour spent reviewing the notes and transcripts of witness interviews, I called Simone.

"Pen," she said. "I heard what happened yesterday. Are you all right?"

"I'm fine. I'm expecting more questions from the police, and I'm trying to get some of the facts straight in my mind. Do you have a minute?"

"Absolutely." We spent about ten minutes going over all the conversations she'd had on the day before the murder. I thanked her and hung up.

Next I called Alicia, who'd stayed home from school. We spent a few minutes talking about the events of the previous day. She and Anita hadn't been allowed to return to the house until early this morning. Andre was still in jail, but Hankinson was negotiating with the county attorney to get him out. "One last thing," I said. "Would you tell me again about the morning after the murder? When you learned Andre had been arrested?"

"Sure," she said, sounding puzzled. After she described again being woken up by Cristina, I asked a follow-up question. She gave me the answer I'd been dreading.

"I have to go," I said. "Let's talk again tonight."

"Okay. 'Bye, Pen."

I clicked off and looked at the phone in my hand. It was decision time.

No, it wasn't. I'd made the decision early on in this case, when I'd committed myself to the truth.

Maybe it wasn't a decision at all. Maybe it was just the way I was wired.

I called Lexi.

Chapter 50

Anita called at eight that night. "Mind if I stop by?" she asked. I was exhausted beyond imagining. "Sure."

I'd exchanged several calls with Lexi during the day. Then I'd tried and failed to take a nap. Now I thought longingly about the wine in the refrigerator, but I knew I had to stay focused and see this messy process through to its messy conclusion.

I buzzed Anita in through the entrance downstairs and went over to the door to admit her. She didn't look too hot herself; the experience had taken a toll on everybody. She embraced me. "You did it."

"Did I?" I had only begun to realize just how little I'd done.

She handed me an unmarked envelope. I opened it and pulled out a check made out to me for a very generous amount. "Hankinson says Andre is getting out in the morning," she said. "Thank you from the bottom of our hearts."

She followed me to the living room, looking around with disapproval. "I never much cared for this place. Pretty impersonal."

"I guess James didn't prioritize decorating."

I sensed there were a lot of things she wanted to say about James, but she didn't comment.

"Drink?" I asked.

"I think I'll pass."

I passed, too. She sat down, and I rolled up across from her.

"So what are your plans?" she asked.

"I haven't thought much about it," I said. "Mostly, I've been thinking about a conversation I need to have with Alicia."

She looked puzzled. "With . . . Alicia?"

"Somebody needs to sit her down and explain to her exactly how this murder happened. And I'm afraid that somebody is me."

"We know the basics of the murder, don't we? We know that Lauren did the deed and that McCort hired her."

"That's what Lauren told the police this afternoon," I said. "She confessed after her alibi fell apart."

Anita looked relieved. "I'm glad that's resolved. I suppose that with McCort dead, there are some details we'll never know. And what did you mean about needing to explain it to Alicia?"

"You know, I've changed my mind about having a drink. Join me?"

"No, thanks."

I retrieved the wine bottle and glass from the kitchen and poured it out as Anita watched me, her expression wary. I sipped from my glass. "I spent all night and most of today deciding whether to listen to these voices in my head. I guess I have a thing about doing what I was hired to do, which was to find the truth. And if you don't believe that, well, you can just consider me an annoying troublemaker."

She looked on full alert now, but didn't say anything.

I fortified myself with another sip. "When Lexi Candiotti told me about Lauren's confession, I suggested that she ask Lauren one question."

Anita waited.

"How did Lauren know Blake was going to be at the Minneapolis house that night?"

She was good. She showed no reaction other than intense curiosity.

"When I searched through the files," I said, "I found that Blake's volunteer driver was the only person who knew he'd changed plans. In fact, that's how the police determined Ellie Ostlund didn't commit the murder—she had no way of knowing

Blake would be there that night. Of course, it was reasonable to assume Blake had told Simone, too. She would have been expecting him out at the lake. Just to make sure, I called Simone. And sure enough, Blake had told her."

Anita still showed no reaction. I drank some more, this time a gulp instead of a sip. "It turns out that Simone told two other people. One was Andre. That was really unfortunate, since that knowledge enabled Andre to go over to confront Blake and set himself up to be charged with murder. But Simone also mentioned Blake's presence there to one other person, a person she talks to on the phone almost every day: you."

Her look went stone cold. "You don't want to go there, Pen, you really don't."

"Sorry, Anita, but I was all in on this case from the beginning. I still am. That's why I remembered that Cristina woke Alicia up the morning after the murder. But Cristina told me she doesn't normally stay over at your place on Friday nights. You asked her at the last minute to stay over that night on some pretext—I called Alicia and confirmed it. And Cristina ended up providing you with your alibi; she was the nameless 'household staff' referred to in the report I saw."

Anita stood up and grabbed her purse. "You're wasting my time—"

"The police weren't yet aware of these facts. And how would they be? I picked them up by hanging around your household. And then I realized there was something else they didn't know: They didn't have a clue that Blake had Andre in a bind. He knew something devastating about Andre, that he had killed his own father and covered it up for thirty years. Knowing that enabled Blake to keep Andre under his thumb, working at AgriMinn and doing Blake's bidding for as long as Blake wanted him to."

"Pen, don't—"

"And you," I said. "You were already furious at Blake's treatment of Andre. His manipulation, his condescension. 'Yes,

Blake, No, Blake.' I sensed serious anger from you. Who wouldn't be mad? And then the crowning touch. Passing him over for the CEO job, yet expecting him to run the company. It was appalling. But Blake was just getting what he'd paid for, in the form of a new SUV. And for you, it was a hell of a motive for murder. A motive, by the way, that explains why Lofton wasn't tortured for the location of Tomlinson's file. The murder wasn't about that."

She stood there, looking at the door and then back at me. Then she slowly sat down. "Pen, I said you shouldn't go there. And I was serious. You're playing with fire."

"You're threatening me? Well, you'll have to take your place at the end of a long and distinguished line of folks."

"You work for me, not the police," she snapped.

"Actually, I work for Andre. But it doesn't make any difference. I haven't told the police anything privileged. If you disagree, you can file a motion to suppress before your trial."

"Trial," she scoffed. "Please. You've got nothing but a bunch of conjecture. Besides, you said Lauren already identified McCort as the person who hired her."

"She did. She was trying to be loyal to you, I suppose. Maybe she was afraid you'd want your money back."

"You know," she said, "I would just bet that the true source of that money will never be found."

"You're probably right. I'm sure you were careful about the payments, just as you were careful in your choice of killer. You picked somebody with access to Blake and a great motive—Lauren had been used, dumped, and humiliated. She also had a cop friend available to give her an alibi. To top it off, she's sort of crazy. Then you gave yourself an alibi. The deed was done, and the whole thing looked good. But then, unexpectedly, you needed a way to clear Andre, who'd blundered into the situation and gotten himself charged with the murder. That's where I came in."

I leaned forward. "You're nothing if not confident, Anita. You were betting that I wouldn't find the truth, or that if I did, I'd keep my mouth shut. You hoped I'd find a way to pin it on McCort or Ellie. And if either of them had gotten Tomlinson's package, that probably would have done it. And in the meantime, you were able to monitor my activities. I gave you a complete update nearly every night. Kind of creeps me out to think back on it. I was dealing with the actual killer all along."

"You can spare me the moralizing. You don't know what it's like to live under the thumb of a man like Blake Lofton."

"No, I guess I don't. But you know what? I don't give a shit."

"Don't you really? Well, that's great, Pen. Because all you have is a theory. All this bullshit of yours adds up to a big fat nothing."

I pulled out my phone. "You're right. Nothing. Nothing except a question." I sent a one-word text: *Now.*

Anita got up and headed for the door. "Well it's been fun," she said. She opened up the door, coming face to face with Lexi Candiotti and two uniformed officers.

She looked back at me, enraged. "You stupid bitch. You think I won't beat this?"

Lexi and her colleagues frisked and cuffed her.

"Actually, you won't beat it," I said. "All I had was that same old nagging question, but it was one Lauren couldn't answer. She couldn't explain how she'd learned Blake would be at the house that night. And she didn't feel like taking the rap herself. So she changed her story—admitted it was you who told her Blake would be there. And that it was you who hired her. You know what else? That money you paid to the Jorgensons will be traced to you, if not by the police, then by Kenny. You won't beat anything, Anita."

Lexi Mirandized her, and the officers led her toward the door. "Wait a minute," I said. I rolled over to the officer holding her purse, took the envelope with the check she'd given me, and stuck it into the side pocket. "Hankinson is expensive."

"Is this what you wanted?" she hissed. "Are you happy now?"

My mind was filled, as it had been all day, by an image I couldn't shake of a fourteen-year-old girl who deserved an explanation.

"No," I said.

After everyone left, I sat by myself, dreading my conversation with Alicia, trying to think of anything positive I could say to her. Sighing, I got my coat, struggled into it, and headed for Deephaven to tell Alicia her stepfather was not a murderer.

Epilogue

I looked around the living room at the Woodruff guest house. I'd packed everything. It was mid-morning, and my flight didn't leave until late afternoon. I didn't know what I'd do until then. And I didn't know what I'd do after that, either.

In courtrooms and law offices downtown, intensive negotiations were under way. Lauren Jorgensen was negotiating her guilty plea in exchange for her testimony against Anita, who was herself engaged in discussions with the county attorney for a plea deal. Ellie Ostlund, recovering from her gunshot wound, had attorneys negotiating a plea to charges of scaling the Woodruffs' fence and sticking me up with a gun. She'd have to drop out of the governor's race. Charges were being considered against Justin Jorgensen, who'd have to explain the money he'd received to redeem his distressed properties.

In Deephaven, the television trucks had returned in force. Several national outlets had joined the local stations, and cable news networks had gone berserk with twenty-four-seven coverage of the crime spree that had upended Minnesota politics and society.

Lip readers reviewing Kenny's video had caught McCort's confession to ordering the murders of Tomlinson, Schott, Hyser, Van Ness, and Sorrel—just about every murder except the one I'd been investigating him for—and multiple law enforcement agencies were now taking a new look at those crimes. No one knew where Brad Van Ness's body had been disposed of, and the men who'd done the deed were themselves dead. In a back room at Together Fitness, police had found an intel operation that employed six people who were engaged in bugging, hacking, surveillance, and other assorted sleazy endeavors. Mark Tomlinson's missing packet of incriminating documents still hadn't been found, and Tomlinson was preparing to release his online copy. He was also planning to return to Minnesota shortly. Lars Hankinson, though deprived of his media circus trial extravaganza, had modestly confided to media sources that "his team" had been responsible for fingering Lauren and Anita.

I was still engaged in heavy navel contemplation when Andre walked in. "Got a minute?" my client asked.

"Sure."

He came in and sat down.

"How are you holding up?" I asked.

"I feel overwhelmed. I just haven't processed the news about Anita yet or accepted the fact that she's going away for good. She did it for me. But now I've lost her, and so has Alicia. And Alicia—I don't know. We're consulting counselors, and we'll see what they say. They might recommend sending her out to live with James. For us, the ordeal is just beginning."

"And for the state?"

He shrugged. "I hope that now, the healing can begin. The Hankinson circus didn't happen. The race riots didn't occur. The news has more interesting stuff to go nuts about, like the second and third shootings of a gubernatorial candidate in less than a month, and which member of the Woodruff family is a killer. But did we resolve anything? Or did we just sweep it under the rug?"

It looked to me as though the brooms were out in full force. The mayor had, via Lexi, extended his thanks, but he had continued to keep my involvement a secret. "He knows you'll understand," Lexi had said. And I guess I did. In a larger sense, the community hadn't really taken to heart all that had happened. A recent poll showed fifty-seven percent of Minnesotans agreeing that protests against police shootings were "a reflection of racism against whites." Fifty-nine percent said all such protests "should be outlawed." Most disturbing of all, a strong majority, as yet ignorant of the evidence, said that if Tony McCort were still alive, they would support him for governor.

"What are your plans?" I asked.

"They've asked me to go back and run AgriMinn. That would be nice, but I just can't do it now. Alicia needs me, and so does Anita."

"What about 1989?"

"I talked to Simone. We agreed that it's time to put the story out. I frankly don't know what the impact will be, but there'll never be a good time. It will be a relief to get it out there. We'll be making a joint announcement with Dave Pawloski next week, and we're holding a press conference afterward."

"Andre, I'm so sorry—"

"It's not your fault. It's ours. You learned the truth. That's what we hired you to do. It was just . . . costly."

"Yeah."

He studied me. "You didn't have to tell the police about Anita, Pen."

"That's true."

"Did you consider not doing it?"

"Not really."

"No, I don't suppose you did." He paused, looking as though he wanted to say more. But then he stood up and left.

With time to kill, I rolled outside to the pool area. The pool had been covered for the season, and leaves had blown on top of the canvas. I reached the gate at the opposite end, toward the lake. The latch was above my head, but I managed to reach it and, after a struggle, got the gate open. I rolled through, and the gate slammed shut behind me. I looked back, saw that the latch was configured differently on this side, and realized I'd never get it open again. I'd have to call for help.

The day was beautiful, almost summerlike. The lawn sloped down to the shoreline, where the water lapped gently against a small line of sand and rocks. Two willow trees, now bare, flanked a stone bench. I longed to go down to the water's edge and sit for a long time and maybe skip a stone or two across the surface, as I'd done with my dad and my sister Marsha when we were little. But the lawn was sloped and uneven. I'd never make it.

As always, obstacles.

I heard the gate close gently behind me. Alicia walked out, a trim, athletic figure with long legs and an easy stride. Me, once upon a time.

"Hi," she said.

I nodded.

Both of us just looked at the lake for a while. "You don't have to feel guilty," she said. "I'll be okay."

"I know you will." I clasped her hand.

"You just did your job, the job Mom asked you to do."

"Right. That's my story, and I'm sticking with it."

She managed a faint smile, and we were silent again.

"Are you going to be on that plane this afternoon?" she asked at last.

"I don't know."

"What's stopping you?"

"I can't go home, Alicia. There's nothing there."

"Yes, there is."

"Now, don't start on me."

She jammed her hands into the pocket of her hoodie. "I've never started on you, Pen." Her voice had an angry edge that I'd never heard before. "I've never nagged you. I've never tried to make you feel guilty. I've just tried to be . . . here."

It was true, I realized. I'd only felt, or maybe imagined, her disapproval, her disappointment. "I imagine that's taken some restraint," I said.

Her smile was thin and sad. "You have no idea."

My gaze shifted toward the lake. "I can't, Alicia. I just can't."

She walked around in front of me, blocking my view of the lake. "You've done amazing things, Pen. You've come a long way on your own. You've coped with having a lot of people let you down."

I nodded.

She leaned down. "You promised me, Pen. BFF's, no matter what, remember?"

"And I meant it."

"I know you did. But you need to take care of yourself first. You have to go back and face your situation. And you have to trust. If you don't, you won't make it."

Trust. If not the opposite of independence, then at least a threat to it. A threat to my control and self-sufficiency, for sure. Most of all, I supposed, a threat to my pride.

Alicia pulled out her phone. "If you won't help yourself, we can't help you," she said. She punched in a speed-dial number and held out the phone. "It's up to you."

I looked at the phone. I could hear it ring. Then another ring. And another.

"Alicia?"

James's voice.

She continued to hold the phone out to me, her face without expression.

"Alicia, is that you?"

I took the phone with a shaking hand and looked at it.

"Alicia, is that you?"

I held the phone up to my face. "It's me."

A brief pause. "Pen." His voice was hushed, stunned.

"I can't give up the things I do," I blurted out.

I waited for the hang-up or the angry rejoinder. Instead, "And?"

Not but. Not either/or.

And.

"And I . . ." I looked at Alicia, looked at the phone, looked at the peaceful lake and the obstacles, trembling, and the tears began to flow. "And I need help."

AN INVITATION TO READING GROUPS/BOOK CLUBS

I would like to extend an invitation to reading groups/book clubs across the country. Invite me to your group and I'll be happy to participate in your discussion. I'm available to join your discussion either in person or via the telephone. (Reading groups should have a speakerphone.) You can arrange a date and time by e-mailing me at brian@brianlutterman.com. I look forward to hearing from you.

THANK YOU FOR READING

Thank you for reading *Nightfall*. I hope you'll take a moment to leave a quick review online. Reviews are an author's lifeblood. To read more about me and my books, and to receive notice of future publications, sign up for my email list at www.brianlutterman.com, where you'll also find news about my appearances and other features related to my books.

Not Sure What to Read Next?
Try these authors from Conquill Press

Jenifer LeClair
The Windjammer Mystery Series
Rigged for Murder
Danger Sector
Cold Coast
Apparition Island
Dead Astern
www.windjammermyseries.com

Chuck Logan
Fallen Angel
Broker
www.chucklogan.org

Brian Lutterman
The Pen Wilkinson Mystery Series
Downfall
Windfall
Freefall
www.brianlutterman.com

Steve Thayer
Ithaca Falls
The Wheat Field
The Leper
www.stevethayer.com

Christopher Valen
The John Santana Mystery Series
White Tombs
The Black Minute
Bad Weeds Never Die
Bone Shadows
Death's Way
The Darkness Hunter
Speak for the Dead
www.christophervalen.com
For more information on all these titles go to:
www.conquillpress.com

CPSIA information can be obtained
at www.ICGtesting.com
Printed in the USA
LVHW09s2154130818
586433LV00008B/6/P